ISBN: 978-1-943728-06-0
Published by Samantha Sabian and Arianthem Press
THE DRAGON'S NIGHT Vol 9 CHRONICLES OF ARIANTHEM, 2020. FIRST
PRINTING.
Office of Publication: Los Angeles, California

What did you think of this book? We love to hear from our readers.
Please email us at: samantha@arianthem.com

THE DRAGON'S NIGHT
SECOND CHRONICLES OF ARIANTHEM I

by Samantha Sabian

Also from Samantha Sabian

FIRST CHRONICLES

THE DRAGON'S LOVER
CHRONICLES OF ARIANTHEM I
(ISBN: 978-0-9885822-0-0)

THE SJÖFN ACADEMY
CHRONICLES OF ARIANTHEM II
(ISBN: 978-0-9885822-2-4)

THE RUNNER THIEF
CHRONICLES OF ARIANTHEM III
(ISBN: 978-0-9885822-4-8)

THE RIVAL'S CONCORD
CHRONICLES OF ARIANTHEM IV
(ISBN: 978-0-9885822-6-2)

THE DRAGON'S ALLIANCE
CHRONICLES OF ARIANTHEM V
(ISBN: 978-0-9885822-8-6)

THE SHADOW GAMES
CHRONICLES OF ARIANTHEM VI
(ISBN: 978-1-943728-00-8)

THE DRAGON'S WAR
CHRONICLES OF ARIANTHEM VII
(ISBN: 978-1-943728-02-2)

SECOND CHRONICLES

<u>THE DRAGON'S NIGHT</u>
2nd CHRONICLES OF ARIANTHEM I
(ISBN: 978-1-943728-06-0)

<u>THE SCINTERIAN'S DREAM</u>
2nd CHRONICLES OF ARIANTHEM II
(ISBN: 978-1-943728-08-4)

visit us on the web at

www.arianthem.com

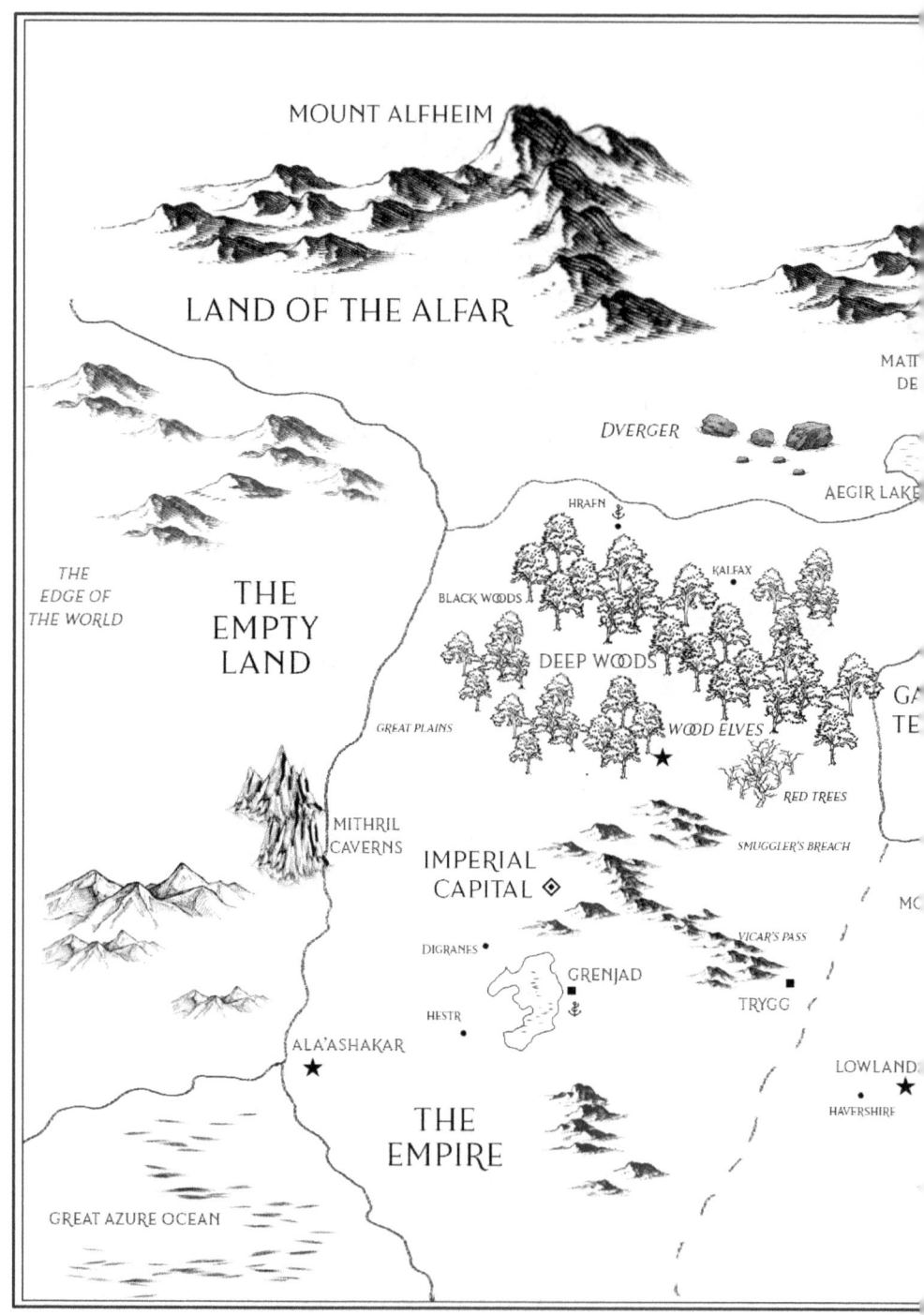

ONS

KYLAN'S
CASTLE
★

BALDUR'S PEAK

DARBY FALLS
REIST KEEP

DVERGER

TER
ORY

GUDRID

HALDIS ◇

THE
SJOFN ACADEMY
★

LAND OF THE
HA'KAN

ARIANTHEM

CIRCA 312 AGW

Chapter 1

The Queen awoke, enveloped in the warmth of the two women entangled in bed with her. Her First General was sleeping soundly on her back, her handsome features relaxed, the fine lines about her eyes barely visible in slumber. Her High Priestess was on her side curled about the General, a shapely white leg flung across her lower body, full breasts pressed against the muscles of her arm.

Halla gazed at the two with love and affection, gently extricating herself from her lovers. Only Gimle was missing, the First Scholar likely lost in some experiments that would end with her in bed with the many lab assistants who revered her for her mind as well as her more physical attributes.

The Queen arose from the bed and pulled on a silk robe, quiet lest she disturb the sleeping women. Senta stirred, the warrior in her alert even in sleep, but she did not sense danger and settled once more. Astrid, the priestess in her alert to the slightest discomfort, pulled the General close.

Raindrops began a gentle pitter-patter on the terrace outside as Halla moved to the stained-glass doors. It was dark, and the rain made it more so, dowsing the many torches on the terrace that were uncovered. She pushed through the doors and stood beneath the overhang that protected her from the rain, gazing out at her kingdom.

Three years of absolute peace. Three years in which the Ha'kan had strengthened their ties with both the Empire and the Alfar, allowing the adjacent kingdoms free and unrestricted access to the trade routes they had acquired by defeating the Garmlain. Three years in which they had bonded with the Dverger, giving the dwarves access to the land beneath the Ha'kan territory in exchange for a percentage of the minerals they so effortlessly acquired. Three years in which her people had grown strong and happy, a record number of births occurring in a people for whom pregnancy was a rare and momentous event.

Torches continued to wink out over Haldis, the capital settling into a darkness broken only by the few torches that were shielded from the rain. Halla smiled, for the Scholar's wing was the only bright spot in the darkness, lit by fires magical in nature that were immune to water. The Ha'kan were not good with magic, but Gimle was a rare exception and she passed her learning on to all who showed the slightest inclination towards the arcane arts.

The front gate, far in the distance, was also well-lit. The pitch that kept those fires burning would fade in a deluge, but nothing less. She could make out the small figures that paced the walls, guarding the capital, grateful for her fearless warriors.

The rain fell softly and Halla's gaze swept the city. She marveled at the pairings that were occurring. The Ha'kan, all-female, were bound together by a sexual energy that astonished other races. Non-monogamous, reproduction by parthenogenesis, the Ha'kan had a caste devoted entirely to sexual pleasure and development, and skill in that forum was as admired and requisite as any other.

The rain increased in intensity, and the lightning and thunder were not as far apart as they were minutes before, the lightning brighter and the thunder louder. The bright flash illuminated the otherwise dark courtyard.

Halla frowned. In that brief illumination, she could have sworn there was a dark figure making its way across the blackened courtyard, one that disappeared as quickly as it had appeared. But that was impossible. There were guards at the gate, and the Royal Guard protected the castle and the three wings bordering it. No one could slip past the elite of the Ha'kan forces.

Still, Halla ventured out into the rain, leaning over the marble wall to peer down into the darkness. Perhaps it was the drop in atmospheric pressure that accompanied every storm, perhaps the electricity that accompanied every bolt of lightning, perhaps the tremble that accompanied every crack of thunder, but the hair on the back of her neck stood on end. She ignored the rain that drenched her long hair, unaware of the rain that ran in rivulets down her back, oblivious to the water that soaked her robe and made it cling to every curve of her body.

The lightning split the sky again, and the thunder followed in an instant. In that moment, Halla again saw the figure, closer to the castle and approaching the stairs that led to her terrace. She felt a finger of fear trace its cold path along her spine, and began backing to the overhang once more, cracking the stained-glass door.

"Senta," she whispered.

In an instant, the First General sat up in bed, crouched, and bounded toward her Queen, every muscle bunched in preparation for battle. The High Priestess also rolled in a graceful movement that left her standing, albeit behind her First General. All Ha'kan were trained to fight, regardless of caste.

"Someone is coming up the stairs."

Senta's sword was already in her hand, for the warriors of the Ha'kan were nearly unmatched in battle, and the First General without equal in their ranks. She understood Halla's words; someone was coming up the stairs, unknown, unnoticed and unchallenged. She took a position slightly ahead of Halla, protective of her Queen, sword at the ready position.

Astrid moved next to Halla, ready to whisk her away at the first sign of danger. All three women waited silently, the steady drumming of the rain as unrelenting as an elevated heartbeat. The darkness was complete, all torches on the terrace having succumbed to the steady stream from the sky.

Halla could hear her own breathing. It seemed louder than the rain, which did not seem possible. Senta was utterly calm, but the tension in her body betrayed her state of mind. And Astrid's possessive clutch on her arm revealed her thoughts as well. All stared at the stairwell.

The lightning flashed, and as when she was a child, Halla began to count to measure the distance of the bolt, but there was not even a second between the lightning and the thunder, because the storm was fully upon them. As was the figure who was fully illuminated at the top of the stairs, a black outline against the momentary nova of the sky. Senta's sword raised and hovered in the ready position.

And then welcome laughter drifted on that unwelcome wind. It was low and sensual, full of dark humor and possessing a familiarity that soothed all.

"You can stand down, First General."

The tone was mocking, but Senta lowered her sword. She knew this one. And experience held that a sword would do no good against the creature who stood before them. Nor was she an enemy.

"Idonea!" Halla exclaimed.

Once under the protection of the overhang, the dark figure became slightly illuminated, and the hood lowered as if by magic. The laughing dark eyes of the most powerful mage in Arianthem were revealed.

"It's been a very long trip, and I seek sanctuary with the Ha'kan."

Her words were curious, but the Queen would answer in only one way.

"You're always welcome here."

"That's good," Idonea replied, "because I bear an enormous weight of enormous value."

This gave all three of the Ha'kan pause as they gazed at whatever burden Idonea bore, for she carried something beneath her dripping robe, something in each arm.

"Whatever it is, the Ha'kan are at your service."

Idonea sighed. "Well, then…"

And as before, as if by magic, her cloak was retracted, and her burden revealed. She held a child in each arm, little more than infants. Both were sleeping contentedly, oblivious to the storm and all who stared enraptured.

"You have children?" Halla exclaimed.

"Not exactly," Idonea said, gazing down at the two with a combination of adoration and exasperation.

One of the little ones stirred, her dark eyes opening to only her twin. She reached out with a tiny fist and grasped her sister, tugging her into wakefulness. The sibling awoke with a protest, lighter eyes opening to gaze upon her other half. And in that instant, both pairs of eyes turned to a beautiful shade of lavender as the twins gazed upon one another.

"By the gods," Halla whispered.

"Yes," Idonea said drily, "that is pretty much how it happened."

Chapter 2

TWO YEARS EARLIER...

The fiery red dragon circled the mountain-top leisurely, using the updrafts to maneuver into position to enter her cave. Sunlight glinted on the dark red scales, giving off an iridescent yellow glow that did indeed make the enormous creature look as if she were on fire. She glided so skillfully along the thermal winds that a single dip of one wing wheeled her about to a straight-line approach to the entrance in the side of the mountain. The wings, each one larger than the sail of a ship, tilted back to slow her approach so that she landed gracefully upon the ledge. The fearsome creature dropped the buck she held in her jaws, the prey still dripping blood but mercifully killed in her first diving strike. This was not for her; she had eaten while hunting. This was for her mate.

This brought a smile to the dragon which revealed rows of sharpened teeth. The fangs disappeared in a brilliant flash of yellow light, as did the rest of the dragon, and when the light faded, a woman only slightly less imposing than the dragon appeared. Tall, long-limbed, silver-haired, she was elegant and regal, lovely and terrifying. Her armor fit her like it was a part of her, for indeed it was, the miniature scales the same color and shape as her dragon plating. When she moved, the scales shifted and curved about her sinewy body, casting the same iridescent, fiery rainbows.

She stepped over the bones of numerous animals, reminding herself she should do some housekeeping later and push those off the ledge. The glow of a warm fire pit drew her, not for its heat, for she could generate that on her own, but for what it contained.

Two large eggs lay amongst the embers, warmed by a layer of hot rocks and carefully positioned sand. They were enormous compared to the eggs of normal fowl, nearly half the height of a man. The amber eyes of the dragon gazed on them proudly, for they were large even for dragon eggs. And when those eyes settled on the woman who also lay amongst the embers, oblivious to the heat and potential for burns, both love and desire was evident in the golden depths. The dragon gazed at the scene for a moment, enraptured with her two unborn children and the love who had given them to her.

The woman in the bed stirred, and the dragon plating beneath her that kept her from burns, shifted. The dragon watched, concerned, to see if the sleeping figure would sustain any injury, but months of practice had taken hold and the woman merely rolled over onto her side to maintain her safe position, never awakening. This gave the dragon a very nice view of the muscular back and intricate blue and gold markings that wove themselves across the skin, up the shoulders, and then down the arms. They were not tattoos, but rather decorative scars of a warrior race that no longer existed. One strong arm wrapped around one egg and a leg hooked gently around the other, holding them both as close as possible.

Weynild settled in behind her young lover, who was young only in appearance. Well over three hundred years old, she was still young to Weynild, who was well over a thousand. Raine stirred again and smiled in her sleep, pressing up against the lithe body that pressed up against her.

"And how was hunting?" Raine murmured.

"I brought you some venison, since you refuse to leave the eggs."

"You've had children," Raine reminded her. "These are my first."

"Hmm," Weynild said, blowing warm air over Raine's skin, an extremely pleasant sensation.

Yes, Weynild thought, she had children, amazing children. Her daughter, Idonea, born from a fling with a human male, an offspring who was not a dragon, but a mage so powerful her gifts were still being discovered. And her son, Drakar, born from a coupling with another Ancient Dragon, the youngster already coming into his own in the dragon hierarchy.

But these two, she thought, musing at the eggs as she ran her hands through Raine's hair, these two were going to be something else. As a gift, the Allfather had turned Raine into a dragon for a day and a night, a male dragon, so that the two of them could mate. And she had delivered not just one, but two eggs, which was almost unheard of amongst dragonkind. Her gestation period had been remarkably short, so the fact +she had delivered two eggs had been even more astonishing.

These two would be dragons, that much was clear. But they would also be Scinterian, the greatest warriors ever known in Arianthem, for Raine, when she was not a dragon, was the impossible offspring of two diametrically different races. The Scinterians were violent, brilliant combatants, living to fight and fighting to live. They had saved Arianthem during the Great War but had suffered such losses their race could not recover and died out.

Raine was also Arlanian, a heritage she often considered more a curse than a gift. The Arlanians were a gentle, extraordinarily beautiful race that were so sexually desirable they were raped into extinction when discovered by the peoples of Arianthem. Neither male nor female until adulthood, they possessed violet eyes for which wars were fought and kingdoms were sacrificed. Her children would also be Arlanian, for as Raine so aptly put it, there were no "half-Arlanians" or "half-Scinterians." Raine was both fully Scinterian and fully Arlanian, an impossibility that now her children would share.

The warm breath reached the sensitive ear canal and had the desired effect. Raine rolled over to face her lover, naked save for the intricate markings snaking over her torso. Her eyes were a dark lavender, a color she hid when around others. But she could not hide them when looking at Weynild, for deep emotion revealed them, and she loved no one more than her dragon.

"Is this really appropriate?" Raine said, teasing. "In front of the children?"

"They're dragons," Weynild said drily. "They'll be born understanding this."

Raine laughed, for that was true. The lust of the dragons was legendary, and really, Weynild's lust was beyond legend. It was only her great love for her Arlanian Scinterian that kept her faithful, not because Raine demanded it, but because Weynild wanted no other.

"Besides," Weynild said, kissing Raine on the neck, "you know, amongst the Ha'kan, bonds are created with the unborn child when having sex with the mother during pregnancy. The degree of sexual intensity between the mother and her partners determines the strength of the bond between the partners and child once the child is born."

Raine rolled on top of Weynild, playfully pinning the dragon, although really, that was impossible given that Weynild possessed all her strength regardless of form. "If that's true with us," Raine said, bending down to lightly kiss her love, then kissing her more deeply.

"Then these children will be more mine than yours."

It was dark when Weynild awoke, the glowing embers the only light in the enormous cave. It was a new moon, so the night sky was filled with stars undiminished by its glow. She lay on her back, gazing up at them through the vast opening in the ceiling. Her golden eyes flicked to her eggs, nestled safely in the warmth, then to the dark figure silhouetted against the entrance to the cave. She sighed and got to her feet.

The arms that embraced her from behind were welcome to Raine, as was the gentle kiss on her neck. Her life was filled with joy right now, the imminent birth of her children, the time alone with the love of her life, and the peace that had settled across the land since their defeat of the Queen of the Underworld.

It was this last thought that caused a shadow to pass over her features, caused the only darkness that intruded upon her happiness these days. Her jaw clenched reflexively. Weynild could feel the tension in her lover and instinctively knew its source.

"Are we ever going to talk about what happened to you?"

It had been almost a year. A year since Weynild had been captured by the Goddess and encapsulated in a tomb of amber from the sap of the Tree of Death. A year since Raine had been taken by Hel and made her Consort, forced to endlessly bear her attentions. A year since the two had outwitted the Gods themselves and taken over the Underworld. A year since relinquishing the fruits of that conquest had yielded the two eggs that lay peacefully in the nest on the far side of the cave.

"You mean with Hel."

Weynild sighed again. "Of course, I mean with Hel."

"I told you my fears," Raine said, "and every one of them came true."

"Your fear was that you would respond to Hel because you're Arlanian. And I told you that I loved that part of you and expected nothing else. And I would rather her seduce you than rape you."

Sometimes Weynild's pragmatism was difficult to bear. "I should have been able to fight her off," Raine said.

Weynild shook her head. "No. You shouldn't have. There are few things in this world or any other that are more powerful than you, and the fact that one of them desires you is not your fault."

Raine's voice was thick with emotion. "I never betrayed you. My body did. But my heart didn't."

Now Weynild's sigh was filled with exasperation as she took her lover by the shoulders and wheeled her about. "Your body didn't betray me, either."

Raine did not appear convinced.

"There's something you should know," Weynild said. "When I was trapped in my tomb, I couldn't see, hear or feel anything. My only connection to life was you. We are one, our souls knit together by the ceremony of binding, which meant that, deprived of all sensation, I felt everything you felt."

Puzzlement appeared on Raine's face. "Everything?"

"Yes," Weynild said. "Everything. I felt your loneliness, your sadness, your helplessness, and your rage as you leaned against my prison. I felt your unwavering love for me, your disgust with Hel, your continual self-recrimination, and," Weynild said, pausing with emphasis, "everything else."

It took Raine a moment to digest this. "Everything else?"

"Yes. Everything else. I felt your pleasure," Weynild said, "just as if it were me. And I can tell you right now, based upon that shared experience, I'm now of the opinion that Arlanians are the strongest creatures to ever exist. Anyone else would die from those sensations."

"Sooo...," Raine said, still absorbing this information, "you were present for all of that?"

"Oh yes, I experienced it just as if it were me. And let's just face it," Weynild said dismissively, "Hel always was good in bed."

An impish grin tugged at the corners of Raine's mouth, one that made Weynild's heart swell for it had been absent for too long. "So, it was more of a threesome that entire time?"

"Hmmph," Weynild said. "Something like that. Although I would have liked to kick one of those three out of bed."

"It was a good thing Hel didn't know that," Raine mused, "I think she would have liked to bed you more than me."

"Hmmph," Weynild said again, "it would've been close. I think the Arlanian would have won. But it's a good thing she didn't know she had us both."

Her words were sarcastic, but Raine's lightened mood made Weynild's immortal heart sing. They had been passionate as always, and it had helped that their first sexual congress had been in dragon form, something completely different than anything that had come before. But Weynild had remained a dragon until the eggs were laid, and a looming shadow had remained over their subsequent lovemaking. Now it seemed that shadow had passed.

Raine took the silver-haired woman's hand and began leading her back to the nest. "So, you think Arlanians are stronger than Scinterians?"

Weynild picked her way through the scattered bones. "Without a doubt," she said, "don't forget it was the gifts of your mother's people that defeated Hel. Although the combination of a Scinterian and Arlanian is frightening."

Raine laughed. "Just think what our children will be like."

Chapter 3

For the thousandth time, Raine leaned forward to peer at the eggs, for the thousandth time, reminding herself she needed to breathe. And for the thousandth time, nothing happened, and she settled back against the rock with a sigh.

"Your constant vigilance will not make them hatch any faster," Weynild said mildly.

"Are you sure it'll be today?"

"I believe so."

And indeed, the birth appeared imminent. The shells of the eggs had grown more translucent of late, the vague outlines of the little creatures inside visible from certain angles. Raine had examined every one of those angles, trying to get a look at the baby dragons. Weynild had watched her affectionately, suppressing her own growing excitement as the shells thinned in preparation of hatching.

"Well, they're certainly taking their time," Raine said.

"They are that," Weynild agreed. "They arrived quickly, but they've spent longer in those eggs than even Drakar did, and I'm certain he set some type of record."

"Do you think they're all right?"

"I'm certain of it, my love. Stop worrying."

Raine settled back into her vigil, convinced that the eggs would never hatch. Then the slightest movement of one of the eggs sent a shock of electricity through her. She watched intently, wary that it had been her imagination, when the other egg also rocked slightly back and forth.

"Did you see that?" Raine whispered.

"I did," Weynild murmured, and she could no longer hide her pleasure.

Raine was rapt as one egg moved, then the other. A hairline crack appeared in the first, spider-webbing outward from a tiny internal blow. Another appeared on top of the second egg, traveling downward like a slow bolt of lightning. Both fissures spread, but at an infinitesimal pace as the baby dragons struggled to free themselves from the sacs that had sustained them.

The Arlanian in Raine wanted to help the dragon chicks out, but the Scinterian stood fast. They needed to fight their way into the world. Weynild, too, stood back to watch her infants struggle. In the first egg, a tiny wing appeared, flapping about with little coordination, but having the desired effect. The crack widened enough that a large, dark eye appeared, the indeterminate color of newborns, and peered out at the world. It was enough to spur the baby forward, and the tiny dragon attempted a roar that made Raine cover her mouth to muffle laughter. The creature smacked its oversized head against the weakened shell wall, causing it to split enough that half the baby spilled out of the egg. Exhausted, the newborn rested for a moment, its head freed, but its limbs, body, and tail still confined.

Raine turned her attention to the second egg. The initial splintering of the shell had been impressive, but now the baby struggled against the many pieces that were still webbed together by the sac. The creature attempted to thrash its way free, then made a honking noise that somehow expressed both irritation and frustration. Weynild rolled her eyes. The personalities of both her children were already on display.

The honking noise drew the attention of the first baby, who gave a growl of encouragement to the struggling sibling. It also spurred the tiny dragon forward, and tiny limbs freed themselves enough to push the clinging eggshell downward and away, allowing the baby to roll over onto its side and use its tail to worm free from the remaining sac. It lay in the nest, breathing heavily.

Not to be outdone, the second baby engaged in a brief frenzy of wing flapping that opened the top of the egg, but also caused it to topple over, sending the baby sprawling half out of the shell. The tiny creature gave another belligerent honk, which caused the sibling to raise its head. Although exhausted, the infant dragon awkwardly pulled itself upright, staggered left, then just as quickly fell over, somehow managing to smash its clutch-mate's egg enough to mostly free it. The two baby dragons chortled, clucked, and cooed at one another.

A brilliant flash of yellow light filled the cave, and then the enormous red dragon lowered her head to her babies. She nudged them gently with her giant head, and the infants stared rapturously at her, instantly recognizing their mother. The magical scene filled Raine with joy.

Weynild gently lifted a baby in her jaws, and the long neck wound around as the gaping, fang-filled mouth carried the little dragon to the lake, dipped it in the water, then gently returned it to the nest. The sinewy neck snaked downward and collected the second to repeat the act. This one honked a little protest at the chill of the water and fluttered happily once returned to the warmth of the nest.

Now that they were clean, freed from the remnants of the egg and amniotic sac, Raine examined them with delight. They looked much like baby birds, giant, scaly, baby birds. Their heads were enormous relative to their overall size, with eyes that were big relative to the head. It was apparent both had difficulty holding them up. Their necks were scrawny and struggled to balance that giant head. Their torsos were also large compared to their limbs and tails. The scales on them were patchy, spots of serpentine skin showing through the immature coverage.

"Ugly little things, aren't they?" Weynild said fondly.

"Don't speak of my children that way!" Raine said with mock indignation. She was as proud as Weynild. She crawled toward the fluttering pair, and their little wings twitched at her approach.

"Hi, my babies," she said softly. The two little dragons raised their heads, and two sets of giant eyes examined her, blinking curiously. Raine could see that one would have light eyes, probably gold like Weynild's. The other's were dark, probably blue like hers. The one with blue eyes also had dark scales, whereas the scales of the other were already flecked with red. Raine smiled, and the two little dragons gazed at her intently.

And then both of their eyes turned purple.

"By the gods," Weynild whispered.

Both baby dragons flapped awkwardly forward, pulling themselves toward the creature they somehow also knew was their mother. Raine gathered them to her, embracing them as lavender tears gathered in her eyes. She lay back against Weynild so they could rest their heads upon her chest and stomach. She softly stroked them as their little wings twitched and they fell into a deep, contented sleep.

Weynild encircled the nest with her enormous girth, then wound her neck around so she could watch her lover and her newborns. The enormous golden eye half-closed with contentment as she stood vigil over her family.

Weynild again wheeled about to make her approach to the mountain keep, bringing food for all inside. She landed, folding her wings so she could fit through the entrance, then stalked forward, her tail scraping along behind her. Raine was babysitting, a bemused look on her face as the infant dragons staggered around awkwardly, flapped their wings, and bit at one another.

"Should I scold them? Or is that normal?"

"Entirely normal," Weynild replied, dropping a carcass to the ground.

Raine picked up one baby to separate them, carrying the darker scaled one several feet away. "They're already heavy," she commented.

Weynild's white teeth appeared. No normal being could lift them up at all. Infant dragons were small relative to her enormous size, but they were already nearly larger than Raine, and growing fast. Weynild tore off a large chunk of meat and dropped it to the little black one, Kai'a. The miniature dragon mauled it ferociously, tossing it about for effect while Raine chuckled. Weynild tore off another chunk and her neck snaked over Raine's shoulder to drop it off to the little red one, La'i'na. This one stalked her prey comically, then pounced on the meat, which caused her to tumble and somersault over it.

Weynild snorted out a breath of hot air, but Raine knew the antics pleased her. The little scamps were already showing their bloodthirsty side.

"I thought Kaia was going to be black," Raine said, "but I think her color is actually purple and maybe a little blue."

The gigantic red head lowered to the baby crunching through a bone, and she nudged the little one, eliciting a trilling noise and a fluttering of wings. When the light hit the scales just right, they did indeed look dark purple. And with her dark blue eyes, it reminded Weynild of the blue orchids that grew in the fields next to her cottage in the wilds. The giant head moved to the other, giving another affectionate nudge, which was greeted with an absent-minded trilling as the baby gorged itself. This one would look much like her. The scale pattern was beginning to even out, and although still dark, there were areas where the red was beginning to peek through. And the eyes were definitely going to be gold. Baby dragons by nature's design were drab, but these two were already showing signs of their future markings.

The long neck pulled back and a flash of yellow light accompanied Weynild's transformation. She stepped through the steadily growing pile of bones that was her children's nursery. She reached out to stroke their ridged brows. When she had first transformed, they eyed the change curiously, but then nuzzled her scaled armor. The little ones knew their mother regardless of form. Weynild picked up Laina as effortlessly as Raine had moved Kaia.

"Let's put you back in the nest, little one."

The baby curled her tail about Weynild's waist while she carried her, and it twitched in happiness when she set her down in the warm sand. She did, however, honk plaintively until Weynild repeated the action and brought her twin to her. The two baby dragons head-butted one another, then curled about each other, cooing and clucking softly.

Raine cut a slice off what was left of the carcass and speared it to cook over the open fire. Soon, the aroma of sizzling meat filled the cave, and coupled with the greens and berries Weynild had also brought, Raine had an exceptionally good meal. Washed down with the ice-cold water she collected from the wall of the far side of the cave, it was perfect.

"Better than anything I could get in Fireside."

This was one of the many reasons why Weynild so loved her Scinterian. Most creatures sought out dragons because of rumors of extravagant wealth, but Raine had been perfectly happy in the mountain keep, and in Weynild's simple cottage in the wilds. Raine herself had quietly owned Fireside for years, an incomparable mansion in the imperial capital where she spent little time.

The two had agreed the children should be kept a secret. Baby dragons were not defenseless, but both Weynild and Raine had powerful enemies who would crush their children given the chance. Or worse, would use the children against them to create a vulnerability that was not present in either. And the keep was a perfect place to house them: private, elevated far above the valley below, and inaccessible except for a near-impossible climb up the sheer face of a cliff wall, or by dragon flight. And even if someone were to somehow access the cave, it was always protected by an enormous Ancient Dragon, or the greatest warrior Arianthem had ever known. And most of the time, by both.

Weynild was lying on her back on a rock sunning herself, which she did in both forms. Raine admired the outline of her body, the firm breasts, the shapely body, the long arm cast carelessly over her forehead, the leg that dangled off the edge. She determined she would join her love and tossed the remains of her dinner in the fire. Weynild would later cleanse the area with a blast of fire that kept the muss at a minimum, leaving only bleached bones behind. One last look at the children, and if they were asleep, perhaps she could join her love for more than a nap.

Everything was quiet in the cave save for the gentle trickle of water down the far wall, and Weynild enjoyed the silence. She frowned a bit, for it had not been this quiet in the cave for some time. She opened one golden eye and it settled upon Raine, who stood at the edge of the nest, frozen.

"Um, Weynild?"

This caught Weynild's attention because like most who saw one another all the time, they rarely addressed each other by name.

"Could you come here a moment?"

The tone was difficult to decipher. Not upset, but strange. Not concerned, but somehow conveying import. Weynild got to her feet.

The soft glow of the embers lit Raine's features as she stared down into the nest. As Weynild came up behind her, the dragon gasped.

"Is this normal?" Raine asked.

There were two infant girls in the nest, not dragons, but humans, or at least human-like. One had silky black hair, golden eyes, and a mischievous expression on her face. The other had light blonde hair, dark blue eyes, and an equally proud expression of what they had just pulled off. Their tiny, perfect limbs kicked, and their eyes glowed with accomplishment.

"Do dragons shapeshift this young?" Raine asked.

"No," Weynild said, shocked. "They don't. Most dragons are incapable of shapeshifting until they become adults. Drakar was extremely talented, and even he could only do it as an older juvenile. And that took decades."

Raine carefully stepped into the nest and reached down and picked up Kaia. She held the baby at arm's length, and the infant simply stuck a fist in her mouth as she grinned. Weynild followed suit and picked up Laina, who reached out her tiny hands to grasp at her mother's hair.

Raine gently drew the child into her embrace, then took Laina from Weynild so that she held them both in her strong arms. There was a feeling in her chest, an explosion of warmth as she was overcome with emotion. It was not that she loved the children any more in their current form, for that was impossible. It was the understanding of what had just occurred. She looked down at them with violet eyes as they looked up at her with the same.

"They—," Raine had to pause, for there was a catch in her voice.

"They did this for me."

"So, they're dragons?" Halla asked.

"Oh yes," Idonea replied. "Absolute little monsters."

"That seems so hard to believe," Astrid replied.

And indeed, it was difficult to believe because the two little girls were barely toddlers, tiny, delicate little creatures, beautiful beyond description. They were content to be passed around amongst the four Ha'kan, the group now including Gimle, who had been summoned posthaste and responded forthwith. She had been as dumbfounded as Halla, Astrid, and Senta, and as enamored. The twins, not identical, but clearly related, were full of personality, and although yet unable to speak, had no need as they were both so expressive.

"Dragons," Halla repeated in wonder.

"Don't let their appearance fool you," Idonea said. She took a sip of tea and adjusted the comforter across her knees. "They possess all the cunning and hellfire of my mother, and all the power and strength of Scinterians. I can only imagine they'll possess all the allure of the Arlanians when grown. These are undoubtedly the most dangerous creatures in all of Arianthem."

"This must have been Talan's heart's desire," Halla said, "this is what she gave up the Underworld for."

"Yes." Idonea took another sip of tea, thoughtful. "I don't think my mother wanted to be Goddess of the Underworld; she just wanted to save Raine. But this is what the Allfather offered her in return for abdicating that throne. Few would have accepted that deal. My mother? She didn't give it a second thought."

Chapter 4

The twins' ability to transform back-and-forth was remarkable, but they preferred to spend most of their time as dragons. They transitioned to human form in the evening, not every night, but at times so they could cuddle with Raine and sleep in her arms. Other times, they slept intertwined with one another in their natural form, tails wrapped about the other, necks resting on the other's torso. Sometimes Raine would join them, and Weynild's girth would encircle the lot.

To Weynild's eye, Raine had the patience of a saint. When the babies first attempted to blow fire, there were several times when Raine was covered from head to foot with soot, as the children were not very accurate, nor very disciplined when they began to attack one another in play. As the skill of the tiny dragons increased, Weynild grew concerned that Raine would be seriously burned, for indeed it was only her extraordinary coordination and speed that had kept her from injury thus far.

Finally, one day, after another near miss, Weynild disappeared for several hours and returned with a satisfied look on her face. Raine was curious at the enigmatic mood and the subtle anticipation present in Weynild. That anticipation seemed to peak when several weeks later, Weynild again set flight early one morning and disappeared over the horizon. Raine played with the baby dragons for hours, running them ragged throughout the cave as they tried to catch her until they at last collapsed on top of one another in the warm sand. Given a moment's respite, Raine went to the entrance of the cave and sat on the cliff's edge, her feet dangling thousands of feet above the ground.

It was not long before the distant figure of the dragon appeared, tiny on the horizon, but distinguishable from birds by the slow, rhythmic up-and-down movement of the wings. The silhouette was also distinguishable by its massive size, which became apparent the nearer the creature came. Raine admired the beauty of the red dragon, a queen among magnificent monsters. It still enchanted her to watch Weynild in flight, the grace evident as the behemoth blocked out the entire sky. The ground gave only a little shake as she tilted her wings and landed.

Raine shielded her eyes from the flash of yellow light, and then her love appeared, gorgeous beyond words.

"I've brought you a gift," Weynild said, pleased.

"A gift?" Raine asked. "For what occasion?"

"Do I need an occasion to give the love of my life a gift?"

"No," Raine said, frowning. "But I've nothing to give you in return."

"That's doubtful," Weynild said, giving her a once-over that communicated exactly how she expected to be repaid. "I can think of many things you're going to give me before the night is over. But this gift is one of necessity, and quite frankly, it's overdue."

Raine's brow again wrinkled as she tried to guess Weynild's intent. But the dragon would not keep her waiting any longer.

"You've been without this for too long."

Weynild unfolded the vestments she held and Raine simply stared. Her throat grew thick with emotion and she was unable to speak. The dragon grinned, knowing it was the perfect gift.

It was a suit of armor, but not just any armor. It was the lightweight and highly functional armor of the Scinterians, unique and unmistakable in design. Hel had destroyed Raine's armor in the Underworld, and although she had little need of it in the mountain keep, at times she missed it keenly. She had spent months re-creating her weapons with materials provided by Weynild's meticulous foraging, shaping Scinterian blades that were perhaps even stronger than her original weapons since these were forged in the dragon fire of the Queen of all Dragons. But she had not recreated her armor and did not think she had the skill to do so.

"It's beautiful," Raine said, stepping forward and reaching out to touch the breastplate. Her previous armor had been leather, specially cured in a process that gave it a bluish cast "But what is this made of?"

The armor was flexible, as soft and malleable as leather. And it was a dark maroon that was almost black. When Raine's hands brushed the material, a shock went through her.

"These are your scales," Raine murmured. "This is made from your dragonplate."

"Yes," Weynild said. "Ground, and then crafted by the most skilled smiths in this world."

"The dwarves," Raine said. "They made this."

"Not just any dwarves. It was the Deep Miners, requiring a meeting that was coordinated by Lorifal."

Raine grinned at the name of her dear friend. "I doubt they required much convincing. You should see the statue of you they have in their underground hall. And of me," Raine said, frowning as she remembered the nude depiction, a memory that then made her laugh.

"Why don't you put it on?"

Raine took no convincing and was stripping out of her clothes before Weynild finished her sentence. This nearly delayed the fitting as the dragon was distracted by the lithe, muscular form that now stood nearly naked before her. She moved the armor away as Raine reached for it.

"You would deny me my gift?" Raine said teasingly.

"No," Weynild said, handing her the armor. "But you're going to give me my return gift as soon as you've tried it on."

"I'll gladly do so."

The armor consisted of a light set of mail that was optional, covering her torso, upper arms, and upper legs if needed. She pulled the mail on, marveling at its light weight and pliability given the material from which it was made. She then slipped on the breeches which fit her snugly but not too tight, allowing for a full range of motion, and then the cuirass which consisted of both the breast and back plate. Finally, there were bracers and greaves which were also surprisingly lightweight given their indestructibility, then a pair of beautiful boots.

"How do I look?"

Weynild was completely silent, but the glow in her amber eyes spoke volumes.

"You're magnificent," she said at last.

Raine grinned, a little shyly, and it made Weynild's heart ache. This creature, who had defeated a Goddess, who had saved Arianthem, who was monstrously powerful, had at times the innocence of a child.

"And now," Weynild said, "let's test it." She scooped a handful of embers from the nest, blowing them to life in her hand, then flung the conflagration at Raine.

It struck the breastplate center of mass and exploded in a fiery burst that went in every direction. When the flames subsided, Raine stood in the center of the burned area, unscathed.

"And now not only are you magic-proof," Weynild said with satisfaction, "you're fire-proof as well. Dragonplate will not burn."

"Now I can play with the children without holding back," Raine said. "But how does it fit me so perfectly?"

Weynild moved to embrace her, pulling her close. "I was able to describe your physique with extraordinary accuracy, although truly, the Deep Miners kept losing concentration for some reason."

The bracers were coming off, as was the cuirass. The boots followed, as did the greaves, the breeches, and then the mail. The dragon was only satisfied when the body before her wore nothing but her Scinterian markings. Her own scaled armor retracted, responsive to her mental command, and firm breasts pressed against that well-developed torso, as hungry for her Arlanian as the very first day they had met on this hallowed ground.

"Do you remember," Raine said, her voice muffled by a passionate kiss, "our first night here?"

Weynild ran her hands down the muscular back. "When you stumbled into my keep? How could I ever forget?"

"I was already in love with you as a dragon," Raine said, her lips working their way down to a breast and suckling it for a moment, eliciting a gasp from the silver-haired woman. "And then you transformed into this, and I was completely lost."

Weynild grasped her hair, pulling her lips to her mouth once more, while a hand dipped to stroke between her legs. "And I thought for sure you would run at the sight of an old woman."

"Old?" Raine said. "Are you joking? It was only fitting, and anything else would have been a disappointment. You're stunning."

It was yet another reason why Weynild adored her Scinterian. She had the ability to transform into anything yet maintained an appearance consistent with her dragon form. And Raine had loved both unreservedly.

The two went to the ground in the soft, warm sand, their lips as one, their bodies entangled, all hands exploring sacred ground. Weynild moved on top of Raine so that she could gaze into the depths of those violet eyes. But the eyes were focused elsewhere as Raine had her head cocked to the side, listening.

Weynild pushed herself upward to look over the rocks that shielded them from the view of the nest. A pair of golden eyes peeked at her over the top of the make-shift embankment.

"Laina," Weynild said, "go to sleep."

The baby dragon honked in disappointment, but the head disappeared back into the nest.

Raine chuckled as Weynild lowered herself once more. "That one is definitely your daughter." She then gasped as Weynild immediately shifted her attention and pierced her with some fortuitous appendage she had just shape-shifted into existence.

"Yes," the dragon said, beginning her rhythmic movement, "yes she is."

Chapter 5

The children scrambled about happily blowing fire at Raine. And Raine, easily able to dodge their clumsy attacks, occasionally let them score a hit so they growled and chittered in delight. Her new armor protected her as designed, deflecting the flame without burning her. The two baby dragons attempted to pounce on her, even growing sophisticated enough to coordinate their attacks, but she laughingly dove out of the way or leaped high above so they collided with one another. Before they grew too frustrated, she would let them tackle her, and they would pin her triumphantly, wings fluttering and tails twitching in elation. The elation would be short-lived, however, because she would send them tumbling with her enormous strength, laughing as they went sprawling in different directions.

"It's a good thing you're unbreakable," Weynild observed from her vantage point on the rock.

Raine's cheeks were flushed with high spirit and exertion. It was a joy to play with the infant dragons. They were growing out of the odd, out-of-proportion bodies that all newborns seemed to share, regardless of species, and were becoming darling little creatures.

They also were beginning to exhibit distinct personalities. Laina was bold, headstrong, rushing into things with an unrestraint that reminded Raine of a young Idonea. Kaia, on the other hand, was measured, thoughtful, at times humorously solemn for one so small. And she would maintain this solemnity right up until Raine would do something that made her curl up into a ball, chortling with laughter. Or her sister would bait her from her seriousness with some antic that also made her wind up in a little reptilian knot, shaking with hilarity.

Kaia's eyes were indeed blue, and Laina's were gold, but that was only when they were not purple, which was most of the time. If they looked at Raine, or at their mother, or at each other, the eyes went to a shade of lavender that astonished Weynild and tugged at Raine's heart every single time. She had known no other Arlanians in her lifetime, so the connection she felt with her children was beyond precious. Anyone else who saw the violet in her eyes felt lust, but her children felt only love. And no one loved as selflessly or as deeply as an Arlanian.

The children were growing tired, evidenced by Kaia's drooping eyelids and half-hearted attempt to parry Raine's mock attack. Laina was even less subtle, nodding off, then jerking herself back awake before she nearly fell over.

"Come on you two," Raine said, "it's time for a nap."

Normally she would lie down with them, but they were so tired they curled about one another in the nest and were instantly asleep, legs twitching, wings fluttering as they joyfully incinerated things in their sleep. Raine stroked the serpentine necks, then got to her feet to join Weynild, who had moved to the entrance of the cave. Raine settled down in front of her and leaned back against that full cleavage while Weynild buried her face in Raine's hair. A comfortable silence descended on them, finally broken by Raine.

"I can almost hear you thinking."

Weynild sighed contentedly and took a moment to reply. "I'm having two distinct, but related, thoughts."

"Go on," Raine said, enjoying the feel of the sunlight on her face.

"You need to get out of this cave."

"What?" Raine said, leaning forward so she could turn around. "Why would I want to leave the keep?"

"Because you've not left since we mated. Not once."

"I'm perfectly happy here with you and the children."

"I know that," Weynild said. "But your friends miss you."

"Lorifal?" Raine asked, returning to her leaning position.

"Yes, and Feyden as well. I saw both when I went to retrieve your armor, and I could fairly feel their reproach."

Raine laughed. "I doubt that. They're both terrified of you. Far too much to show any reproach."

"Then perhaps it's my own guilt," Weynild said, nuzzling her hair in a manner that reminded Raine very much of her dragon form. "I've traveled far and wide while you've been a prisoner here."

"A prisoner?" Raine exclaimed. "First off, I'm hardly a prisoner. I do everything of my own free will. Second, if I were a prisoner, I can't imagine a more glorious way to be held captive."

"Okay," Weynild said, taking a deep breath, "we're getting off topic."

Raine could tell by the rise of the breasts at her back that her dragon was becoming aroused. It was only by the greatest self-discipline that Weynild brought the conversation back on track.

"Even so. I think it would be good for you to get out with your friends. Go hunting. Go destroy a tavern somewhere."

Raine frowned. "And how would you and the children eat?"

"You're not going for that long," Weynild said. "Don't think I'll allow you apart from me for more than a few days."

At this proclamation, Weynild ran her hands possessively through Raine's hair, which thrilled her, for they had been apart far too many times, and each time, for far too long. She never wished to be apart from her love again.

"But it'll take me a day just to climb down this mountainside," Raine said, "and at least two to climb back up."

"No," Weynild said, "I'll fly you down."

Raine shook her head. "Absolutely not. We agreed the children would never be left alone."

"Well, that brings me to my second thought."

Raine was both skeptical and curious. "Which is?"

"Perhaps it's time the children met the rest of the family."

Raine stood expectantly at the edge of the cave, watching the horizon for the unmistakable silhouette that was her love. She glanced back at the nest, frowning at the two pairs of eyes that peeked over the top. The eyes promptly disappeared and there was much rustling as the baby dragons returned to their agreed hiding places.

When Raine's eyes readjusted to the sunlight, she could see the dark outline in the west that indicated a dragon was coming. And because a dragon's wing motion was as distinct as a gait, she knew that it was Weynild. Another silhouette appeared behind Weynild, this one sleeker, smaller, the wings moving slightly faster, and it brought a smile to Raine's face. She knew this one as well.

The outlines of the two dragons grew larger, and because she was looking for it, Raine saw the deviation in the outline of the second dragon that indicated it had a rider. This brought about a full grin, for riding a dragon could be an enormously sensual experience. And Idonea had chosen to ride her brother, a decision that had likely brought Drakar both pleasure and pain. The poor boy had an unnatural crush on his sister that Weynild constantly sought to deter, and one which Idonea exploited without end.

The two dragons maneuvered skillfully so that Weynild alighted first, and Drakar shortly thereafter. The ledge was just wide enough for the two enormous dragons. Raine gave a quick glance over her shoulder, frowning at the two wide-eyed babies who stared out at the black dragon. They caught their mother's glare and ducked back down into the nest with a flurry of rustling.

With a brilliant flash of yellow light, Weynild transformed. As per her usual custom, she greeted Raine with a lengthy, passionate kiss that caused Idonea to roll her eyes as she sat atop Drakar. Raine caught herself and pulled away so she could assist Idonea to the ground. Once the chivalrous move was accomplished, a flash of red light made the black dragon disappear, and a dashing dark-haired young man dressed in black stood in its place.

"Drakar," Raine said, "you're as handsome as always."

Drakar smiled a brilliant smile, every hair on his head in place, his thin, stylish moustache twitching at the compliment. He took Raine's hand and kissed it, lingering an inappropriate amount of time.

Weynild cleared her throat and Raine retrieved her hand.

"Idonea," Raine said, and that was all she needed to say as she embraced the young woman with the laughing dark eyes. Firm breasts threatened to spill from an ensemble that was surely held together by magic.

Weynild sighed, for both of her children had dragon's blood running through their veins, which meant that lust and sensuality was imbued in them as much as the dark magic that fed their power. Drakar would become an Ancient Dragon, seeking to bed just about anything that moved, and Idonea was already a mage of vast power, who could and would seduce anything that brought her pleasure.

"I haven't seen you in ages," Idonea exclaimed to Raine. "I knew you two would hole up, fucking one another's brains out for the Divine knows how long, but really, this was longer than I expected."

"I'm so proud," Weynild said dryly under her breath.

"Well," Raine said, "it's been a different type of pleasure that's kept us from your company."

Raine's tone caught the attention of both Idonea and Drakar.

"There's something I want you both to see."

Drakar looked at Idonea, and Idonea looked at Drakar. Raine motioned for them to follow, and Weynild fell in behind the group. Idonea, for whatever reason, found herself holding her breath, and Drakar felt a strange tension that made him want to run but also never leave.

They approached a make-shift berm, where sand was pushed upward at the edge of a rounded-out bowl. Heat was emanating from the bowl, created by the embers that lined the edge of the soft sand. The four stopped at the edge of the berm.

"By the gods," Idonea said at last.

Two little dragons stared at them, frozen in indecision. A little dark, blue-eyed dragon gazed at them, flicked a glance to Raine, then stood steadfast. A golden-eyed baby flicked her gaze to her twin, to Weynild, to Raine, then back to the strangers, then also stood resolute. And then both their eyes turned violet.

"By the Divine," Drakar murmured.

Raine stepped into the nest to reassure her little ones. But they had already sensed the bond with these two, hence the color of their eyes. Their wings fluttered, their tails twitched, and they fairly shook with restrained excitement.

"The gift from the Allfather," Idonea said, "your greatest heart's desire."

"I already had two perfect children," Weynild said, "I just wanted one more. And I was given two."

Idonea sat on the edge of the berm and swung her legs over so she was in the nest. Laina scurried over and put her nose on her lap. Idonea stroked the little ridged brow, marveling at the golden eyes.

"Hello, little sister," she said softly, then laughed. "I know what you're going to look like when you grow up."

Drakar also slid into the nest and moved toward Kaia. The little dragon observed him warily, then bounded to the left, crouching. Drakar also crouched, grinning, and the little dragon pounced on him. The two wrestled playfully, then Kaia skittered away again, gaining enough momentum to make it up the berm and leap out of the nest. Drakar followed her, laughing the entire time. Laina could not help herself, and bounded away from Idonea, following them up the berm and then out into the cave to join the fun.

"He's probably never been around a baby dragon," Weynild mused. "Hopefully, his relationship with them will be a little more 'normal' than his relationship with you."

"Well," Idonea said, "it will help that he actually knows they're his sisters. And that he's met them as infants."

This conversation caught Raine's attention. "What happened with you?"

Idonea's low, sensual laugh reminded Raine very much of Weynild. "Drakar met me when I was a young woman—"

"You were still a child," Weynild corrected.

"Well, were I human, I would have been a woman—"

"You are not human," Weynild said drily.

"Are you going to let me tell this story or not?"

"You clearly cannot tell it right," Weynild said, turning to Raine. "Drakar was born over a century before Idonea, but because dragons age so slowly, he was still essentially a juvenile. When I realized I was 'with child' with Idonea, no one was more surprised than me. I isolated myself in the wilds so I could remain in human form and give birth to her naturally. Idonea also grew very slowly, no doubt due to her dragon blood, and she was a little girl for a very long time. When she was finally beginning to blossom, Drakar just so happened to decide to visit me. They met, neither knowing anything about the other."

"So, he fell in love with you," Raine said slowly, "not knowing who you were."

"And I admit, I had something of a crush on him," Idonea said.

"He was a toy to you," Weynild said. Her words were not harsh, nor judgmental. They were very matter of fact. "He was something new and shiny, and you played with him. But his feelings were very real. He was devastated when he learned that Idonea was his sister. He compensated for his heartbreak by fucking everything that moved."

Idonea bestowed a knowing look upon her mother, and Weynild relented. "Very well. He is my son, so he probably would have done that anyway. But I hope by introducing them now he'll have a far more traditional relationship with Laina and Kaia."

And as Raine watched Drakar with the two little ones, any misgivings she might have had eased. He was joyful with them, running about the cave, splashing through the shallows of the lake as they chased him. And when Laina prepared to blow fire at him, he sent a well-timed spray of water in her direction that left the tiny dragon emitting nothing more than white smoke. Kaia curled up in a ball, her little sides heaving in the dragon's equivalent of doubling up with laughter.

Idonea watched her brother fondly and when he caught her eye, he winked rakishly and blew her a kiss.

Weynild sighed. "Two steps forward, three steps back."

"Well, two-and-a-half steps back," Raine said. Although it seemed his improprieties with Idonea would continue, Drakar was perfection with the babies. Playful, gentle, protective, full of fun, he was going to be a very good big brother.

"So, now I can transport you to your friends," Weynild said. "The children will be guarded by a dragon and the most powerful mage in Arianthem. And they'll be fine for the few hours it will take me to go and return."

"Are you sure?" Raine said doubtfully. The thought of being away from the children and Weynild filled her with dread, although that dread was offset with the thought of seeing her friends again.

"Yes," Weynild said. "It'll good for you to get away for a few days."

Chapter 6

Raine splashed water over herself as Weynild watched her naked form languorously from the shore. The sunlight glinting off that perfect body was glorious to behold, and were they not already late, she would have taken her to the ground once more.

"I think I missed that almost more than anything," Raine mused, drying herself as best she could.

"You mean flying on my back?"

"Of course, I mean 'flying on your back,'" Raine said. "There were times while the eggs were incubating, I debated having you fly around the cave just so I could enjoy that."

Dragons were enormously proud and allowed few to ride them. The first time Weynild offered the honor, the sensation of that sinewy neck between her legs, the rhythmic movement of the wings, and the very pleasant pressure created by the two nearly caused Raine to climax on top of Weynild. The two often joked that dragon-flight was not necessarily faster than walking for them. Raine was relieved that no other dragon elicited the same response; but Weynild elicited it just about every time.

"Get up, you," Raine said, holding out her hand, then pulling Weynild to her feet. "We're already late."

"I'm surprised the wood elves aren't hiding in the bushes," Weynild said wryly, "they do enjoy watching us."

Raine grinned at the reminder. She and Weynild had engaged in epic sex atop one of the mountain shrines dedicated to the Queen of all Dragons, and when they were done, collapsed to the sight of two stunned elves standing at the bottom of the stairs, mouths agape. Raine was certain that episode was already woven into elven lore somewhere.

She gathered the small armory she carried with her: a long sword, two short swords, and two daggers. Once her ensemble was back together, Weynild mentally shrugged her own armor back into place.

"That must be nice," Raine commented, and the two were off.

The walk was not far, for Raine had almost made it to the wood elf encampment before she succumbed to the sensation of Weynild's flight. It was likely the scouts had seen Weynild's approach.

They exited the forest into a clearing, and the sights and sounds of a fairly permanent settlement greeted them. "Fairly" was accurate, however, because if the need ever arose, the wood elves could disappear into the forest within hours, leaving little sign behind of the dwellings that had been there for decades.

A hue and cry greeted them, pure joy from a people that adored Raine, and pure reverence from a people that worshipped the Queen of all Dragons. If it had been Raine alone, she would have been smothered with hugs and back slaps without end, but the dragon kept everyone at a respectful distance as the two made their way through the camp. But the delight was palpable, for they had not seen either Talan or Raine since the epic battle in the Underworld.

Raine approached two enormous stone pillars that bordered a platform serving as the entrance to a cave, the only permanent part of the settlement. And here, "permanent" was perhaps an understatement, for these pillars were older than time, engraved with elven glyphs that few could even still translate. But one who could read those markings stood at the bottom of the stairs between the two pillars. A tiny, ancient elf dressed in dark green robes leaned on a gnarled staff. She had waited with great anticipation for the two that were now before her.

"Matriarch," Raine said, kneeling not in submission, but out of respect, to get on the same level as the diminutive elf. Wise green eyes examined her.

"Hello, Dragon's Lover," Y'arren said, and a smile split that wizened face.

Raine also grinned, for Y'arren addressed her with the title from a prophecy, a prophecy she had turned on its head to defeat the Goddess of the Underworld. Y'arren turned gravely to Talan and bowed. "Talan'alaith'illaria."

Weynild nodded, and it gave Raine something of a thrill, reminding her exactly who her lover was, the Queen of all Dragons. She experienced this, of course, with no sense of her own revered position amongst these people, something that gave Weynild an equal amount of pride.

"You will stay with us awhile?" Y'arren queried.

"I cannot stay," Weynild said. "I'm needed elsewhere. But Raine may stay as long as she likes."

"A few days," Raine said, "no more. But I promise those days will be filled."

A searching gaze probed Raine's blue eyes, and Raine inwardly sighed. She could hide nothing from Y'arren.

"We should go inside," Y'arren announced, and Raine and Weynild clasped hands as they obediently followed.

The interior of the cave was considerably cooler than outside, and a firepit exuded warmth. Many candles provided light, and the air was full of a woody incense, probably something derived from the Santalum plant that flourished in the nearby forest. Y'arren settled on a wooden bench cushioned with numerous hides, and Raine and Weynild settled across the fire from her on a similar bench.

Weynild stretched out her long legs, amber eyes reflective mirrors that gave no clue to her thoughts or emotions. She was vastly different around mortals than when she and Raine were alone, and Y'arren would not address her out of respect. But Raine, Raine she had known for nearly three hundred years, and she would speak to her as she willed.

"You are well, my goddaughter?"

Raine smiled at the endearment, for Y'arren had indeed adopted her many, many decades ago. "I'm very well, thank you. We both have healed, physical and otherwise."

Y'arren now turned that very probing gaze on the dragon; she was not certain that was the case, for the dragon exhibited signs of a fatigue she had not seen in centuries. Those amber eyes swung around to her with a knowing, meaningful look, one demanding her silence. Y'arren obeyed and returned to Raine.

"But I sense a luminance about you, something new."

As if on cue, the attendants who were ever at Y'arren's side disappeared, and the three were left alone. The silence grew pronounced in the cave, for Raine was not ready to speak of her secret. Y'arren filled the silence by leaning forward to tend the fire.

"Would you like some tea?" she offered.

The tea was dispensed with great ceremony, and the three sat sipping it mindfully.

"Ah," Y'arren said with satisfaction, "the Camellia has bloomed beautifully this year. As apparently, have many things."

Raine's eyes slid sideways to Weynild, who at last spoke.

"Yes," the dragon replied. "Many things have bloomed this past year."

"I see," Y'arren said, then fell into a contemplative silence.

The silence grew extended, and Raine helped herself to more tea to somehow fill the gap in conversation. She offered it to Weynild, who declined, her golden eyes on the elven seer who stared into the fire.

"Maeva's little treasure, the one with eyes like yours," Y'arren said, changing the subject, "sent me a scroll just last week."

"You speak of Kiren," Raine said, and Y'arren nodded.

Kiren was a young human, an imperial noble who owned the entire border between the Empire and the land of the Alfar, the high elves that occupied Mount Alfheim. Maeva was the powerful Directorate of the Alfar, and in an incident that seemed almost humorous in hindsight, had kidnapped Kiren because she had become enamored with her. It was fortunate for everyone that Kiren had fallen in love with Maeva or it might have set off a diplomatic firestorm. It was also fortunate that Kiren, a gentle little soul, also possessed a brilliant mind and a spine of steel, for it entertained many that Maeva had met her match in the little woman-child.

The reference to Raine's eyes meant Y'arren shared Weynild and Raine's belief that Kiren had an Arlanian ancestor in her lineage, something that should have been impossible.

"Kiren believes she's found another prophecy."

"Another prophecy?" Weynild said, shifting in a subtle movement that spoke volumes.

"Yes," Y'arren said. "It's one that I've not seen, but bears similarities to the first."

Raine and Weynild exchanged glances, for the first prophecy was about Raine. And Weynild and Raine had turned that prophecy upside down to defeat Hel.

"What do you mean 'another' prophecy? There was only one, the one that referred to me as the 'Dragon's Lover.'"

"Yes," Y'arren replied, then repeated the mantra. "'The Dragon's Lover, felled by the closest of allies, carries into death without dying, that which saves all worlds. And then the final line," Y'arren said, turning to Weynild, "which it appears you knew before anyone."

The amber eyes were again reflective mirrors, revealing nothing. "Whose destiny it is to be the Consort of the Queen of the Underworld. Yes, I knew the translation, hence my desire to become Queen of the Underworld, at least temporarily."

Things were getting off track for Raine. "Yes, we dealt with all of that. We had a plan that miraculously worked, with a last-minute intervention from a few Gods, but what's this about a new prophecy?"

"This language is even older than that before. It was written in stone, on an artifact hidden and forgotten for centuries. Only a scholar of Kiren's depth could have found it."

"And what does this artifact say?" Raine demanded.

"Patience," Y'arren counseled. "It's uncertain, and little has been translated. The language it's written in no longer exists, and Kiren seeks to piece it together from languages that are themselves dead."

"What has been translated?" Weynild asked.

"Only one line," Y'arren said. "To defeat that which cannot be defeated."

"Well that doesn't sound very good," Raine said, and her understatement made Y'arren laugh, relieving some of the tension.

"No, it doesn't. But without the rest of the prophecy, it means nothing. That's the third line of four. But there is one other word in the first line that's been deciphered."

"And what is that?" Raine and Weynild asked in unison.

Y'arren's eyes glowed in the soft light from the fire.

"Child."

It was with enormous relief that Weynild glided into her mountain keep to find all her children safe and sound. False and insignificant prophecies abounded, but the elven seer Y'arren was not one to sound the alarm without cause. It was all she could do to talk Raine into staying in the forest for a few days, convincing her that the words were obscure, unconfirmed, and possibly entirely unrelated to anything and anyone they knew.

Still, as the sleek black dragon romped about the cave with his baby sisters, and the dark-haired mage laughed at their antics, Weynild's thoughts wandered to the black days through which they had passed. Truly Raine had borne the brunt of those events, drawn into the Underworld through trickery and deception. She had endured the attention of a Goddess who was obsessed with her, and Hel's obsession was made worse by the fact that revenge played a role, for Weynild had spurned Hel as a lover hundreds of years before Raine was even born.

"You've been very serious since your return," Idonea commented.

The firelight flickered on Weynild's fine features, highlighting her cheekbones and causing her amber eyes to glow.

"It was hard to leave Raine in the forest," Weynild admitted. "We've not been apart for any length of time since she returned from the Underworld."

Idonea nodded her understanding, silent for a moment. "You know," she said, "when you first sent Raine with us on that quest years ago, I wasn't impressed. I thought her lazy, even a little cowardly. And then she took off the head of that Marrow Shard without even trying."

Weynild laughed, for she had heard the tale many times from Raine's comrades, and it never ceased to entertain her.

"But I knew her far better by the time I realized you two were bound together, and when she expressed regret that you, an immortal, had tied yourself to her, I told her I thought you might have gotten the better end of the deal."

Weynild was not insulted by the observation, mainly because she shared the opinion. "I bound myself to her because I loved her and wanted to protect her. I also sought to circumvent that prophecy. But it's been she who's protected me. She gave me her lifeforce when my enemies sought to drain it, and that's the only reason why I'm here today. And," Weynild added, "because my daughter is the most powerful mage in Arianthem and was able to break the bonds that were killing me."

"Thank you, mother," Idonea said, for a compliment from Weynild was rare and momentous. Perhaps the infants were softening the old dragon. "My point is this, I know you worry about Raine, but I can tell you this…" Idonea's tone was casually ruthless.

"If the Goddess comes for her again, Raine will take off her head as easily as the head of that Hyr'rok'kin."

The words comforted Weynild, as did Idonea's brutal nonchalance. "You know," Weynild said in her low, husky voice, "despite your physical form, you're as much a dragon, perhaps even more so, than any of my children."

The words brought warmth to Idonea. For much of her life she had been angry and rebelled against her mother for not having been born a dragon.

"I don't know," Idonea said, watching the twins. "Laina is going to be a handful."

"Yes," Weynild replied. "She reminds me a lot of you."

"Really? Because she reminds me a lot of you."

Weynild turned her amber eyes upon Idonea and looked at her pointedly.

"Both of those statements are correct, in case you haven't noticed."

A slight flush of pleasure reddened Idonea's features, a once-in-a-lifetime event Weynild pretended not to notice.

A comfortable silence ensued, but Weynild broke it when at last she spoke her mind.

"When Raine returns from the forest, I'd like you and Drakar to go to the land of the Alfar."

"The Alfar?" Idonea asked. Here was the burden that was on her mother's mind.

"Yes," Weynild said. "It might be nothing. But I need you to speak to Kiren. It's possible she's found something."

Chapter 7

aine was with a group of wood elves, admiring a rack of finely crafted bows, when the "thunk" of an axe in the earth at her feet caused several of the elves to leap aside and draw weapons. Raine merely sighed, examining the beautifully crafted weapon, one so heavy it was unlikely that any of the elves could have lifted it, let alone wielded it in battle. And yet Raine pulled it from the earth with one hand, hefted it as if it were a dagger, then flung it back in the direction it came.

It was caught, also one-handed, by a belligerent-looking dwarf who was accompanied by a handsome, slender elf who merely rolled his eyes at what was about to unfold.

"And that is how you greet me?" Raine demanded.

"It is," the dwarf said angrily. "What do you expect when you abandon your friends?"

"I expect a little understanding," Raine said, "a little leeway for the things that might occur in life."

"You'll get none," the dwarf announced, and prepared himself to charge.

"Very well," Raine said, bracing herself, "so be it."

And the dwarf charged, an unstoppable force of muscle, momentum, and determination. But the unstoppable force met an immovable object, and the collision was epic, sending spectators flying in every direction. When the dust settled, Raine had the dwarf in a headlock and was rubbing her knuckles vigorously across the top of his head.

"I yield, I yield!" Lorifal exclaimed, his ruddy cheeks bright with pleasure.

"Fine," Raine said, releasing her beloved friend with laughter. She gasped as the dwarf lifted her off her feet and nearly broke her ribs with his enthusiastic embrace.

"And, how are you?" Raine said, turning to one she loved equally.

"I'm well," Feyden said, smiling, an unusual gesture for the taciturn elf. He, too, embraced Raine, with slightly more decorum, but no less emotion. It was clear these three possessed a unique bond; the type that was forged in blood and combat. Although many had now been to the gates of the Underworld, almost none had been there twice.

Lorifal examined Raine's armor with appreciation. "That is beautiful."

"I understand you had a hand in its creation."

"Not a physical hand," Lorifal said, "more of a hand of influence. One of the benefits of being on the Dwarven Council. Although," Lorifal added, "the Deep Miners would have done it for Talan with or without my help."

"Yes," Raine said, "I saw her statue, and mine, underground."

Lorifal guffawed. "Then you know they worship you both."

"That is beautiful," Feyden said, echoing Lorifal. He had seen it before, but not on its wearer as he did now. "Is it heavy?"

"It's surprisingly light," Raine replied. "As light as my Scinterian armor."

"And I imagine almost indestructible, if it's made from Talan's dragonplate."

"It is," Raine said, "although I doubt we'll meet anything in the forest that will require such protection."

"Speaking of which," Lorifal said, "I have another gift for you. And this one I did have a hand in crafting."

This caught Raine's attention, for Lorifal's clan did not forge armor; their expertise was weapons.

"Granted," he began, "this was a difficult project, almost doomed to failure from the start. We had to research scrolls, tomes, finally even fairy tales to get any sort of detail. Our first effort was a disaster, as was the second and third. There were so many problems and mechanical issues to overcome, in the end we didn't think we would be successful. But fortunately, I'm one of the few who has actually seen this thing in action, so I was able to fill in the blanks here and there."

Raine was baffled, and Lorifal's anticipation was palpable.

"I made you this."

The dwarf's features were ruddy with pleasure as he brought the device from his knapsack. Raine stared in disbelief at the shiny object.

"Is that—?"

"Here," Lorifal said, "take it."

Raine reached out hesitantly, first merely touching the strange item, then taking it into her hand. The weight felt good, well-balanced, promising.

"Go ahead," Lorifal said, "try it."

A deep breath came from Raine as she held the weapon, then snapped her wrist forcefully in one direction, then immediately the other. The bow snapped out to its full length in a smooth motion, and Raine stared at the Scinterian bow in wonder.

Lorifal sighed in relief. "None of us were able to accomplish that maneuver, so I wasn't sure it would work."

The bow delighted Raine. The leading edge was wickedly sharp, hence part of the reason it was carried folded. The only place it could be held with any degree of safety was the center, and just snapping it to a ready position required enormous skill. It was a weapon that few could even open, let alone wield, and it could serve as much as a melee device as ranged.

"It's beautiful," Raine said, breathing out. She carefully folded it, then snapped it out once more with a flick of her wrist. She repeated this act several times.

"She makes that look easy," Lorifal said, his prodigious eyebrows lowering in a frown.

And Feyden had to smile, for it was easy for a Scinterian to wield a weapon that was designed for no one but them.

"It's a testament to your skill, my friend," the elf said, "that no one can wield it but her."

They left the wood elf encampment, promising to leave their game at specified intervals for their followers. It was high hunting season and they hoped to bring in enough food to last the wood elves through the colder season. The wood elves were perfectly capable of hunting their own meat, but right now they were dealing with an anomaly. Like many of the people of Arianthem, they had experienced an increase in the number of births after the war. Although this was a blessing, it brought difficulties. The little ones required protection, and their parents were reluctant to leave them, all at a time when there were more mouths to feed than ever. Raine was overjoyed to help them with such a wonderful problem. Between her, Lorifal, and Feyden, she thought they could stock them with stores for the entire winter.

Raine breathed in the fresh air of the forest. As much as she missed Weynild and the children, she realized she had also missed this. Her friends, wandering through nature, the thrill of the hunt, all reminded herself of a part of her she had put aside to raise the infants. She could not wait to bring the little ones down and teach them to hunt. She would make them their own Scinterian weapons and teach them to use them the way she had been taught, at least while in their human form. Weynild could teach them dragon tactics, and they would be able to utilize the best of both.

Feyden observed his friend's sunny disposition and it warmed his heart. He feared for what she had suffered at Hel's hands, but something was bringing a smile to her face right now, that was for certain.

They hunted for hours, leaving behind two bears, an enormous panther, six elk, and a particularly venomous lizard that was about six feet long and had given them an incredible fight. This kill was doubly useful: it was a violent and dangerous beast that needed to be purged, and it would give Y'arren and her acolytes a supply of poison that could be used for everything from weaponry to antidotes.

It was starting to get dark and Feyden was going to suggest they make camp when Raine raised her hand, and the elf and the dwarf froze and went silent. Raine did not look concerned, however, merely in a state of deep concentration.

"Do you smell that, Feyden?"

At first, he did not, but gradually he detected the faintest aromas: a campfire, various noxious odors that suggested alchemy, and the more welcome smell of some type of stew.

"Hmm," Raine said thoughtfully, "Juniper. Bloodroot. A little bit of Primrose and Black Hawthorn."

"And a little bit of garlic," Feyden said, tilting his head to one side.

Lorifal smelled nothing. Had it been a vein of ore, gold, silver, even iron, he would have detected it first. But in this he was required to rely on his friends. And Raine did not appear worried at all.

"I think I know who this is," she declared.

It was about a third of a league through the forest, and in about a quarter of an hour, they approached a campfire that now glowed brightly in the dark. Raine did not seek to disguise her approach and made enough noise to announce their arrival.

Three women raised their heads to the intruders, but once they identified Raine, the intrusion became no imposition at all. A beautiful witch with pale green irises gazed upon the now-welcome guest with little-disguised lust in those striking eyes.

"Hello, Raine."

Lorifal and Feyden exchanged glances at the sultry greeting, for Raine had admirers spread throughout Arianthem who did not hide their desire. Somehow, Raine always managed to take it in stride.

"Valka," Raine said. "It's a pleasure to see you."

The beautiful witch would take what liberties were allowed, and as Raine neared, Valka leaned forward to kiss her on the cheek, a kiss that just managed to brush the corner of Raine's mouth and cause the slightest flicker of purple in her eyes. Valka observed the purple with pleasure.

"It's a good thing your dragon's not here. I'm sure she would bite me in two for that."

"She is a bit jealous," Raine said, shrugging off the impropriety. Valka was an extraordinarily powerful witch who could be a valuable ally, so Raine allowed her a certain latitude. She turned to the other witch, Valka's sister. Unna was plainer, a bit rounder, but sweeter in disposition. Raine clasped Unna's hands to her chest, which brought a flush of pleasure to Unna's eyes.

"And you remember...?" Unna said.

Raine examined the young woman before her, half the age of the other two but with the same pale green eyes as the first. "No," Raine said. "And yes. I believe she was a deer the last time I saw her."

"Yes," Unna said, drawing her niece close to hug her. "You saved her life."

Raine bowed to the young woman in a chivalrous manner which reddened her cheeks. "I'm pleased to see you've recovered."

"It's only because of you that I live at all," the girl stammered.

Valka watched the exchange with her mocking gaze. It was a long story, but she was the one who had turned her daughter into a deer as a punishment, and then asked Raine to rescue her when poachers had endangered the doe.

"And why have you graced us with your presence, Scinterian?"

"No reason," Raine said. "This is Feyden of the Alfar, and Lorifal of the Dverger. They're my friends, and we're simply out hunting."

Valka's pale eyes examined the two, unblinking. "They are your comrades and allies that have twice accompanied you to the Underworld. The elf is the twin brother of the Directorate of the Alfar, and the dwarf sits on his people's High Council."

"Yes," Raine said mildly. "But they're also my friends, and we're simply out hunting."

Valka examined them a moment longer, then relented. "Then you'll join us for dinner and stay in our camp tonight."

Lorifal slowly released his breath. This witch was sparring with Raine as surely as had both been wielding swords. Only now did she sheath her weapons and lower her guard, and Raine nodded for the two to relax.

Feyden, too, felt the tension drain from him. The witch's demeanor was unnerving, a combination of frightening power and a lust for Raine that was palpable. But Raine, as always, seemed to control the situation with an insouciance that was supernatural.

The stew the witches provided was delicious, flavorful with a bit of heat and spice to it. Feyden deigned to take seconds, and Lorifal downed four bowls. Raine would have liked to follow Lorifal's lead, but politely mimicked Feyden.

"Still hungry?" Valka said across the campfire.

"No, no," Raine said in a manner that suggested anything but.

"I wouldn't want you to leave dissatisfied."

Feyden coughed into his hand and Lorifal stopped his spoon halfway to his mouth, where it hovered.

"I assure you I'm fine," Raine said, and Valka made a noise of disappointment. The Arlanian was completely unobtainable, this she knew. But it would not stop her from flirting unmercifully. And although she knew the woman was immune to magic, she often wondered if any of the various potions she had at her disposal were enough to immobilize, even if temporarily, the enchanting creature.

Almost as if Raine followed her train of thought, Raine's conversation became more direct, albeit still polite.

"I can't help but notice that all of you seem a bit more powerful than last I saw you."

Unna beamed with pleasure and her niece blushed. But Valka's pale eyes caressed her across the firepit. "Yes," she agreed. "It's the strangest thing. But I have felt something stirring."

Feyden assessed this response. Unlike mages, witches seemed a part of something larger, ebbing and flowing with unseen events, tied to forces that had nothing to do with them individually. Although Raine was completely immune to magic and could not wield it at all, she seemed to have some sort of connection to it that was beyond understanding. He had sensed nothing.

"I saw a sprite at the water's edge earlier today, and I would swear I saw a nymph off in the distance."

"A nymph?" Unna blurted out, then blushed.

Raine grinned. "Yes, down the creek to the south, just where it bends to the east, and where the four rocks are stacked to look like an altar."

It was a deliberately specific description, and Feyden knew why. Nymphs were magical creatures doomed to sexually satisfy anyone who demanded their services. That said, they were positively obnoxious about it and generally reveled in their fate, which is probably why Raine felt no remorse about revealing the creature's whereabouts.

"I see," Unna said, memorizing the location.

But the revelation was not enough to deter Valka from her desired prey.

"I'm not sure why, but I've seen an explosion of magical creatures in the forest. I saw a centaur the other day."

Raine nodded. "I saw a satyr, something I haven't seen in over two decades." She mulled this sighting. "Do you have any idea why?"

It was a question fraught with meaning, and although Valka was speaking to an Arlanian she desired more than anything in Arianthem, she was also speaking to the Scinterian who had saved them not just once, but several times.

"I've seen this on two occasions," Valka said. "I saw it over two decades ago when the Hyr'rok'kin began to vomit from the earth, and you and your band stopped them." With these words, she gave a subtle nod to Feyden and Lorifal, respectful, but also reinforcing the fact she knew exactly who they were.

"And I saw it recently, several years ago when again the Hyr'rok'kin began to appear."

Raine considered these words as Valka continued. "That time, the manifestation stopped rather abruptly."

Raine's jaw clenched, and Valka did not miss the involuntary response. It had stopped because the Goddess of the Underworld had taken this one captive and instantly lost all interest in the mortal realm. Consistent with the mercurial, unpredictable nature of witches, Valka was both grateful for Raine's sacrifice and aroused by the fact that Hel had likely fucked this one without mercy.

"And now?" Raine asked quietly with venerable control.

"I'm not certain," Valka said. "It's the same surge of magical power, but this time there's no Hyr'rok'kin invasion. I haven't seen them at all."

Raine settled into silence, staring into the fire. She had been apart from Arianthem for well over a year in her mountain cave, but she had noticed the differences instantly upon her return. They were subtle, but to someone who had seen them before, the signs were recognizable. Something was happening; it just was not identifiable yet. Magical creatures were appearing in number. The only thing that was missing was the Hyr'rok'kin. Granted, the Allfather had forbid Hel to meddle in the mortal realm, but it was only a matter of time before she found a way around that edict.

Raine sighed. She really thought it would have been longer.

The Raven sisters retired to their tents, and Raine, after declining one last invitation from Valka, joined Feyden and Lorifal on her bedroll before the fire. It was cold, but the fire emitted a welcome heat that left the three drowsy. Raine gazed up at the stars, tracing her beloved constellations as her eyes grew heavy.

She frowned. The constellations had changed. They were strange, foreign, and filled her with a deep foreboding. How could this be?

She tried to turn her head and found she had difficulty moving. Her limbs felt leaden and her mouth would not move when she tried to speak. Try as she might, she could not even raise a finger. She could only stare up at the unwelcome, alien stars.

She did not sense either Lorifal or Feyden, and felt like she was no longer outside, but rather inside in some infinitely large space, despite the presence of the stars. She tried to control her breathing, but her chest was tight. And more than anything, she was so cold she was freezing. Her body began to tremble.

And then she felt it. A malevolent, obscenely powerful presence, one filled with equal parts lust and rage. It was angry with her, no, furious at her, for her disobedience, her sacrilege, but most of all for her betrayal and infidelity. Then the eyes appeared in the darkness, blood red with a slit pupil, much like a snake. And they resolved into emeralds, glittering with malice and desire. Then the lips appeared, as blood red as the eyes had been, and they resolved to the dark red of a rose on the verge of corruption.

"Hello, little one."

The words of the Goddess were crushing, arrogant, vicious, triumphant, and petrifying. She loomed over Raine, her pale skin the only thing visible in the blackness, her full breasts heaving with the depth of her fury. And Raine's eyes involuntarily flicked to those breasts because she had only one weakness outside her love, and it was this being.

Hel laughed an awful laugh, pleased that the Arlanian still desired her. It did not diminish her fury, for this one had humiliated her as none other. Defeated in her own realm, her throne taken, she had been disgraced in front of the Allfather himself. Her own brother had chosen this one over her, and all of Arianthem had disobeyed her edict to come to her aid.

"Where am I?" Raine muttered through gritted teeth, her jaw clenched to keep the teeth from chattering.

Hel ignored the question. "You have no idea how much I've missed you," she said sarcastically. Her hand moved to the prone figure, for she wanted to punish the Arlanian in the most brutal and effective way possible.

Raine tried to pull away, but she was still immobilized. The hand settled on her lower leg, and the fingers began to trace their way up her calf, then to her inner thigh, then hover expectantly before they settled between her legs. The touch caused Raine to jump which came out more of a twitch since she was so restrained. The hand lingered possessively, preparing to enter what it considered its eminent domain.

"No!" Raine screamed, and began to struggle wildly, all her mobility and strength returning. But it was little use, for the strength of the Goddess was overwhelming, and even a Scinterian could not overcome it. Hel just laughed as Raine helplessly flailed against her.

"Raine! Raine!"

The voice was distant, and she thought she recognized it as a friend, but still she struggled mightily.

"Raine!"

Finally, she recognized this far-off voice as Feyden, her friend and comrade, which did not cause her to cease struggling, but slowed her fight.

"Raine!"

Raine opened her eyes to find herself pinned by Feyden and Lorifal, Feyden struggling to control her upper body while Lorifal desperately sought to contain her legs. Lorifal had a bruise on his forehead and Feyden had a trickle of blood running down from his lip.

"Raine!"

At last the panic and plea in her friend's voice penetrated her terror and she stared dumbly up at him while her body slowly went limp. Feyden himself had to struggle for control because her eyes were the most beautiful shade of violet he had ever seen, and even he was not resistant to the charms of the Arlanians.

"Feyden?" Raine said uncertainly as her eyes phased back to a dark blue.

Feyden was grateful for the color change as his control returned.

"Yes," Feyden said, "yes, it's me. It's me and Lorifal."

He released her and leaned back on his haunches while Raine pulled herself to sit upright. Lorifal still had a death grip on her lower extremities, and she patted him on the back.

"I think I'm okay, old friend."

Lorifal released his hold even slower than had Feyden, as if testing her. She patted him again.

"No, I'm fine. It's okay."

Raine took stock of her surroundings. Apparently, she had put up quite a fight because the campground was in total disarray. Pots and pans were strewn about, the embers from the fire were spread wide, and the remains of the stew were spilled on the ground. Three pairs of eyes stared from the tent openings, two wide with surprise and one narrowed in contemplation.

"Sorry about that," Raine stammered out. "I seem to have had a nightmare."

Unna clucked sympathetically, and she and her niece disappeared back into the tent. The pair of light green eyes, however, stared a bit longer, assessing, then they, too, disappeared into the blackness of the tent.

Raine sat back on her bedroll, trying to control her breathing. She never had nightmares. Her dreams were always pleasant, of her love and the children, or of nothing at all.

"So, what was that about?" Feyden asked, settling back onto his own pack. He watched Raine carefully. In all the years he had known her, he had never known her to have nightmares. Lorifal, too, gazed at his friend, troubled.

"Nothing," Raine said, crossing her arms over her chest and hugging herself. She rubbed her arms. "Just a bad dream."

The elf and the dwarf exchanged looks and said nothing.

But Feyden had felt how cold Raine's body was in the struggle, and even now he could see the bluish cast to her skin. And as her breathing calmed and her eyes paled to a gray blue, he could see the condensation in the air as she breathed out a stream of almost pure frost.

When Feyden awoke, the campground was cleaned and Raine sat sharpening her swords. He marveled at how quietly she had moved, for she had straightened everything without making a sound. He wondered if she had slept at all. She was in the process of scratching out a note on a piece of parchment, a "thank you" to the Raven sisters, when Valka came out pulling a shawl about her shoulders against the chill of the morning air. She approached Raine, and those pale green eyes again assessed her.

"A bad dream?"

Raine's stony silence told Valka all she needed to know. "Mages and witches have so much in common," she began, watching the Scinterian gather her things.

"They both use magic, most of the time dark. Certain forms, such as necromancy, are used mostly by witches whereas others, such as mechanical, are used mostly by mages. Mages tend to use objects such as staves or magical artifacts to augment their power, whereas witches tend to use alchemy and potions. But there's one distinct difference between witches and their magical brethren."

Feyden found himself holding his breath for the conclusion of the impromptu lesson.

"Dreams are exclusively the domain of witches."

Raine's head was bowed for a moment. "Tell your sister I said goodbye, and thank you both for your hospitality," she said quietly, then turned on her heel and left. Lorifal and Feyden followed Raine from the campsite.

"Take care, Scinterian," Valka called out after them.

It was a far more subdued group that hunted that morning, and Feyden wondered if they were going to deplete the entire forest, so efficiently did Raine kill. Before the sun even peaked in the sky, they had brought down more game than the entire previous day. Fortunately for the remaining animals, she decided to take a break while they fled in all directions.

Raine settled on a rock and took a long, preoccupied drink from her flask of water. Lorifal sat down next to her and took a long drink from his own flask, but it was not water he was drinking. When he offered it to her, she raised an eyebrow at him, for it was early in the day, but then took the container. The licorice-flavored liqueur he carried with him burned all the way down but felt good. Lorifal then offered it to Feyden, who always refused, but he surprised them both by accepting the flask. He took a deep drink and welcomed the fire that settled into both his cheeks and his stomach. The three sat in a comfortable silence and some of the tension seemed to leach its way from Raine's taut frame.

"Good god," she said at last, "there must be a herd of pigs trampling through this forest."

This startled both Lorifal and Feyden, for Raine appeared to be addressing no one, and they had no idea what she was talking about.

"Or perhaps piglets," Raine said disapprovingly, "squealing through the underbrush."

Feyden was afraid that Raine's dream had so affected her she had grown addled, but a low-to-the-ground, slinking form caught his eye. It froze as if to avoid detection, but Raine just shook her head.

"Too late, I saw you. And I can hear the rest of you. It's a wonder you're able to feed yourselves with all that noise. Come out now."

And a pack of wolves bounded joyfully from the shadows, hopping about in a pup-like frenzy of happiness. Even the large ones dodged about playfully, crouching down on their forward paws with their haunches in the air, tails wagging furiously. Raine slid from the rock and greeted her friends.

"By the gods," Lorifal murmured. "That still surprises me."

"And I heard nothing," Feyden murmured back, "so who knows how long they've been stalking us."

"A little over an hour," Raine said, her hearing as acute with them as it had been with the wolves. "But I have a little more practice detecting them. They constantly try to sneak up on me."

The wolves yelped and barked and yipped in a flurry of conversation, as if they were trying to explain their shortcomings to the one they adored.

"Mm-huh," Raine said, "uh-huh. I see."

Lorifal grinned, for this was the Raine they knew and loved, the light-hearted warrior who enchanted even the fiercest of beasts.

And then Raine's smile grew, for there was one coming through the forest whom she dearly loved, one who perhaps had the ability to comfort her at this moment when few could. A gigantic wolf walking on his hind legs entered the clearing, and he was a head and shoulders above even Raine. Both Lorifal and Feyden bowed low, while Raine simply ran to her friend and hugged him.

"Fenrir!"

The wolf growled her name in a voice like thunder.

"Raine."

The embrace went on for some time, the contact expressing love, gratitude, admiration, so very many things. Finally, Raine pulled back but not away, unwilling to let go of the warmth of his fur.

"It got back to me that you were here, and then I received word you were unleashing a reign of terror most unlike you."

"That's why I stopped hunting," Raine said. "I'm done for the day."

"Then let's make camp here," Feyden suggested.

It was an excellent proposal, for they were on a plateau that received full sun, provided an unobstructed view of the valley below, and would be protected come nightfall. Not that they needed much protection, the stout dwarf, the skilled elf, and the lethal Scinterian, surrounded by a large pack of wolves and accompanied by the Wolf God himself. They made camp quickly, and Lorifal again brought forth his flask.

Fenrir transformed into a moody, brooding, muscular specimen of a man with flowing brown hair and dark brown eyes.

"And what's this?" Raine asked. She never asked Fenrir to change from his natural form to one in which he was less comfortable.

"Your dwarf is gripping the handle of his axe in a way that tells me he's not entirely at ease."

"What?" Lorifal sputtered. "No, no, I assure you I'm fine."

Feyden just laughed at him, and Lorifal took another swig from his flask.

Raine eyed the gorgeous creature before her. "I understand you created quite a stir in the Ha'kan capital when you appeared like that. They are an insular people and attracted only to women, but there were several who considered making you the exception."

The wolf god blushed and Raine wondered if he did that all the time underneath his fur.

"And I've not had the opportunity to truly thank you, my friend," Raine continued.

"For what?"

"For defying your sister and coming to my aid in the Underworld."

Raine had not seen Fenrir since her return to the mortal realm. He grew serious at the reminder of all that had transpired.

"You would have done the same for me."

"I would," Raine said firmly. "But still, you took a great risk. And Hel will seek to punish you for that."

The mane of hair swung around. "Not as much as she'll seek to punish you. You and Talan were the ones who defeated her. Something that has never been done before."

Raine sighed. "Then let's hope the Allfather keeps watch on this realm, as well as keeps his word."

Fenrir was not optimistic. The Allfather had forbidden Hel to meddle in the mortal realm, but he had seen the eddies of dark magic in the forest that indicated Hel was already attempting to find a way around that edict. And the Allfather could be both impulsive and inattentive, easily distracted.

"I dreamed of her last night," Raine said, her eyes distant. "It wasn't pleasant. I curse the effect she has on me."

Feyden recalled how cold her skin had been, a byproduct of the collision of purity and evil, but he did not think that was what Raine was talking about. Nor did Lorifal, but he sought to lighten the mood. "Your eyes turned purple the first time you saw that blue dragon. Dragons and Gods, would that I had only those two weaknesses."

The thought of Kylan made Raine smile, and she wondered how the Ancient Dragon was doing.

"Then why is it that I don't have that effect on you?" Fenrir said, teasing, but also a little morose.

"I'm guessing it's because, like the Ha'kan, I'm Ana'kari."

"Ana'kari?" Feyden asked, leaning forward. As long as he had known Raine, there were still things she was circumspect about.

Raine reached for Lorifal's flask, which he eagerly proffered. She took another swig and enjoyed the burn.

"My people, or rather my mother's people, are either Ana'kari, Ina'kari, or Ono'kari, meaning they are sexually attracted to women, men, or both."

"And this is determined when?" Fenrir asked, still hopeful.

"It seems from birth and fairly immutable," Raine mused, "which is saying something considering our sex is undetermined until we become of age."

It took a moment for Raine's words to sink in. Although all had heard the legends and tales of the Arlanians, most of the time they just did not see Raine in that light. And to hear her speak of her mother's people in the first person was most unusual.

"So," Fenrir said carefully, "you were neither male nor female before you became an adult?"

"No," said Raine. She marveled on the seeming impossibility. "Neither of my parents knew whether they had a daughter or son before they died."

"Would it have mattered?" Lorifal asked. For the dwarves and elves, it mattered not at all, although males were seemingly favored with the imperials. And for the Ha'kan it was not even an issue.

"No," Raine said. "Neither sex nor sexual preference made any difference to my people."

Again, it was a novelty to hear Raine address the Arlanians as "her" people as opposed to her mother's people. It seemed Raine was coming to grips with both sides of her identity.

"If I were female," Fenrir began, "you would react to me the same way you do my sister?"

Raine laughed. "Well, how am I supposed to know that?"

With a wave of his hand, Fenrir transformed into a gorgeous, earthy, buxom woman with long brown hair, deep cleavage, and fabulous skin. Beautiful brown eyes were framed with long, curly eyelashes that blinked fetchingly, and the lips were full and luscious. Long, lovely limbs pulled into a more delicate seating position, thrusting those breasts skyward.

Raine's eyes immediately turned purple.

Lorifal choked on his drink and nearly spewed it out, his love for the liqueur the only thing keeping him from wasting it. Feyden's mouth dropped open with an uncharacteristic lack of composure. The wolf god made a stunning woman.

"You will turn back now," Raine said, fighting to keep her tone even.

Fenrir laughed a booming laugh as he transitioned back to his male form. He could barely contain himself. "Oh, would that I knew that trick before you met Talan," he said with regret, still laughing.

"I'm glad you didn't," Raine muttered. It was unnerving the effect the gods, well, goddesses had on her.

"Oh my," Fenrir said, delighted with Raine's discomposure. Perhaps it was the fact those purple eyes had finally turned upon him, but more likely it was the comfort she was no more attracted to Hel than him, the difference being a mere artifact of biology.

"I'm sorry," Fenrir said at last, wiping the tears from his eyes. "I shouldn't have done that to you."

"No," Raine said thoughtfully. "I'm glad you did. It makes me feel a little better about my weakness towards her, knowing it's something more general than specific." It also warmed her that Fenrir would not dream of using the trait against her.

"Like I said," Lorifal commented, taking another swig from this flask. "Would that my only weaknesses were Dragons and Goddesses."

The wolf god left the following day, after a promise from Raine that she would be more accessible, and the three resumed their hunt. Finally, according to schedule, the little band returned to the wood elf encampment. They were greeted enthusiastically by all, perhaps even more so than usual since they had provided stores that would last for months. The wood elves were skilled hunters, but these three were in a category all their own.

"Y'arren'ikad'qeri," Raine said, playfully addressing the matriarch by her full, revered title.

"Raine'estania'illaria," Y'arren replied, returning the honor.

Raine smiled at the moniker. Her first name gave homage to her mother, the second to her father, and the third tied her to the Queen of all Dragons.

"I like that," Raine said, flashing a wolfish grin.

As if to punctuate the tie, a roar split the sky as Talan'alaith'illaria circled, then settled in a nearby clearing with an enormous thud and cloud of dust. When the dust cleared, a silver-haired woman in dark red dragon scale armor strode toward them. Raine drank in the sight of her lover, grateful for the time with her friends but desiring to be reunited with her soulmate above all else.

All bowed or went to a knee, but the dragon was oblivious as she had eyes only for her lover, and she took the young woman in a crushing embrace and kissed her with a searing passion. At last, the golden eyes flicked to the elven matriarch, one she would deign to acknowledge.

"And did my love provide you with food for all your young ones?"

"She did," Y'arren said, bowing low. "My goddaughter has blessed us."

The golden eyes then flicked to Lorifal and Feyden, two she would acknowledge because of their close friendship with Raine. "And did you keep her out of trouble?"

Feyden nodded smoothly but Lorifal blanched, thinking of the encounter with Fenrir.

"Really?" Talan said, the amber eyes sliding back around to Raine. "I look forward to hearing all about this."

Raine blushed, but Talan knew it was likely some minor incident Raine would feel the need to confess, like when her eyes turned purple upon first sight of Kylan. She would not let her off easy, however. "Hmm," was all she said.

"Could I speak with the two of you privately before you leave?" Y'arren asked.

The request was unusual, for Raine had determined she would leave as soon as Weynild arrived.

"Of course," the dragon said.

The interior of the cave was cool as always, lit by candles and smelling of herbs and spices that calmed and focused. Y'arren settled before the fire, adjusting her robes about her while Raine and Weynild sat down across from her. Weynild draped one long arm about Raine's shoulders, and Raine pressed against her love. A prolonged silence ensued while Y'arren chewed her lip thoughtfully, a sign that Raine recognized. The elven seer had something significant to say.

"Two nights ago," Y'arren began, "After you left, I had a dream."

Weynild felt the tension in her lover. Outwardly, Raine displayed nothing, but the stiffness in her body was unmistakable. Y'arren noticed nothing, or perhaps was too preoccupied with her own vision to observe Raine's involuntary response.

"It had no beginning and no end, and I can't place it any sequence. I can't identify a place or a circumstance, or even determine if it was the past or the future."

"What did you see that could have been the past?" Weynild asked. Y'arren was the only being in Arianthem nearly as old as she was, so there was much the two of them had seen that no one else had.

The ambiguity in Y'arren's vision was something of a frustration to her, which was evident to Raine and filled her with foreboding. This vision was incredibly important, for frustration was a foreign emotion to Y'arren.

"I saw a rip in the Veil," Y'arren began, "I saw demons pouring forth. I saw witches coming into power. And I saw the Aurg'el'mir."

"You saw the Titans?" Weynild asked in disbelief. "They're a myth. Even in my long life, I've seen nothing to suggest they were real."

"Nor mine," Y'arren agreed.

"Who are the Titans?" Raine asked.

"The El'mir are allegedly the ones who created the Gods," Weynild said dismissively. "I've seen no proof of their existence. They're a fairy tale, meant to explain the unexplainable."

Y'arren's relief was evident. It was clear she wanted the dragon to discount her vision, every part of it. "And in the realm of fairy tales, I also dreamed of Ba'kun U'ra'buros."

"Were you smoking Loph'o'phora?" Weynild asked. She was referencing a plant often used in spiritual ceremonies, and less often for recreational pleasure. It could be dangerous if misused, and carried a nickname associated with its religious purposes. The 'divine messenger' could bring insight, or it could just bring hallucinations.

The words bordered on insulting, but again, they brought comfort to Y'arren.

"You'll have to pardon my ignorance," Raine began uncertainly, "I don't know who U'ra'buros is."

"Another myth," Weynild said. "Ba'kun is the creator of all that is, every realm of existence. It's symbolized by the circular serpent that eats its own tail, and is represented in many ancient cultures. But again, without proof. Once the gods made themselves known, those cults disappeared."

"I can make no sense of it," Y'arren said. "Perhaps the rip in the Veil, the rise of the witches, maybe that was all part of the past."

Amber eyes captured those of the elven seer. "That is how the Great War began," Weynild reminded her.

"Of course," Y'arren said. Perhaps it was as the dragon said. All of it in the past. Witches. Demons. A rip in the veil. All of this had happened before. There were times when her mind dreamed visions, and other times when it dreamed to repair and organize itself. Clearly the dragon thought this was one of the latter.

"I'm more concerned with this new prophecy," Weynild said. "And I intend to send my son and daughter to the Alfar when we return."

Y'arren nodded at the wisdom of this action.

Raine, however, sat brooding while staring into the fire, witches and demons very much on her mind.

Chapter 8

It was only her incredible desire to see her children that kept Raine from misbehavior while riding Weynild back to the mountain keep. Y'arren's strange vision also successfully dampened her libido, and Weynild was very aware of the preoccupation of the youngster on her back.

Still, Raine's excitement grew as they neared the mountain, and Weynild wheeled about to make her approach. The fiery red dragon had barely alighted on the ledge when Raine bounded from her back and sprinted towards the baby dragons, who were in a flurry of delight at her arrival. They bounded about, jumped up and down, chased each other's tails, then tackled Raine with utter joy. Raine hugged the serpentine necks, pinned to the ground by the tiny monsters, her heart exploding with happiness. All three had eyes so dark purple they were almost black.

"They do love her, don't they?" Idonea said.

The scene filled Weynild with as much joy as her little ones. "They certainly do."

"And how are Lorifal and Feyden?" Idonea asked, addressing Raine.

Raine sat up, spilling the two dragons into the warm sand and starting another round of wrestling. Kaia and Laina tried to coordinate their attacks, but they were no match for the Scinterian. They backed off and circled her warily. Raine watched Laina out of the corner of her eye as she replied to Idonea.

"They're well, and they send their love." Valka had recognized Feyden and Lorifal as Raine's comrades from her forays into the Underworld; she would have recognized Idonea as such as well.

As Raine spoke, Laina attempted to ambush her from behind, and at the last minute, Raine stepped aside. The little dragon's misjudged jump sent her flying towards the lake, and all the frantic flapping of those little wings did nothing to alter her trajectory. She landed in the water with a great splash, and Raine doubled over with laughter. Kaia bounded over to make sure her sister was all right, then charged Raine with mock ferocity.

"Really?" Raine said. She caught the little dragon mid-leap and rolled backward, sending Kaia flying, this time towards a pile of soft sand. Again, a frantic flapping of wings was no help at all as the tiny reptile went head-first into the hill of sand. She came up coughing and sputtering, as indignant as her sister.

"Uh-oh," Raine said, her eyes gleaming, recognizing the dangerous glint in her daughter's eyes.

Kaia let loose a funnel of flame, much better than any she had produced before. Previously Raine might have allowed it hit her, counting on her dragonplate armor to protect her, but this one actually looked dangerous. Raine leaped skyward and the fire shot harmlessly beneath her. She landed, dodged right, then rolled toward the miniature dragon. Kaia, for her part, had frozen, astonished at the flame she had produced. She didn't know if she was in trouble or not.

Raine picked her up and hugged her. "That was amazing!"

The little dragon curled her tail about Raine's waist and laid her head on her shoulder, trilling softly. Laina came careening over, encircled Raine's legs, and Raine leaned down to encourage her as well.

"And you are very close to flying," Raine whispered, stroking her little ridged brow. "I saw you!"

Laina trilled in pride and happiness. They had worked very hard while their mother was gone.

Weynild picked up Laina and kissed her. "They always try to impress you."

Idonea marveled at the little ones, for it did seem like they were trying to prove themselves to Raine. She wondered if that was the Scinterian in them, for although both she and Drakar had spent their lives trying to make their mother proud, they certainly wouldn't have let her know it, and as youth had done it in a most counterproductive manner.

"Well, we should get going," Idonea said.

"So soon?" Raine asked.

"We're heading off to the land of the Alfar."

"Ah," Raine said, understanding. "Your mother is sending you to Kiren."

"I enjoy that little scholar's company."

"And I enjoy the elven women," Drakar said. Elves looked upon most other races as inferior and therefore dalliances outside their own kind were rare. Dragons, however, were an exception. Gorgeous, seductive, with rapacious sexual appetites, the only concern was for the fragility of the non-dragon participant.

"Don't kill any of them," Weynild said drily, addressing this danger.

"I'll do my best, mother."

Weynild kissed them both. The baby dragons hopped about, saying their goodbyes to their brother and sister. Idonea hugged them both, and Drakar, upon transforming, leaned his great head down and nudged them gently. He then leaned down so Idonea could mount him, which clearly gave him great pleasure.

"Drakar," Weynild said with mild exasperation.

"Don't worry mother," Drakar said as he moved to the entrance. "I haven't learned to fly quite as 'rhythmically' as you have." That great head turned about and gave Idonea a wicked look. "Not yet."

And then the black dragon leaped skyward, shooting out from the mountain and wheeling about in a pinpoint turn. The black wings caught a thermal updraft, and the dragon glided upward before he turned west towards another mountain range in the far-off distance. Idonea's laughter drifted back to them.

Weynild sighed.

After Raine had completely tired out the little ones and they were curled up in the nest sound asleep, she joined Weynild at the firepit. They had hollowed out a space, much like a couch, where they could sit comfortably. The space was lined with soft furs and was just wide enough so their legs could intertwine as they sat facing one another. They held hands in the warm glow of the fire.

"Tell me of your journey."

Raine exhaled, knowing this moment had been coming, both dreading and welcoming it.

"The first day was uneventful, the hunting was good, the weather was beautiful. The only thing I noticed was an increase in the number of magical creatures in the forest."

"I had noticed that myself," Weynild agreed, "on my last few forays. Fairies, pixies, even a faun."

"Yes," Raine mused "and speaking of magical creatures, I ran into the Raven sisters."

"And how is Valka?"

The aridity of Weynild's query made Raine chuckle. "About the same."

"You're lucky you're immune to magic. Otherwise, that one would use all her power trying to kidnap you."

"You're something of a deterrent," Raine reminded her. "But you're right, my immunity serves me well with that one." She grew thoughtful. "And that was something else I noticed. The Raven sisters, even the young one, seemed more powerful than the last time I saw them."

Raine fell silent and amber eyes settled on her young lover. Here was the point in the story she was waiting for, the cause of the disquiet she sensed in a creature who feared almost nothing.

"The night I spent in the witches' camp, I dreamed of Hel."

Weynild said nothing. This had been the same night as Y'arren's dream. Although she herself had dreamed of Hel many times; her dreams involved destroying the Goddess in a myriad of creative ways. She did not think Raine had dreamed of her in that context.

"It was as if I was back in the Underworld, paralyzed, helpless. I even saw the foreign stars above my head. She…" Raine stopped, then cleared her throat, "she was about to do horrible things to me when Feyden and Lorifal woke me up. I had pretty much destroyed the entire camp in my sleep."

Weynild squeezed the hand she held and pressed her calf to Raine's thigh. She waited patiently for Raine to work through her thoughts, and when it seemed Raine could not voice her fears, Weynild did it for her.

"Was it just a dream?"

"I don't know," Raine said. "It felt so real. I could feel her, I could even smell her, and—"

Weynild steeled herself.

"I was freezing cold."

Weynild breathed out, and Raine was grateful for the warmth the dragon could exhale even in human form.

"Perhaps it was the clarity of the dream," Raine continued, "but I've never had that reaction to something that wasn't actually there."

Weynild squeezed her hand again and the two fell silent. Weynild was very aware of another unique characteristic Raine possessed. When absolute evil met absolute purity, it produced an icy cold. When Raine was confronted with pure evil, her body grew very, very cold. It could be a warning mechanism; it could even be used as a weapon. But in extreme cases, it could be a debilitating handicap as it slowed Raine's movement and reactions. Being around the Goddess had nearly frozen her, and Weynild always went out of her way to keep Raine warm. She wondered if that was why Raine welcomed the dangerous experiences with the children, for their flame wasn't merely warmth, it was a sign of purity.

The silence was growing oppressive, so Weynild sought to move the story along.

"What happened the following day? And what made the dwarf choke on himself?"

This brought a smile to Raine's face, and some of Weynild's tension eased.

"I was killing everything in the forest, so we stopped early. Then Fenrir and his pups showed up."

"And how is the Wolf God?"

"He's well and sends his regards. I thanked him for his help."

Weynild held her opinion on that matter. She feared the Wolf God would suffer greatly for defying Hel, but she did not want to return Raine to her previously brooding state.

Raine was thoughtful. "In our conversation, I was regretting my involuntary response to Hel, and Lorifal made a comment about 'dragons and gods' being my only weaknesses, since my eyes turned purple on first sight of Kylan."

"Hmm," Weynild mused, "perhaps it's only Ancient Dragons."

"Hopefully, since there are so few of you left. But anyway, Fenrir wanted to know if I had a weakness for the Gods, then why didn't I respond to him? I told him that I was Ana'kari, explained what that meant, and said perhaps it was only Goddesses that the Arlanian in me responded to. He then transformed into a woman."

"A woman?" Weynild said, arching one fine eyebrow.

"A very beautiful woman," Raine admitted. "Stunning."

"And...?"

"My eyes immediately turned purple."

Weynild laughed the low, throaty laugh that Raine so loved. "Ah, would that I could have seen that, and the blush on your face."

"I was the color of a beet, from Feyden's description. I told him to turn back, and fortunately he did so. But I was relieved. It seems my response is not to Hel, but something more general. And Fenrir was relieved, I think perhaps because he's a touch jealous of his sister."

Weynild would not correct her lover. "Touch" was not even close. It was a good thing the Wolf God was respectful in all things; otherwise, she would be battling two gods for Raine.

At last, most of the tension drained from Raine, and she felt the contentment of her family settle upon her. Her babies were sleeping, warm and safe, and she was sitting across from the most beautiful woman in all of Arianthem.

"Mmm," Weynild murmured as the light purple turned to dark lavender. As she was around Raine so much, she was the only one to observe the full range of her Arlanian eyes.

Raine was wearing only light clothing, having shed her armor once the children went to bed, and the pants and shirt came off easily. Although the improvised "couch" was enjoyable for more acrobatic positions, it was too confining for what Weynild wished to do. She rolled Raine onto the soft ground before the fire, kissing her ardently as her hands explored what was so beloved and familiar with a passion that made it feel always new. And Raine responded in ways that she would never respond to another, with a hunger and craving that went far beyond the Arlanian proclivity for sex, driven by the strength of a Scinterian and a love that was boundless.

"So, you've been riding me," Weynild said, "and now I wish to ride you."

Raine grinned, for this was truly one of her favorites. With the heat of her flame, Weynild could shape a sexual toy out of nothing but earth and was skilled at doing so. She demonstrated that skill now, as Raine reached over her head to pull the harness from her pack. The Ha'kan were so very good at making these devices, and Weynild was so very good at modifying them for her use. And the assembly was donned and adjusted with a dexterity that would have impressed even the Ha'kan.

"There we are," Weynild said, straddling her love and allowing the device to sink deep within her. And Raine loved this position because she could stare into the golden eyes of her lover, which, although not possessing the range of her own, still clearly expressed pleasure and desire. And those wonderful, full breasts were a sight to behold, at times, tantalizingly out of reach, and then in perfect position for her mouth to kiss and suckle with abandon. Weynild's hips moved with a rhythm that Raine matched, gentle at first, but with increasing urgency. The muscles of her torso were mesmerizing to Raine, and she caressed them before placing her hands on the hips and began to lift the woman on top as she thrust deeply into her.

And this always amazed Weynild, the strength of this one. She was fully capable of taking her own pleasure, pinning that gorgeous, muscular body beneath her. But to watch those muscles rhythmically contract, to see that sheen of sweat appear on that lovely skin, to watch as the girl fought for control as she lifted with the force of her own increasing passion, that was what pushed the dragon to orgasm. But she would never go alone, riding on the edge of that wave of pleasure until she was certain the one beneath her was going as well, then released with an utter and total abandon, riding her in manner that would have ground most mortals into a powder.

"Ah," Raine exhaled, collapsing. Her heart was thudding in her chest and the warmth and weight of Weynild lying on top of her was glorious. She could feel the dragon's heart slow, the breathing return to normal, and she traced gentle patterns on the silky skin of her back.

"Mmm," Weynild said, her voice muffled as her face was buried in Raine's hair. She turned to kiss her neck, then the raised blue and gold markings on her shoulder. "I wonder why your Scinterian markings always appear when we make love?" she murmured

"Do you really need to ask that?" Raine said, her voice for once as dry as Weynild's.

The low, throaty chuckle told Raine that Weynild knew exactly why the markings appeared. The Scinterian scars always responded to danger, and there were few things as dangerous as mating with a dragon.

The chuckle continued and Weynild rolled onto her back, carrying Raine with her. Raine was content to lie next to her, hip-to-hip, her head on her shoulder, her cheek resting against those lovely breasts, her leg flung across her thighs. It was not long until the warmth, the contentment, the exertion, and the previous lack of sleep took their toll, and Raine began to drift into sleep.

Weynild absent-mindedly stroked her hair. Raine's breathing deepened, and little time passed before she was asleep, for which Weynild was grateful. She had noticed the fatigue that Raine hid from her comrades and wondered if she had slept at all on her trip after the first night.

This caused Weynild's thoughts to wander to Y'arren's vision, and given Raine's dream, she now considered the vision in a different light. She had given the seer's words far more credence than she would openly admit, and although the elven matriarch had welcomed her disregard, Weynild knew that Y'arren also saw through it. Events were eerily parallel to those leading up to the Great War. Magical creatures were growing in abundance, vortexes of power were appearing in the forest, the only thing that was missing were the Hyr'rok'kin. She thought the rest of Y'arren's dream, Ba'kun and the El'mir, were likely allegorical, but she could not think of what they might represent. She was half-tempted to fly across the Empty Land to see if the Veil had thinned. But she was not willing to leave Raine right now.

Her grip inadvertently tightened, and Raine let out a groan of protest in her sleep, so the dragon relaxed her embrace. She returned to her absent-minded stroking of the hair, knowing that as tired as she was, sleep was unlikely to come, because something was bothering her above all else.

Although Raine had not repeated Valka's words, Weynild was fully aware that dreams were the domain of witches.

Chapter 9

The Alfar had entertained many guests of late, unusual for the proud people who forbade most from entering their lands. But when the new Directorate had assumed the position as head of the High Council, a soirée of historical proportions had been held to celebrate the event. Dignitaries from all the lands of Arianthem had attended, even the Queen of the Ha'kan, who had deigned to leave her country to welcome the new leader of the elven people. And of course, the guests of honor had been the Ancient Dragon, Talan'alaith'illaria, and her lover, the Scinterian-Arlanian Raine.

Even amongst this renowned crowd, the dragon's children had stood out, admired both for their startling good looks and offhand, scandalous behavior. It was for this reason that the approach of the black dragon, once identified, was welcome and greeted with much excitement.

Both Maeva and Kiren stood on the balcony that Talan had landed upon when arriving in the city. It had no access from outside, situated hundreds of feet above ground, except to creatures capable of overcoming that limitation. And if it was large enough for the Queen of all Dragons to alight upon, then it was certainly large enough for her sleeker, smaller son.

Maeva admired the ebony creature as he landed, for he was a gorgeous specimen. And when he disappeared into a flash of red light, an equally gorgeous creature emerged, a rakish fellow dressed in black with a stylish moustache, a trace of a goatee, and the manner of a courtier. And on his arm was his female counterpart, a dark-haired vixen whose blouse plunged to her navel, revealing breasts always seemingly on the verge of exposure, a creature who swirled with as much dark magic as her dragon brother.

"Idonea," Maeva said, stepping forward, "and Drakar."

Idonea took Maeva's hands and proffered a cheek which Maeva kissed, as she did so, lightly pressing her body against the breasts that strained to free themselves. She then offered her own cheek to Drakar, who grinned, took her hand in his, and gracefully kissed the cheek, straying just close enough to the lips to provide a flush of pleasure to the Directorate.

"And you know Kiren?"

"Of course," Idonea said, "And how are you, little one?"

Kiren blushed, her dark blue eyes bright with joy. She was well-aware of Maeva's weaknesses and possessed not a jealous bone in her body. But these two were worthy of that attention, children of the dragon she admired, and adopted children of the one she adored.

Idonea gently kissed Kiren on the cheek, tempering her constant state of seduction for a number of reasons. First off, she suspected that Kiren had an Arlanian ancestor, an impossibility that meant the young woman deserved the gentlest of handling. Second, although Kiren possessed not a jealous bone, she was certain the Directorate's entire skeleton was composed of such. And finally, she respected Kiren too much to toy with her.

"I'm well," Kiren said brightly.

"That's good," Drakar said, also exceedingly gentle with the little one, and Idonea eyed him. Perhaps the baby dragons were having an effect on him. He leaned down to kiss her on the forehead, as polite and non-sexual a gesture she had ever seen him deliver.

Idonea returned her attention to the Directorate, who had watched the proceedings carefully, but with satisfaction.

"My mother sends her regards, as does Raine."

"I would love to see them," Maeva said.

"Well..." Idonea replied.

"Yes, yes," Maeva said with a brushing motion, "I'm certain they're fucking non-stop."

Drakar grinned. The bluntness of the Directorate was always welcome. She could be nefariously indirect, so to anyone who knew her, her candor was a compliment.

"They are," Idonea admitted. "It's almost disconcerting to visit them."

"I can only imagine," Maeva said.

"But we're here at my mother's request," Idonea continued. "I understand Kiren has discovered something of import."

"Possibly," Kiren said, biting her lower lip. She did not want to be wrong on something that could be crucial. "I'm glad you're here. I'd like you to look at it, and I've already sent it to Gimle in the Ha'kan capital. I'm hoping we can come to some sort of consensus on what it means."

"We'll do our best," Idonea said, putting her hand on Kiren's shoulder as they proceeded from the balcony. Maeva and Drakar trailed them.

"So," the Directorate said, "the ladies of my court are in a veritable frenzy at word of your arrival. I trust you'll not disappoint them?"

"I don't have as many talents as my sister," Drakar said with a rakish grin, "but there's a reason my mother sends me on these quests."

"So, that's what I received from Kiren," Gimle said.

"Yes," Idonea replied. "It was an artifact within an artifact, which is why it went undiscovered for so long. An engraving beneath an engraving, seen only because an elven servant dropped it, shattering the tablet, and revealing one beneath it."

A tiny fist distracted Gimle and she caught the infant's hand playfully, kissing it, then returning it to the hand of the High Priestess, who held Kaia in loving ecstasy. The Queen was doting upon Laina, who had enchanted both her Majesty and the First General. And Senta made silly, whimsical faces to the infant that likely would have astonished all who knew her.

"I confess I haven't made any more progress than Kiren, although I was able to verify her initial findings," Gimle said.

"Then you agree the third line should be interpreted, 'to defeat that which cannot be defeated?'" Idonea said.

"Yes," Gimle replied, "that much is clear. And the second line has the same pattern as the third, but I don't recognize any of the symbols."

Halla's attention shifted from the infant in her arms, communicating to Idonea she was paying far more attention to the conversation than was evident.

"The word 'child' in the first line, you believe it refers to one of these?"

All four Ha'kan grew silent at the Queen's question, and both babies turned their gaze upon Idonea. Although they looked like infant children, and indeed that was their age of development, they more followed the path of dragon growth. Although in human or Ha'kan terms they were infants, their mental acuity surpassed that.

"I don't know," Idonea said, "I pray that it doesn't. I saw Raine bear the weight of the last prophecy and saw the price that both she and my mother paid. I wouldn't wish that on anyone, but especially not these two."

Chapter 10

The tiny reddish-brown dragon crouched low, slinking up behind the Scinterian, who fully knew she was coming. Still, Raine allowed the little one to pounce on her, rolling about in the sand as the small reptile sought to pin her. A small dark dragon leapt from a nearby rock, joining the frolicking melee. Tails thrashed, small jaws latched onto dragonplate gauntlets, and it seemed Raine would be defeated until she shrugged the two off as if they weighed nothing. The dark red dragon honked in frustration while the little blue dragon's brow furrowed.

"Okay," Raine said, relenting, "we can practice, but you have to skim over the water."

The two baby dragons hopped about. Their little wings were growing, still nowhere near strong enough to gain any lift for their stout little bodies, but they could glide for short distances if given a little help. Raine picked up Kaia, put her on her shoulder, and then began sprinting toward the lake. Right as she reached the edge, she sent the baby sailing, and between her momentum and the push, Kaia glided over the water a good distance until she plonked down in the shallows, splashing about in a frenzy of excitement. She bounded out of the water and began sprinting back toward her mother, just as Raine was preparing Laina.

"Now no silliness," Raine cautioned, "just a straight line, like Kaia."

Raine repeated the sprint and sent the little dragon sailing, and Laina's wings fluttered in a frenzy of incoordination, causing Raine to hide a smile. She doubted the frantic flapping was helping at all, but the tiny dragon was giving it her all.

This pattern was repeated for some time as Raine sent both girls sailing over the water, strengthening their wings in exercise, much as a human would teach their offspring to walk. Any normal being would have collapsed in exhaustion, but Raine lifted each tiny behemoth and sent them flying repeatedly without effort.

The same could not be said of the two little ones. They were clearly in ecstasy over the experience of flight, but their bliss was tempered by the fatigue that was setting in.

"All right, my babies. One more turn apiece, and then it's nap time."

Raine launched Laina, then jogged back to Kaia. The girls were getting better; Laina was extending her flight time and was still gliding by the time Kaia was in the air.

"Laina," Raine called out sternly, "knock it off."

The little red dragon was experimenting, tilting her wings one way, then the other, which caused her to change direction in unexpected ways. It was a novel feeling, and as much as Laina wanted to obey her mother, a prisoner to her impulses, she could not. An updraft caught her at just the right moment, and in delight, she wheeled about in a quarter turn, gaining more altitude.

"Laina!"

Concern was creeping into Raine's voice. Laina was getting higher and higher in the cave, and the drafts were stronger near the opening. One such draft caught Laina, and she trilled in delight.

Until she realized she was heading toward the cave opening.

"Laina!" Raine yelled as she began sprinting toward the opening, trying to close the gap between her and the baby dragon.

Kaia, recognizing the peril that her twin was in, wheeled about in a maneuver that would have made her mother proud had she seen it. The tiny dragon flapped her wings with monumental effort, utilizing an inborn skill to catch another draft that sent her sailing towards her sister at an angle. Raine saw the little blue dragon coming in and knew what she was trying to do.

"Kaia!"

The little blue dragon caught and collided with her sister, redirecting Laina back into the cave. Unfortunately, the collision also redirected her and sent her tumbling out the entrance. The tiny dragon was no longer gliding but in total free-fall.

"Kaia!" Raine screamed as she leapt off the mountainside.

The tiny dragon was desperately trying to right herself in a flurry of limbs and wings, so Raine was able to streamline her body and catch her in a headlong dive. Once she caught the baby, she did a barrel roll, so the baby was on top, then went spread eagle, trying to balance with three of four limbs to slightly slow their descent.

"Spread your wings little one!" Raine shouted above the roar of the rushing air, talking as fast as she could. "Keep them close to your body and angle towards the horizon. Open them slowly, to slow yourself, then begin to glide as you near the ground."

Kaia's wide eyes were purple with terror, not for herself, but for her mother, who had no wings.

"I'll be fine," Raine said with the confidence of a Scinterian who was about to die. "Just go. Now!"

Raine pushed the baby away in the perfect position and attitude for her to stabilize and maintain control. And the little wings opened just slightly, as instructed, not enough to tear at the fragile appendages, but enough for the baby dragon to begin slowing as Raine fell away. And Raine stared upwards at her daughter with enormous pride as the baby followed her instructions exactly, began to level off, and truly flew for the first time. She was glad that she had no time for sadness.

A furious roar echoed through the valley and shook the mountain itself. It was a roar that declared it had battled fate before and would defeat it again as the red dragon dove straight towards the ground in a sleek profile that would have put her son to shame, with a swiftness that would have beat a meteor to the earth. And Talan'alaith'illaria swooped from that dive with an agility that few dragons possessed, driven by a technical mastery of flight acquired over a thousand years. And the fiery red dragon caught her companion in jaws capable of crushing iron, with a gentleness that would not crush an egg.

The abrupt change of direction was jarring and took Raine's breath away, but she did not have time to consider her injuries. She grasped the scales above her love's eye and pulled herself onto Weynild's neck as the dragon wheeled about and went after her child.

Kaia was terrified but roared a tiny roar to her mother as the great red dragon came up beneath her. Weynild's flight was so skillful, Raine was able to reach up and gently guide the tiny dragon down in front of her onto her mother's neck. Once the baby was secure, Raine grasped her tightly, pinning her to her mother's warmth with her body weight, she herself clinging to Weynild's plating.

Weynild's great wings rotated back as she glided into the entrance of the cave, and she landed with a skillful thud. Laina was in a frenzy of anguish and guilt that told Weynild everything she needed to know. No sooner had Raine dismounted with Kaia in her arms than Laina smothered them both in mortified concern, scurrying over both, gently head-butting them and nudging them with anxiety and tenderness.

"We're alright, little one," Raine said softly. She couldn't be angry with the little dragon. She was who she was, and she hadn't meant for it to happen.

Kaia seemed a little shell-shocked, but as reality returned, she gathered herself. She took inventory of her twin with mutual head butts and nudging to ascertain her safety and condition, an action so typically Scinterian that Raine hid a smile. Her father's people often dealt with their own fear by taking care of others.

"Come on you two," Raine said, lifting both baby dragons. "It's time for your nap."

The girls intertwined with one another so tightly in the nest they appeared as one. And as two pair of purple eyes turned upon her, Raine had only one response.

"I'll be back in just a moment, and we'll sleep together."

It was only then, as Raine turned away, she realized every bone in her body hurt. And as a brilliant flash of yellow light filled the cave and a set of amber eyes gazed upon her with a baleful look, she hurt even more.

"What," Weynild said with emphasis, "were you thinking?"

"I was merely helping the babies fly," Raine began.

"I don't mean that," Weynild said, "I'm certain Laina did something foolish that started this chain of events. She's far too much like me for that to be in doubt. But did you really think you were going to survive that fall?"

"Actually," Raine started, then stopped. "I didn't really think about it at all."

"Of course, you didn't," Weynild said, taking her in her arms. Their children were in danger and Raine would sacrifice her life for them without a second thought.

A long embrace ensued as both considered what had just occurred.

"I probably wouldn't have died," Raine said, her voice muffled because her head was buried in Weynild's shoulder. "Your life would have sustained me."

"Yes," Weynild said, her voice muffled as her face was buried in Raine's hair, "it's likely my life source would have kept you from death. But every bone in your body would have broken in that fall. I can't imagine the pain."

"It would have been nothing compared to the pain of losing Kaia."

Weynild raised her head and gazed into lavender eyes that she loved. "I know," she said simply.

And the two walked hand-in-hand to the nest, where they climbed in and gathered the two little ones into an embrace. And once the adrenaline faded, they both quickly yielded to sleep.

Chapter 11

I've been thinking."

Raine turned to Weynild across the campfire, this phrase usually yielding something momentous.

"Perhaps this is not the best location for the girls to learn to fly."

Raine remained silent, this fact so self-evident in the face of the recent fiasco it required no comment. Were it just Kaia, it might be manageable. But the two of them made it difficult, and Laina was hopelessly headstrong.

"We could take them to the Wilds," Raine mused, "but even as remote as that is, they could still be seen."

"Yes, and word of the sight of two infant dragons learning to fly would spread very quickly throughout Arianthem."

Raine silently agreed. There were many remote parts of Arianthem, the Deep Woods, the Great Plains of Enire, the Endless Azure Sea, but there was no guarantee of secrecy, and no place as private as the keep.

"And the increase in magical creatures throughout the land," Weynild continued, "makes it even more difficult. No one gossips the way those pests do."

"And they likely answer to Hel."

"Most of them, yes."

Weynild came to a conclusion, debated it with herself a while longer, then finally articulated the thought.

"There is one place that's completely isolated. It's not as habitable as here, but the cold will little affect the girls. And there's another Ancient

Dragon there that will protect the little ones with her life."

The thought of Kylan brought a smile to Raine's lips and a flash of purple to her eyes. Weynild caught both inadvertent responses.

"Hmph, it's a good thing I trust Kylan."

The comment was wry but without sting, because regardless of whether she trusted Kylan, Weynild never doubted Raine.

"You wish to go there? At the top of the world?" Raine asked. "How is that better than here?"

"First off, although it's at great altitude, the southern descent is gradual, and the huge snow drifts will soften any hard landings."

"Hmm," Raine said, trying to imagine the layout and area of what was once Weynild's castle.

"Second, that castle was made for dragons, and it's much larger than this keep."

"Hmm," Raine said again as she imagined the great rooms in her mind's eye. The infants could fly about the castle before they were ready to launch outdoors.

"And finally, no one, dragon or otherwise is allowed in that place without an invitation from Kylan."

"Which means it's probably overflowing with young, beautiful dragons of both sexes right now."

Weynild frowned. That was likely true given her last visit to the frozen keep.

"I'll go tomorrow, then. Tell her we intend to take up residence there for a while."

"Will you tell her about the children?

"No," Weynild said with a smile. "I want that to be a surprise. I'll make it a short trip, clear the area, then come back for you and the girls as quickly as possible."

"Perfect."

Chapter 12

A "short" trip to the top of the world was anything but, this Raine knew. Although Weynild left at daybreak, Raine did not anticipate the dragon's return until late the following evening. She played with the babies in spurts all day long, short bursts of activity punctuated by naps and eating. Indeed, it seemed all the children did at this point in their development was eat, sleep, and ferociously play. Raine mused that being a dragon child and a Scinterian child were much the same.

Night fell, and as Raine climbed into the nest with a book that Y'arren had given her, she found two infants crawling about in the warm sand, not dragons, but little Arlanians. Or so they looked to her, with their perfect little features, happy little expressions, and lovely purple eyes. Raine wondered if she had looked like Kaia as a child. Both children shared the androgynous beauty of young Arlanians, but unlike her at that age, they were both undoubtedly female. She marveled at how they were able to garb themselves in simple dragon skin clothing, copying the short pants and shift she herself wore.

Raine took a stick and stoked the embers in the center of the nest. A cheery fire sprang to life, casting shadows all over the cave and warming the surrounding sand. She dropped the stick next to the firepit, then moved to the edge of the small bowl. She reclined against the sand berm, stretched out her legs, and the two little ones scooted over to crawl onto her lap.

"I have a wonderful treat for you," Raine began, opening the tome. "My godmother Y'arren gave this to me. It's a book for elven children."

Kaia looked up at her somberly. She did not know what an elf was. Her head swiveled toward her twin, who neither knew nor cared, already gasping in delight at the elaborate, colorful illustrations in the book. Kaia leaned over to peer at the pictures, and her eyes grew wide as well. Her tiny hands reached out to touch the fine paper.

"Now this is a very special tale," Raine began, "it's a story about the Great War, and about the Queen of all Dragons," Raine paused for effect as she slowly turned the page.

Kaia's eyes grew round and Laina's mouth dropped open. On the page was a dramatic rendition of a fiery red dragon blowing fire at an army of Hyr'rok'kin as she swooped across a bloody battlefield.

"And her name was Talan'alaith'illaria."

The twins were awake far longer than usual, fascinated by the book of legendary tales. Whoever had illustrated the tome was an incredible artist, capturing the different stories with a style of savage beauty. Raine wondered if it was indeed a book for elven children because it surely would have given any normal child nightmares. It was, however, perfect for a pair of baby dragons who were also Scinterian, making Raine wonder if Y'arren had prepared it especially for them. Which meant she had suspected their presence long before Raine had told her, because this book had been no simple project.

At last the two fell asleep, visions of bloody skirmishes dancing through their dreams as they swooped into battle with their mothers, and Raine set the book aside. She leaned back, completely comfortable, a child in each arm, and as she drifted off to sleep, her last thought was that everything was perfect save for the absence of her love.

It was cold. And it was dark. She was sitting half-upright on the ground, leaning against something, and she could not move. She was in a position that she had been before...

But she could not finish that thought. Before what? And where was she now?

It was not completely dark, because she could see her breath come out frigid in the air in front of her. She could hear her heartbeat pound in the silence around her. She slowly became aware of a presence, not through sight, but through the anger that emanated outward from this being like something alive.

"And here you are again."

It was the voice she feared above all others, the voice that began as dry as a dead reed rattling in the wind, that moved to the hissing sibilance of a snake, then transitioned to the low tones of one who claimed ownership of her. The Goddess of the Underworld stepped from the darkness, her blood red eyes resolving to two glittering emeralds, hardened by her fury. Hel examined the prone woman in front of her, the air of satisfaction about her as frightening as it was dangerous.

"Where am I?" Raine demanded, clenching her jaw to keep her teeth from chattering.

The demand angered Hel, for it was disrespectful, but the chattering of the teeth was soothing. She knew it was not from fear; it was the cold produced by their proximity, and it reminded her how delightfully cool that skin was when the girl was pinned beneath her.

Hel waved her hand derisively. "Where do you think you are?"

In desperation, Raine's eyes sought the extents of the space she was in, finding no rocks, no walls, no windows, no doors, no discernible features of any kind that would give her a clue to her location.

"I'm dreaming," Raine said.

"Really?" Hel said. She waved her hand and a throne-like chair appeared in front of Raine in which she settled comfortable, smoothing her black robe. "Then why do I have so much control over your dreams?"

"Who knows?" Raine said, straining to move her arms.

The dismissive tone did not sit well with the Goddess and with a motion of her hand she yanked Raine forward so that she was on her knees before her, the collar of Raine's shirt bunched in her fist. Raine again shivered at the proximity.

Hel examined the subservient position, and the emerald eyes drifted over those chiseled features. "Ah, the things you've done for me on your knees."

Raine stared steadfastly at the ground, or what should have been the ground were it not utterly black.

"Mmm," Hel said. Even her anger, as great as that inferno was, tempered under the influence of her lust. Such perfection. Those muscular arms, the firm breasts. The full lips, pronounced cheekbones, long eyelashes that sought to hide the lavender beneath. "No," Hel said, placing her index finger beneath Raine's chin and tilting her face upward. "I don't think so."

Blood-red lips closed upon Raine's mouth, parting unresisting lips with a dominating tongue. So deliciously cold, just as she remembered, perhaps even more so now. The kiss grew deeper and she felt the Arlanian relax, begin to yield, just as she always did. Hel's rage would not dissipate any time soon; but it could be slowly released through the absolute sexual domination of this one. The things she would do to this girl, the humiliation she would force her to endure...

Raine stiffened.

"What was that?" Hel asked, pulling back and looking around her at the blackness. She turned her attention back to Raine, whose eyes were now an opaque, reflective ice blue.

"I don't know what you're talking about."

Hel's eyes narrowed. Something had just happened. The Arlanian had disappeared and only the Scinterian remained. And as mirror-like and inscrutable as the Scinterian was, Hel still knew her well.

"You're hiding something."

"I don't know what you're talking about," Raine calmly repeated.

Hel sat back, enraged. But then her expression altered, became contemplative as she assessed the woman on her knees in front of her. This turn of events was not entirely unwelcome. The Scinterian was indeed hiding something, something of enormous importance to her. Something so important it was capable of, at least momentarily, breaking Hel's spell on her.

And that meant leverage when she discovered it.

The strong jaw clenched. "Goodbye."

The muscular body flickered as Raine began to awaken, but Hel merely leaned upon the arm of her throne and placed her hand beneath her chin thoughtfully.

"I will find it, you know. You have to sleep sometime."

"Goodbye," Raine said firmly.

Light grew visible behind Raine's closed eyelids, and she became conscious of being both very cold and very hot at the same time.

"Hot" was perhaps inaccurate, because, really, she was on fire.

She jumped to her feet. There were two baby dragons in the nest, paralyzed with fear, wide purple eyes on their mother. They were unharmed, and that was all Raine needed to know as she began sprinting toward the lake. She leaped and dove beneath the surface, the water warming the parts of her that were frigid and extinguishing the parts that were on fire.

She broke the surface, sucking in the air as if she had not been breathing for days. She floated for a moment, staring up at Arianthem's stars through the cave opening, then slowly began paddling back towards the shallows. The two little dragons stood on the shore, trembling with fear.

Raine waded from the water, then knelt to hug the babies.

"It's okay," she said softly as they trilled and nudged her. "It's okay. Come here."

She hoisted them up onto her shoulders and carried them back to the nest. She gently set them down, then examined the scene around her to decipher what had occurred. There was an outline of blackened sand in the form of her body.

"Let me guess," Raine said, "I became very cold."

Kaia's wide eyes told her she was correct.

"And you decided to fix that."

Laina's expression confirmed that as well.

"So, you lit me on fire."

The two little dragons looked at one another. It didn't sound so good a plan now.

"Thank you," Raine said at last. "You saved me."

The two little ones settled in protectively beside her, their wings and tails twitching alertly for danger for at least the quarter of an hour they managed to stay awake. Raine stroked their little brows as she leaned back against the berm, sleep not even an option. The burns hurt, very, very much, but that was not what kept her awake.

She had no idea what had just happened, but she was not sleeping until Weynild returned. She didn't know what would be worse: if she fell asleep and the children lit her on fire again…

Or if she fell asleep and they didn't.

The babies hopped about, wings fluttering with excitement as the massive red dragon hovered in the cave entrance, then came to a graceful landing, causing only a slight shake of the mountain top. They fell over one another trying to gain their mother's attention, butting her tree-trunk legs joyfully. Her wings draped over them in affection, and the giant head leaned down to gently nudge them both.

Their excitement did not wane when the dragon transformed, but Weynild's attention to her young ones was now absent-minded as she noted the dark circles beneath Raine's eyes, then the burns on her extremities. They were already bright pink with new skin, consistent with her companion's preternatural healing, but there was a story here.

"Should I dare ask what happened?"

The two little dragons hunkered close to the ground, still uncertain of their previous actions, and skittered over to Raine, encircling her legs with serpentine necks and tails. Raine rubbed the bridge of Laina's nose and the back of Kaia's neck.

"Yes, but you should tell me yours first, and we'll get to mine when the children are asleep."

Weynild took another long look at Raine, then picked up both children, carrying them over to the main fire pit with the excavated furniture. The baby dragons crept about uneasily, restless, until Weynild and Raine settled across from one another in the make-shift lounge, at which time they jumped up onto their parents, desperate to be close to them.

"We should have made this larger," Raine said with a groan. She shifted Laina's weight so that she not pressing on her diaphragm, then breathed deep. "That's better."

Weynild shifted Kaia so that the two infants sat on their laps between them. The baby dragons were in heaven, close to both mothers, warm and safe. Raine felt Laina's soft little snort of heat on her leg, knowing that the two would likely be asleep within moments.

"And how is Kylan?"

Weynild's teeth were brilliant in the waning light. "She's well, and intrigued, to say the least, at our upcoming visit. She senses something, but I don't think she knows what's coming."

Raine grinned, her teeth as white as the dragon's. "She'll love these little ones."

"And they'll adore her. I can't wait to see the look on her face. She pretended some reluctance at clearing her court, but I could tell she's looking forward to our return. I told her we would be there in a matter of days."

The picture of Kylan seeing the infants for the first time pleasantly occupied Raine, and Weynild did not wish to interrupt her reverie. But the burns on Raine's arms and her obvious fatigue concerned her. A gentle snore from Kaia and the rhythmic expansion of Laina's ribcage told her the girls were asleep.

"So, will you tell me what happened while I was gone?"

Weynild almost regretted the question as Raine's countenance darkened. It was some time before she could gather her thoughts.

"I dreamt of Hel again."

Weynild had known this before it was said. She interlaced her fingers with Raine's but remained silent.

"It felt like she was looking for me."

"And she found you."

"Yes," Raine said slowly, "I don't know how. She has some power over me in my dreams, some control, but it's not complete."

"What happened?"

Raine was lost in the horrible image. "She yanked me towards her, then kissed me."

Weynild suppressed her own jealousy and rage, knowing Raine would feel guilt over even an imaginary infidelity.

"And then—,"

"What?"

Raine sought to decipher what had happened, and Weynild held her breath at the slow-growing horror on Raine's face.

"I think she sensed the children."

"What?"

Weynild's anguish mirrored and amplified her own. "She didn't see them," Raine said quickly, "and she didn't find them. She merely sensed them when they tried to draw me back into this world."

"You never left this world," Weynild said firmly. Despite her fear for the children, she needed to disabuse Raine of any notion that Hel had power over her. "Hel has found a way to enter your dreams, but that's a weak connection of last resort, a desperate act of one with few options."

Weynild's matter-of-fact pronouncement had the desired effect, and some of the tension drained from Raine's body.

"I know," she said. "I just felt so exposed, as if she could sense, maybe not them, but something, something I cared for. And she started looking for it."

Weynild stroked the healing burns on Raine's arm. "So, let me guess. You turned ice-cold, as you always do in the presence of pure evil, and my little ones, not knowing what else to do, attempted to warm you."

"They lit me on fire," Raine said dryly.

This caused a bout of prolonged, throaty laughter from Weynild, which Raine so loved. Kaia's tail twitched happily in her sleep, and Weynild quieted herself.

"I wish I could have seen that," Weynild said, "the flurried debate between the two of them, together coming to perhaps the worst possible solution."

"I don't know," Raine said, stroking Laina's back. "It was effective."

This brought forth another chuckle from Weynild.

"Although," Weynild said thoughtfully, "I think if I were here to see it, it might not have happened. It might not have even been necessary."

"What do you mean?"

"It's been almost two years since we defeated Hel, and she's not come to you once. Twice now, she's come to you, invading your dreams. And both were under similar circumstances."

Raine sought the commonality, and then it was obvious.

"Both times I was apart from you."

"Yes," Weynild said, leaning forward to kiss her love. "And those are the only two times we've been apart. I imagine that my dark magic protects you, even in your sleep. The solution to this problem is simple and desirable."

"We must never part," Raine said, leaning forward to kiss Weynild again.

"Never."

Chapter 13

The cerulean dragon perched upon the parapet. Her scales were a dark sapphire at the base, transitioning to a more opalescent blue at the tips, creating a twinkling illusion when she moved, as if she were made from stars. Deep blue eyes scanned the horizon for One she both sensed and expected. Her Queen was coming.

Kylan shifted, swinging her tail around and thumping it once on the balcony. Despite the fact she was nearly as old as Talan, she had none of the red dragon's patience. Although in physical manifestation, she was ice to Talan's fire, she was just as hot-blooded as all dragons, and looked forward to the presence of her liege and that gorgeous Arlanian Scinterian. Really, just looking at Raine was entertaining, although she wished Talan had not made her send everyone away. It would have been better had she some outlet for the lust that both her Queen and the Arlanian inspired.

Still, the blue dragon thought, it would be enjoyable, for she had not seen the two of them since the battle in the Underworld. And she was enormously curious about Talan's enigmatic mood, a mixture of happiness and sly anticipation she had not seen in her in centuries.

At last the awaited silhouette appeared, the leathery wings rhythmically beating against the air, propelling the gigantic creature forward and upward so skillfully the steep ascent appeared effortless. As Talan neared, she could make out the small figure on her back, who appeared to be carrying bundles of supplies. Kylan grinned, several rows of pearly white fangs displaying. Although she had more than adequate stores for guests, that meant the two were staying awhile, which greatly pleased her.

The red dragon landed with a light thud, causing no quiver to a castle which had been designed by and for such creatures. Kylan bowed her head low.

"My Queen," she said respectfully with a trace of the sensuality innate to all dragons.

"Kylan," Talan said, "thank you for having us."

"It's your castle," the blue dragon said. "I've always considered it on loan."

Raine slid off the back of Talan behind her, then came around the massive body that was her love. Kylan prepared to transform so she could greet her in human form when Raine raised her hand.

"Wait, wait. Greetings, Kylan, but don't transform just yet."

Kylan's curiosity peaked and she furrowed her scaly brow. Raine turned back, motioning to something behind Talan. Apparently, what was going on behind Talan was not going exactly to plan because Raine raised her hands in exasperation.

"I'm sorry," Raine said, "they're a little shy." She disappeared behind the girth of Talan.

"What is a little shy?" Kylan asked Talan. The red dragon simply grinned, displaying rows of bright white fangs.

There was a great deal of low, murmured conversation coming from Raine, and finally she reappeared.

"Okay, let's try this again. Come on out."

Kylan cocked her great head to one side, her curiosity now overwhelming. But out of everything she could imagine that might be behind Talan, she never would have guessed the truth.

"By the gods," the blue dragon said in astonishment.

Two tiny dragons bounded from around Talan, desperately trying to be brave, but only managing to get as far as Raine until they curled about her legs. They stared up at the gigantic blue dragon, excited, fearful, thrilled, and terrified. Little tails were low to the ground as they peered around Raine. Talan leaned down to nudge them with encouragement.

Kylan had frozen, so great was her amazement, but as she took in the sight of the two little ones, she settled down onto her belly, making herself as low to the ground as possible, and laid her great neck down so that her head rested on the tiles of the courtyard. The two little ones circled Raine, trilling and growling and honking uncertainly.

"Go on now," Raine said, giving them both a gentle push.

The two little ones crept towards Kylan, padding quietly as if that somehow disguised their presence from the monster in front of them. But this monster drew them as no other, with a presence that was as mesmerizing as their mother's. And the fact that the creature remained still, waiting patiently for them to approach, encouraged them. Finally, both broke into a sprint, and happily leaped upon the blue dragon's serpentine neck, little bodies and tails wrapping themselves about her in a flurry of delight.

And Kylan was in heaven, for these little ones were precious beyond belief. And there was no doubt that these were the children of Talan and her lover, for the little red one had eyes as gold as the Queen's, and the little dark one as blue as the Scinterian's.

And then Kylan gasped again, for the tiny dragons' eyes were not blue or gold, but purple, and they were undoubtedly the most beautiful eyes she had ever seen.

"I see they've inherited that weakness as well," Talan said drily.

Raine chuckled. "Yes. I had no doubt their eyes would turn when they saw Kylan."

"Hmph," Talan said, but Raine could tell she was pleased the infants adored Kylan.

The great blue dragon played with the two tiny ones, far more careful with the precious cargo than either of their parents. And the two little ones scurried over her in ecstasy, flapping their wings, thumping their tails, and running up and down and around the length of her body. Finally, they were growing weary, and Talan transformed.

"Come here, you two."

The babies were submissive to their mother regardless of form, and after a head butt apiece to the great blue dragon, they scurried off her back down to Talan and Raine. Kylan took that opportunity to transform, and with a white flash, she appeared in her human form, and the two tiny dragons gaped at the vision of loveliness. Like Talan, Kylan's human-like form was similar in age to her actual. Her long dark hair was streaked with silver, her features aristocratic, her blue eyes twinkling with laughter and her gown twinkling as if covered in diamonds. Raine sighed as she felt her eyes turn as purple as her children's.

"Kylan," Raine said, bowing.

"So formal," Kylan said, then pulled the Arlanian to her. She kissed her full on the mouth while Raine turned bright red, and where such an action would likely result in death to most, it elicited only a sigh from Talan. Kylan turned her attention back to the two baby dragons.

"I can't wait to hear how this happened."

Once inside the great walls, the two little ones seemed to gain a second wind, and Raine set them loose. They romped down the hallway, nipping at one another until they careened around a corner, disappearing.

"I assure you there's nothing they can get into," Kylan said.

No sooner were the words out of her mouth, then a large clatter came from the direction the twins had disappeared. There was a pronounced silence, then two little heads poked from around the corner, peering down the hallway. Raine frowned at them.

Kylan waved her hand airily. "Probably some armor or a few weapons, no matter. There's nothing they can hurt. And if they're anything like you," Kylan said, assessing the frowning muscular specimen in front of her, "there's nothing that can hurt them, either."

Raine relented and waved them off. The two tried to appear contrite, but Laina could not maintain the farce and chortled. Then with a flip of their tails, they were gone. A more distant clatter sounded, but this time the twins did not return, fleeing from their collateral damage.

"That little red one is trouble," Kylan noted.

"Hmmm, yes," Talan agreed. "Although the little blue one is just as much trouble in her own way."

"I hope you're right there's nothing they can get into," Raine said. "Other than one, brief, accidental flight by Kaia, this is the first time they've been out of the cave."

"You were holed up in your keep?" Kylan said, motioning for them to follow her.

The two women followed the blue dragon into the common area of her suite, a luxuriously furnished room that reflected the personality of its occupant. Various plush seating areas were arranged in circular fashion, and Kylan settled into the largest of these circular couches.

"It seemed the safest place to hatch the eggs," Talan replied. "It's almost inaccessible save for dragonkind."

"And none of our kind would dare disturb you there," Kylan said with approval. "But that had to be boring for you," she said to Raine.

"What? Of course not. I could read, swim, train," Raine paused, "train some more."

"You really are Scinterian," Kylan said. "And I imagine once Talan laid the eggs, she kept the Arlanian part of you more than busy."

"You can't imagine," Talan said with a sultry glance at her companion.

"No, but I would like to!" Kylan exclaimed, laughing. "But two eggs! Whoever heard of such a thing!"

"Well, we had a little help from the Allfather himself, so none of it was normal."

The conversation was interrupted by a distant clatter that echoed in from the hallway, followed by a muffled "boom."

"I'm going to go find my children," Raine said.

"I'm certain they're fine," Kylan said, unconcerned.

"I'm not worried about them. I'm more worried about this castle. They're remarkably destructive."

Both dragons laughed as the figure set off jogging down the immense hallway. Kylan watched the lithe form disappear, then turned back to Talan.

"So, now you must give me the details," Kylan said.

"About?"

Kylan leaned forward and swatted her liege's knee. "Don't play coy with me. I want every single part."

The low throaty laugh confirmed Talan knew exactly of what she spoke. "Well," she began, "my heart's desire was to have children by Raine, which clearly the Allfather knew."

"I wondered what could possibly prompt you to give up the Underworld, having defeated Hel. It's not every day you become a Goddess, my dear. And you looked marvelous in that raiment."

"Being a god is overrated," Talan said dismissively. "And what I gained is beyond measure."

"Agreed," Kylan said with a glance to the doorway through which Raine had disappeared. "Go on."

"The Allfather transformed Raine into a dragon, a beautiful male dragon, for a day and a night. And then nature took its course."

"Took its course!" Kylan said, swatting her again. "It had to have been epic. A male dragon who was also Scinterian and Arlanian, by the Divine, I can't even imagine."

"A male dragon who was also the love of my life, so yes, it was epic."

Kylan paused, examining her Queen closely. "The Allfather transformed Raine into more than a mere dragon," she said shrewdly.

Talan's amber eyes glowed. "Perhaps."

"Perhaps nothing. Those two little ones are both Ancients. I can tell already."

"They will be," Talan said, "in half a millennium or so." Her casual manner did not hide her pride or pleasure. "Do you know they can already shapeshift?"

"No!" Kylan gasped. "Into infant form?"

"Yes. I believe they do it for Raine. And they're as darling as baby Arlanians as they are dragons."

"Oh, I must hold them in all forms."

"I'm glad you desire to do so. We may be here for a while."

"You may stay as long as you like."

"You might regret that offer."

Raine spoke these words as she strode through the doorway, a baby dragon underneath each arm. Kylan took a moment to admire the bulging biceps that had trapped each rascal, also admiring the strength it took to cart the two mini behemoths around. Raine released them and they scurried to Talan, flowing over her in a reptilian embrace. Bright blue and gold eyes peered at Kylan as they wrapped about their mother.

Talan, however, had eyes only for Raine. The warrior was covered in soot.

"You smell like brimstone."

"Does that turn you on?" Raine said, brushing at the black ash.

"You know it does."

Kylan recognized the tone of her liege. It spoke of needs that all dragons shared.

"Why don't I watch the children for a bit?" she suggested.

Talan stood, gently disentangling herself from the babies. They scurried to the open arms of Kylan, who reveled in the tiny reptiles. They trilled and honked as she hugged them to her.

"I'll take them into the great room," Kylan said. "It's large enough for some basic flying lessons."

"That would be divine," Talan said, taking the hand of her love.

The dragon's heart thudded in her chest as she sunk back into silken pillows. The exertions of sex with her partner were far greater than the entire flight up the mountain range.

Raine rolled over, also gasping for breath, enjoying the aftermath of their lovemaking, and enjoying the freedom from worrying about the children. This was a benefit she had not anticipated. There were few beings she would trust so absolutely with Kaia and Laina.

"As much as I could spend the rest of the afternoon," Raine paused, "this evening, all of tomorrow, and probably all of next week—"

A raised eyebrow told her to get on with it, "—in bed with you, I really would like to see their flying lessons."

"I guess I can let you up for a little while."

Raine was not fooled by the casual tone. "You want to see them, too."

Both sprang from the bed and took a quick rinse in the bath. Talan's armor formed about her and Raine donned cloth breeches, a leather tunic, and some soft leather boots.

"Willing to take your chances with the little firebrands?"

Raine appreciated the double meaning and added her own. "Yes, I'll have to be mindful of the little hotheads without my armor."

Both smiled at their jests, then walked hand-in-hand through the enormous doorway, then through the vaulted hallways.

"So, this was once your castle?" Raine asked.

"It was," Talan said. "I spent many centuries here."

"Ah, if these walls could talk."

Talan squeezed her hand at the teasing tone. It was a good thing her Arlanian was not jealous. She had enjoyed an endless array of lovers before meeting the girl. To her credit, she had been faithful ever since, a fact that astounded all who knew her.

"The architecture is unique, clearly designed by dragons for dragons."

Talan nodded as they kept walking. The castle was built for gigantic occupants, and everything was outsized. In their current form, they were dwarfed by passageways wide enough that two dragons could pass one another, ceilings high enough that a dragon could walk fully upright, and ledges large enough that a dragon could perch or lie down. In her mind's eye, Talan could see the many dragons that had traversed these passages, feel the many ghosts that lingered still.

Raine stopped. "Now that's an odd expression on your face."

Talan could hide nothing from her love.

"Kylan utterly deserved this castle for her faithfulness to me, but there were many reasons why I gave it away."

Raine was quiet, allowing the dragon to sort through her reminisces. She understood the disconnect of time, at least in a relative sense. She herself was over three centuries old, and had a different experience of time than say, the sons of men, who generally lived less than a century. She related more to the dwarves and elves, who shared similar lifespans to Arlanians and Scinterians, and even the Ha'kan who, although not quite as long-lived, could survive well into their second century.

But dragons could live millennia, and Ancient Dragons longer than that. Talan'alaith'illaria was the oldest creature in this realm, and only Y'arren was even close. Memory could be a terrible taskmaster.

"There were many dragons I knew that lived in these halls, young ones, elders, even an Ancient or two. The halls were very empty after the Great War."

Raine was quiet, respecting the silent echoes of the past. The faraway look in those golden eyes hurt her heart.

"That was when I retired to my keep, which seemed far less lonely, even when I was completely alone."

Raine examined the walls around her, trying to imagine it filled with dragonkind. "I've often wanted to visit the Ala'ashakar," she mused in empathy.

This brought Talan from her reminisce abruptly. The Arlanian next to her had felt her pain, but the Scinterian knew it intimately. Although the dragons had been depleted in the Great War, the Scinterians had been annihilated, unable to recover as a race. The creature next to her was all that remained of their sacrifice. And Raine's quiet musing had inadvertently made that clear.

"I'm sorry," Talan said, taking her in her arms, "I'm being selfish."

"What?" Raine asked, "you most certainly are not. Your kind suffered great losses during the war."

"And yours was destroyed."

This quieted Raine. She had not thought about it in those terms. The recent dreams of Y'arren seemed to stir up a great deal. Ala'ashakar, or "The Field of Honor" in the common tongue, was the graveyard of the Scinterian race. It was the site of the end battle of the Great War.

"No," she said, shaking her head. "My race is not dead. I have two beautiful children. And when they're old enough, we'll go to Ala'ashakar so they'll know their legacy."

"And because they're Arlanian, they will have suitors without end."

Raine smiled at the sly tone of her lover. "And because they're dragons, they will mate without end."

"Perhaps ensuring the future of all races involved, dragons, Scinterians, and Arlanians."

Raine grinned, the somber mood passing. "Do you think we're putting too much on their shoulders?"

Talan made a rude noise, much like the snort of a dragon. "You've seen Laina. She'll embrace this role without hesitation."

And the two walked hand-in-hand down the hallway.

Kaia had a very determined look on her face. She had listened intently as the blue dragon explained how to run and leap into flight from a level surface. Laina, although slightly more fidgety, also listened closely to the lecture. The only flight they had experienced, outside of Kaia's accidental one, was gliding over the water in the cave, and all of that momentum had been generated by Raine. It was far more difficult for them to generate their own. The great hall was very long and the ceiling very high, and both had taken several runs across the room, gliding for short distances, running, then hopping up to glide some more.

"Very good," Kylan said. "Now that your wings are warmed up, let's get you to the next step."

Talan and Raine settled across the room, draped over one another, content to watch Kylan in her dragon form instruct the young ones. The great blue dragon spread her wings, and they went wall-to-wall across the hall as both Kaia's and Laina's eyes grew wide.

"The next time your feet leave the ground and your wings are carrying you, tilt them back slightly like this."

The great wings rotated at the shoulder, tilting them only a few degrees.

"If you don't tilt them enough, very little will happen." Kylan demonstrated the position by rotating them forward. "But if you tilt them too much—" at this, she rotated them rearward so they were perpendicular to the ground, "—it will slow you and you will fall unless you can flap your wings to maintain altitude."

Both tiny dragons digested this information, then looked to one another.

"Laina, why don't you go first?"

The little red dragon took a ready position, crouched to the ground, then began sprinting across the stone floor. She leaped, glided for several feet, and Talan leaned forward in anticipation. Laina tilted her wings, but as in all things, far too much, which stalled her out. No amount of frantic flapping could stop her rotation as she nearly somersaulted backwards, her tail high in front of her, then landed with a thud. She righted herself, then shuffled back to the starting line with a wounded look on her face.

Kaia nosed her sister to make certain she was unhurt, then took her own ready position. She began sprinting, then leaped upward with purpose. Unfortunately, she had taken her sister's lesson too much to heart and barely tilted her wings at all. This resulted in her landing, hopping, skipping, jumping, gliding, then landing, hopping, skipping, jumping, repeatedly all the way across the hall.

Talan cleared her throat and placed her hand over her mouth to hide her smile. Kylan transformed in a flash of white light, and walked over to the two of them, soliciting their assistance with a shrug.

"Well, I tried."

"I can fix this," Raine said. "Kaia, Laina!" she called across the hall.

The two little ones were circling one another, intertwining necks and tails in commiseration of their failure, but they snapped to attention at the commanding tone of their mother.

"Stand next to one another," Raine instructed, "wing-tip to wing-tip. When I say go, you run together, when I say launch, you launch together. When I say tilt, you both tilt your wings backward, and when I say tilt again, you tilt your wings forward and land, running until you can stop. Understand?"

Both tiny dragons nodded, all trace of despondency gone, focused on the words of their mother.

"Ready? Go!"

The two little dragons began running side-by-side, in perfect stride.

"Launch!"

Little leg muscles corded, and the red and blue dragon glided in a perfect, level position.

"Tilt!"

The baby dragons tilted their wings in unison, Kaia slightly more than before and Laina slightly less, the maneuver popping them up several feet before they instinctively leveled out and glided at the higher altitude.

"Tilt again!"

The babies tilted their wings forward, lowering themselves several feet until they were again gliding just above the ground.

"Stop!"

Both babies instinctively rotated their shoulders rearward, so the wings acted as a brake, as they had seen their mother do so many times coming into the cave, and they gracefully came to a stop with only a few steps required.

Raine could not contain her grin as the two little ones scurried over each other in excitement at the far end of the hall.

"How is it that someone who can't fly is able teach them better than I?" Kylan said with a sideways glance at Talan.

"She's spent decades riding on my back," Talan said drily, "so I imagine she has a good grasp of the mechanics."

Raine leaned over to kiss Talan. "I'm so distracted by your flight I can't imagine that's true." She eyed the frolicking babies. "But it's their destiny to balance one another, this I know."

"I see," Kylan said, "that's why you had them do it together."

"Yes," Raine said. "They'll make progress much quicker if they train at the same time."

Raine jogged over to the starting line as the babies bounded toward her. In no time, they were repeating the exercise at her command, each time better than before.

"There's another reason why Raine is such a good teacher."

Kylan eyed her liege, given her significant tone.

"I didn't know her father, Garik Estania, well, but if the Scinterians had kings rather than only generals, he surely would have been their king."

"Then why didn't you know him better?" Kylan asked. "You brokered the alliance with our former enemies. You brought the Scinterians and the dragons together to defeat the Sinister and the Hyr'rok'kin in the Great War."

Talan's gaze was distant. "Garik was a magnificent warrior, one without equal, a trait inherited by his daughter. But when not on the battlefield, Garik felt he had a calling, which was to train the Scinterian soldiers. It's said that Garik Estania, during his lifetime, was the lead instructor for the entire Scinterian army."

"So, Raine has inherited that from her father as well."

"Until I saw her with the children, I wouldn't have even thought about it. She has his tactical brilliance, his diplomacy, and obviously his skill in battle, but I never would have known she had his ability to teach until I saw her with these little ones."

Kylan watched the Scinterian with the two baby dragons that were now flying across the hall, experimenting with different altitudes and even occasionally attempting more complex maneuvers. Kaia was managing reasonably tight turns, and Laina was at times near the ceiling of the great room.

"Your children are going to be dangerous," Kylan commented.

"Yes. Yes, they are."

Chapter 14

ow that is a beautiful set of armor."

The sun glinted off the armor, revealing the deep burgundy color that appeared black in darker light.

Raine grinned. "This was a gift from my love, forged by the Deep Miners."

"I can tell it was made by the dwarves," Kylan said, "just by the craftmanship, and it resembles your Scinterian armor in style. But what is it made of?"

"Touch it," Raine said, extending an arm.

Kylan reached out to finger the fine mesh material, then could not resist stroking it. It was maddeningly familiar, and when Raine moved in the sunlight, it gave off iridescent flickers that resembled flame.

"This is Talan's dragonplate," Kylan said slowly, astonished.

"It is!" Raine exclaimed. "She saved the scales she shed and had them ground into material which the dwarves forged. It's the most remarkable armor I've ever seen! And it's fireproof, so I have no idea how the dwarves were able to do it."

"Fireproof?" Kylan asked.

"The children like to set me on fire."

Kylan burst into laughter. That didn't even surprise her. The cloud that passed over the Scinterian's face, however, did.

"And what's that about?"

Kylan was as shrewd as Talan when it came to certain things, and

Raine would not lie to her.

"Most of the fireballs sent my way are in play or training, but the one time they truly did set me on fire, I was asleep."

"Asleep?"

"I dreamed of Hel," Raine said darkly, "and it felt so real I became cold as ice."

"Ah," Kylan said, "so the children attempted a rescue."

"Of sorts," Raine said, a grin tugging at the corner of her mouth, chasing the dark expression away. "It worked."

Kylan was reluctant to bring the darkness back, but Talan had mentioned the dreams to her. "Do you think the Goddess was really here?"

A muscle in Raine's jaw worked as she wrestled with the question.

"I don't know," she said at last.

Just then, Talan came out onto the enormous open courtyard with the two little ones scurrying about her legs. In the few days they had been in the castle, their flight had improved dramatically. They were able to fly down the long corridors, at first making wide turns but gradually tightening the radius until they were swooping around corners at a fair speed. They chased one another, and other than a few scraped wingtips and claw marks on the walls, the flight was without incident.

Which is why Raine was ready to take the next step. The interior of the castle was safe and controlled, but real flight required dealing with a multitude of factors.

"You think they're ready for this?" Talan asked mildly.

"Well, no," Raine said, and both girls frowned. "Which is why we're going to hedge our bets, so to speak."

Raine withdrew what looked like a tangle of leather straps from a bag near her feet. "I had these made while I was in the wood elf camp. I described what I wanted, and they were able to craft them like magic." She held the straps up, adjusted their length, then smoothed out any remaining twists or knots. "Kaia, come here."

The little blue dragon bounded over to Raine, then obediently stood still while Raine pulled the harness over her head, then fitted it about her sturdy little body. There was ample room for the wings, and after some additional adjustments, the harness fit snugly about the torso without binding neck, tail, or legs.

"Does that feel okay?"

Kaia nodded solemnly while Laina sniffed, then nudged at the straps.

Raine pulled two rolls of flaxen twine which had metal buckles at the end that snapped into the harness just underneath each wing.

"What is she doing?" Kylan whispered to Talan.

"I have no idea," Talan whispered back.

Raine just grinned, giving one last tug on the straps and patting the harness. She stood upright.

"Now I'm going to give you all the slack you need," Raine said, addressing both miniature dragons. "When you feel a slight tug, don't resist but go with the tug. If you feel like you're about to fall, don't panic, just spread your wings a little and I'll take control."

Both Kaia and Laina nodded.

"These first few times, you'll go alone so I can help you, but when you get better, you can go together."

The girls again bobbed their heads in unison.

"Okay, come along now."

The two women followed Raine curiously as she walked to the edge of the balcony, then up onto its wide ledge. The two little ones fluttered up to perch on each side of her. Kaia stared down the mountainside nervously, and Raine stroked the back of her neck.

"You're not going down there," Raine said, flashing her a brilliant smile. "You're going up there."

The little blue dragon looked up into the pristine sky and felt an excitement and longing she could barely contain, as well as the surge of courage her mother imparted. Laina shifted from one foot to the other, her excitement growing as well.

"I want you to just jump, spread your wings, and I'll do the rest."

Kylan elbowed Talan. "Do you want to transform just in case this doesn't go as planned?"

"No," Talan said, "I think I know what she's doing."

"Okay, Kaia. Ready? One, two, three!"

The tiny dragon's legs bunched with muscular effort and the baby leaped into the sky. Although she was able to level out, she was not gaining any altitude other than from the land falling away below. Raine allowed the twine to slip through both hands, giving her some length to work with.

"And here we go," she murmured, then skillfully tugged on one line, removing the slack, while separating her arms to raise the second line.

The effect was instantaneous, causing Kaia to pop upward and wheel about. The tiny dragon roared with excitement as she gained altitude, giving a few experimental flaps, then gliding as she tested the updrafts.

"She's flying her like a kite!" Kylan exclaimed.

And the red dragon smiled, for indeed the Scinterian was flying the little dragon as skillfully as she flew a kite, a past-time for which the wood elves were renowned, and one that Raine had clearly mastered. Raine gave the little dragon more and more line, moving along the ledge when she needed to take in slack, coordinating the lines together so that Kaia could turn, dive, and attempt maneuvers the baby never would have managed on her own. She allowed her to fly for a prolonged period of time, and when Kaia started to show fatigue, she gradually pulled in the lines, stepped backward to the center of the courtyard, then brought the little one to a graceful, gentle landing.

Kaia bounded about in ecstasy, beside herself with excitement. Laina could barely contain herself, and Raine struggled to extricate the wriggling Kaia, then struggled equally to equip the little red dragon.

"You're not helping," Raine admonished her, and Laina desperately tried to still her fidgeting so it would be her turn

"Was that fun?" Talan asked as Kaia bounded over to her, somersaulted, then leaped about the two of them. She blew smoke, then fire, then ran back to Laina to encourage her. Raine again took a position on the ledge, and in no time, Laina was also wheeling about, gaining altitude, and engaging in ridiculously advanced acrobatics, testing the various wind conditions with glee.

"They'll be flying by themselves in a matter of days," Kylan said in disbelief.

"Yes, they will," Talan agreed. Under normal circumstances, a baby dragon would learn to fly much like a baby bird. The problem was that dragon flight generally advanced much slower because their wingspan to girth ratio was not advantageous, at least not as babies. Birds gained lift as their feathers came in, but dragons had to wait for their wing membranes to grow large enough.

Unless, of course, your mother knew how to fly you like a kite. Raine was teaching them all the things that normal dragons could not learn until they could gain lift, at the same time strengthening their wings so that "lift" would come much sooner. And Talan could already see the instinct of her children taking hold as they adapted to the various conditions, updrafts, downdrafts, gusts, even high winds.

Finally, Raine reeled the final flight in. She kneeled to counsel the two as she removed the harness from Laina.

"So, eventually, we'll try the two of you together. When we do that, you'll have only a single line each, so you'll be responsible for your own maneuvers. I'll still be able to help you, but I have less control with one line, so you're going to have to work really hard to get to that point."

The two baby dragons, tired as they were, hung on her every word. Both nodded gravely, causing Kylan to hide a smile.

"Now you need to go eat a lot of meat."

Raine emphasized the last three words, and the girls yelped in agreement as both were starving. They sprinted off towards the castle, chasing one another and nipping at each other's tails with little razor teeth that grew sharper each day.

"And drink water!" Raine called out after them.

"You," Talan said, leaning down to place a kiss on Raine's forehead, "are amazing."

"That was incredibly fun," Raine said, "I dreamed about doing that even before they hatched."

Kylan just shook her head. "I wouldn't have believed it had I not seen it with my own eyes."

The twins gorged themselves on half an elk that Kylan had once frozen with her breath, and that now, Talan thawed with hers. While the children ate, Raine busied herself over the fire, cooking up some fine rare steaks for the adults, although hers was a little less bloody than those of the dragons. Talan, after eying the ample pantry that Kylan possessed, chose a few items and created a salad and side dish of seasoned grains that caused Kylan to raise her brow at the heretofore unknown domestic skills of her liege. And the blue dragon disappeared to peruse her nearly endless wine cellar, returning with a vintage selection worthy of the occasion.

The three women sat about a small fire pit that was more ornamental than functional. The gigantic oven at the far end of the room did the heavy lifting and heated the entire castle, but it was unlikely that any but Talan could withstand that heat with any degree of comfort. This heat was necessary because, although Talan could create her own heat due to the nature of her dragon breath, Kylan had no such ability, and had stocked her castle accordingly. As a frost dragon, she was more tolerant of the cold, but the freezing temperatures of the castle were not comfortable even to creatures who breathed ice. Therefore, there was a wing of the castle devoted entirely to the storage of fuel for heating. Wood, oil, even the strange rocks taken from the volcano K'ran'a, were stored there. The firepit inside the oven was lined with these rocks and, once heated, they would retain their temperature for days. Throw a little wood on the firepit, blast it with dragon fire, and the entire castle would be heated comfortably.

Still, the flickering flames of the fire that was not actually doing any work were pleasant, and the three women sat around them and ate their meal and drank their wine while the twins settled drowsily in front of them.

"Have you heard anything of Volva?" Talan asked, ripping a piece of meat from the bone with incisors that were no less sharp in her human form.

"No," Kylan replied. "I would think it would take decades for that tail to grow back, and she can't fly, well, not with any skill, without it."

Dragons did not possess external ears, rather just openings in their skulls where sound passed through, but Raine saw the twitching of the tails of both twins that indicated they were listening.

"Come on you two," she said, rising to her feet. "You can sleep in here tonight, but I want you a little closer to the big fire."

The babies padded after her, disappointed they would not hear such an interesting conversation but pleased that they could sleep nearer the flame that brought them so much bliss. Kylan observed their departure with curiosity.

"She enjoys the Similitude with them, doesn't she?"

Kylan was referring to the mental bond that all female dragons had with their offspring while the dragons were in infancy. It was an ability to communicate that went beyond speech or even thought, almost a pure transmission of understanding. It did not last long, fading as the infants matured, although whispers of it could remain into adulthood.

"She does," Talan agreed, "to a far greater degree than I do. In fact, I've never seen anyone possess it to the degree that Raine does with these little ones. Sometimes, I feel she's speaking aloud simply as a courtesy to everyone else. But they seem to understand exactly what she's saying."

Once the tiny dragons were settled on a pile of furs, wrapped about one another in the radiating heat of the gigantic forge, Raine returned to Kylan and Talan.

"You don't think Volva will return for decades?" Raine asked, settling next to Talan.

Kylan took a sip of her wine, laughing. "If you could have seen the tail that was left behind when that Tavinter chopped it off, you would think centuries."

Volva was the only remaining Ancient Dragon outside of present company. She had aligned herself with Talan's enemies in an attempt to defeat the Queen of all Dragons and bring back the darkness that the Hyr'rok'kin brought upon the world. Her plan had nearly succeeded, but Raine had sustained Talan with her life force while Idonea had broken the bonds with which Volva had imprisoned the great dragon. And in retaliation, Kylan and Drakar had enlisted Skye, a young Tavinter of enormous power, to battle the gold dragon. Skye's magical gifts tended towards stealth, and she had mastered the ability to make objects "ephemeral," essentially nonexistent until she said they were.

In the battle with Volva, Kylan had been snared by her traps, and Skye had been forced to flee, but in an act both desperate and brilliant, she commanded the castle gate to become ephemeral, then manifest right on top of Volva, severing her tail.

"She'll nurse her wounds for a while," Talan agreed. "I don't expect to see her anytime soon."

This brought a palpable sense of relief to Raine. Everything had changed with the birth of the little ones. She felt little if any fear for her own safety, and her love was immortal, the most powerful creature in this realm. But the babies were vulnerable, defenseless against the horrors arrayed against them. Until they were grown and became the Arlanian-

Scinterian-Dragons they were meant to be, they were exposed not only to natural enemies, but to the host of adversaries she and Talan had acquired in their lifetimes. And that list, like their lives, was both long and distinguished.

The conversation waned as the three were content to sit before the flames. The fire's crackle and pop was soothing, and the food and wine made Raine a little drowsy.

"You look tired, my liege."

The words were innocuous, benign, a simple courteous observation, applicable as much to Raine as Talan. And yet the words hung in the air.

"I assure you, I'm fine."

The comfortable silence grew oppressive.

"Well," Raine said, "I'm a little tired myself. I think I'm going to go lie down with our children. Would you care to join me?"

The two rose as one, and Raine bowed to Kylan. "Thank you for a most enjoyable evening."

The tall, lean dragon and her muscular companion walked across the room towards the great forge. Kylan watched them go, a thoughtful look on her face.

Chapter 15

The twins bounded up and down the courtyard, tackling each other and rolling about in an energetic frenzy. Their flying lessons had been progressing quickly, and today they were going to advance yet another step. Raine busied herself preparing their harnesses, this time using only a single metal buckle centered on each harness, as opposed to two spread equally apart, as before. She carefully snapped a single line to each center strap.

"Are you sure they're ready for this?" Kylan asked, expressing aloud the thoughts Talan was keeping to herself.

"No," Raine said, "they'll crash within minutes."

"Then perhaps it should wait a few more days?" Talan suggested.

Raine continued to busy herself with the straps. "Failure is an important part of Scinterian training. It builds character, instills humility, and most importantly, it teaches one to learn from mistakes."

"That will be important for Laina," Talan said dryly.

Raine yanked on a strap to test it. "Kaia will make as many mistakes, just different ones."

This intrigued Talan, for both widely recognized themselves in their two children, Talan in Laina, and Raine in Kaia. She wondered what mistakes Raine had made in her early life, because as long as she had known her, Raine had made few.

The sun was bright in the courtyard, the sky a pale blue without a cloud in the sky, unlike the previous three days in which it had stormed unceasingly. And Talan realized that was another reason Raine had chosen this day. The weather was clear, the winds were mild, and the slope was covered with loosely packed snow drifts that would cushion any hard landings.

"Come here you two!"

The two baby dragons galloped across the stones at Raine's command, wings fluttering in excitement. Raine patiently maneuvered the squirming little bodies into the harnesses.

"The sooner I get this done, the sooner you can fly," Raine murmured, which was enough to still the fidgeting and let her finish the job. She tested the straps on Laina, adjusted them, tested them on Kaia, then patted the soft leather in satisfaction.

"Now," she said, snapping a line into each harness, "today you'll have only one line apiece, so you can fly together. But that means I have far less control over your flight. I can help, but you two are going to be responsible for most of it."

Laina nipped excitedly at Kaia, and Kaia returned the gesture with a head butt. Raine sighed. This was going to be interesting.

"Alright," she said, giving them some slack on the line and motioning for them to follow. "You're going to fly only on the south side over here."

The south side had a gentle decline, unlike the north, which had a precipitous 1000-foot drop. The south side would be forgiving were there any mishaps.

"I want both of you to jump off into a glide," Raine said, stepping up onto the ledge. "I'll give you some slack, then pull up so you can gain altitude. Kaia, you stay to the west, Laina to the east. Ready? Go!"

Little legs flexed and the babies leaped off the ledge and began gliding. They followed the slope downward a ways as their lines spooled out, then Raine lessened the rate of spooling and took up the slack. The babies popped upward away from the ground, their strong little wings giving them lift as they instinctively maneuvered about. Tiny roars drifted back to the women on the huge balcony. Raine controlled each line, giving a tug here or a pull there, but for the most part, the girls were doing the work, and Raine's movements were little more than suggestions.

Talan watched her little ones with pride, thinking perhaps Raine's assessment was too pessimistic, right up until it was proven completely apt. The tiny dragons were so excited about flying with one another they forgot their mother's caution to stay east and west. The flew nearer and nearer, swooping at one another playfully despite Raine's tugs to keep them apart.

"And here we go," Raine muttered.

Emboldened by their new freedom, the two seemed to forget that Raine was helping them and overrode her line control. That worked well for a brief time until they both wheeled about and collided head-on with one another. Both stunned, they separated, and all the frantic flapping in the world could not stop them from plummeting to the ground.

Were it any other group of women on the balcony, the reactions would have been markedly different. But given that two were Ancient Dragons, and one was Scinterian, the dramatic collision drew little reaction at all. Raine simply sighed, holding a slack line in each hand, while Talan gazed in bemused consternation at the two little wriggling tails sticking up out of the snow. Kylan muffled laughter.

"Shall I go retrieve our children?"

"You shall," Raine replied.

The silver-haired woman disappeared in a flash of yellow light and the gigantic dragon leaped from the parapet and glided the short distance down to the fiercely wiggling tails. She landed gently near them, sweeping up great gusts of snow with her wings. The tails stopped squirming when they felt the earth shake. The serpentine neck lowered, and the great jaws gently clasped one tail and pulled a baby free from the snow, then grasped the other and did the same. She nudged them both in the direction of the castle, and Laina hunkered down to the ground and honked in protest. Even Kaia barked plaintively. Neither of them could generate the lift from their present position to fly back to the castle, and it would be a very long walk.

The great dragon felt her heart swell for her little ones, but she would not let this lesson go unlearned. She shook her head, nudged them again, and with a sweep of her great wings, levitated, then powered upward with a few thrusts. She wheeled about to gain altitude, then wheeled about again to land gracefully in the courtyard once more. To the girls, she looked very small in the distance, as did the castle.

The two little dragons began padding morosely up the snowbanks towards the keep. They castigated one another with head butts, tail smacks, even snorts of fire that bounced off one another harmlessly. The nipping and chipping left a meandering trail in the snow from the dejected dragging of their tails. The journey took them twice as long because of their meandering, but they were at last at the base of the wall. Raine looked down at them, her legs dangling off the edge as she sat patiently, reeling in their lines.

"Are you ready?" Raine asked, standing, and both little dragons braced themselves within their harnesses.

"Would you like me to pull them up?" Kylan offered.

It would have been effortless for the blue dragon to transform and pull the two little ones up the wall, but Raine would have none of it.

"That's alright," she said as she turned about, flinging a line over each shoulder. "I don't want to get soft."

Kylan did not see how that was possible as the Scinterian flung a line over each shoulder, leaned forward, then began marching across the courtyard, leg muscles straining as she pulled the two little monsters slowly upward. When they reached the top edge, Raine was all the way across the large square. Talan leaned down and grabbed one harness while Kylan grabbed the other, pulling the tiny dragons up over the wall.

Raine jogged back over, and neither of the babies could meet her eye. Laina was studying the cracks in the tiles and Kaia was staring off to the left at nothing.

"And what did we learn?"

The mild rebuke told the little dragons that Raine was not angry, and they swarmed over her in repentance. Their fluttering, twitching remorse made Raine laugh.

"Tomorrow we'll try again."

And on the next day, the little dragons listened to Raine, kept their distance, and soon were flying as acrobatically as they had with the dual line control. As days passed, Raine allowed them more and more slack, and their control grew accordingly. After a week, little wings strengthened and unbeknownst to them, Raine was doing little if anything. About three weeks into their training, a beautiful day under a clear, blue sky, Raine walked out onto the courtyard in keen anticipation. Both little ones posted up on their sturdy little legs, posturing for the donning of the harness.

"I don't think so," Raine said, "not today."

Little tails drooped in disappointment, but their mother's mood was curious, and they perked back up, sensing her excitement. She put a hand on each little scaly brow, stroking them, then slid the hands beneath their chins, tilting their heads up so they were all eye-to-eye.

"Today," she said, pausing meaningfully, "today we're going to fly without them."

A fierce roar split the heavens and the Queen of all Dragons wheeled about and swooped down into the courtyard, followed by her right hand, the stunning blue frost dragon. The two giants thundered onto the platform, and the two babies were in a frenzy of excitement and fear. Their mother was enormous, but the two Ancient dragons together took up most of the courtyard. Awe and terror, but mostly exhilaration caused the babies to hop about, snap at one another, chase their tails, and blow fire. Raine had anticipated this reaction and wore her full armor, which deflected the results of their rambunctious enthusiasm.

"Come along now," she said, striding towards the parapet. "Laina, you, there," she said pointing to the left. "Kaia, you, over there. No, farther apart."

The two little dragons inched apart on the low wall, and Raine stood between them. "Your mother is going to need more room than that."

The two little ones understood as Talan's neck snaked past Raine. They moved with far more alacrity, balancing atop the wall.

Raine could not hide her grin as she looked upon her love. She had been dreaming of this from the day she learned Talan was with child.

"Might I have the honor of a ride?" she requested formally.

"You'll have to behave yourself," Talan said, feigning disappointment. But Raine was not fooled. The Queen of all Dragons was taking flight with her children for the very first time, and her excitement rivaled, even surpassed that of Raine.

The lithe Scinterian grasped the ridged scales just forward of Talan's body and pulled herself upward. It was the strongest part of the dragon's neck, although Raine could ride all the way forward, just back of Talan's head and the dragon would barely feel it. But it was Raine's experience that, especially in battle, Talan could whip her head about in a manner that could send her flying if she wasn't prepared. Riding close to the body eliminated some of that whiplash movement and allowed for a more comfortable ride. She settled into the space between thorny spikes, stroking the scaly skin in the gaps between the armored plates. The touch sent a shock of electricity through Talan as the dragon lumbered up onto the low wall.

"And so, my love," Raine said, leaning down close, "I turn their training over to you."

Another thunderous roar split the heavens, and it was answered by two tiny roars that made Raine grin ear-to-ear. The great red dragon leaped into the sky, and without hesitation, the two tiny dragons leaped after her, gliding free and on their own for the very first time. They paralleled their mother, gliding when she glided, flapping when she flapped, and making wide graceful turns at her wing tips. And as Raine watched, other than the fact that the little ones required thirty flaps to their mother's one, they imitated her beautifully. They flew slightly forward of her great wings, so they weren't swamped by her turbulence.

The two little ones were so ecstatic at the experience that, for once, there was no tomfoolery. The only difficulty that Raine could see was that it was a strain for Talan to fly so slow, being so large. With little wind, she could only glide so far. But Raine had anticipated this problem, noting the differences even in Drakar's flight from his mother's. She turned about and gave a nod to Kylan, who swooped near in response.

"Come here little ones," she rumbled, and the two babies slowed as their mother pulled ahead.

"If you want to keep pace with a much larger dragon," she instructed, "you must fly here."

Kylan swooped down into the draft of her liege. The two girls followed her lead and positioned themselves just behind the rhythmic up-and-down of their mother's tail. They were astonished at how flying suddenly became much easier, almost as if they were pulled along in their mother's wake.

"And," Kylan said, tilting her right wing down and moving to the right and rearward of Talan's wingtip. "If you're flying long distances in a group, you must fly in a 'V' formation, because it's more efficient."

Kylan wheeled away and the two little ones obediently split off, so they formed a "V" behind their mother, and again they were struck at how the lift from her wings propelled them forward. They roared in excited discovery.

And Talan's heart sang, for other than Drakar and Kylan, she had not flown with other dragons in centuries, and when her children were fully grown, they could fly in a full draconic phalanx, which she had not done since the Great War. Every time she had watched the geese migrate, she felt a twinge, but the fact that the great and terrible movement of the dragons could be revived filled her with an emotion she could barely contain.

Raine leaned down and kissed the reptilian skin beneath her, feeling the emotions of her lover. The Queen of all Dragons possessed the largest heart in the realm in pure physical size, that was indisputable. But most would be shocked to learn that, metaphorically, it was also true.

Of course, Raine had known this all along.

Chapter 16

Every day was filled with joy as the two Ancient dragons and the two baby dragons leaped into the sky together, traveling further, higher, and faster, each and every hour. And Raine rode astride her love, thinking no Scinterian in all of history could have felt greater happiness. Although once enemies, Scinterians and dragons were two halves of a single whole, and to be bound to an Ancient, then have children by her, was an indescribable gift.

The children were a wonder, larger each day, their extremities beginning to catch up to their overly large heads and stocky bodies. Still tiny compared to the two Ancients, they were at least more proportional, and their flight improved as a result.

Raine's lessons had achieved a profound result, and Kylan determined that, whenever she got around to re-contacting the rest of their kind, she would recommend the method. The two little ones jetted about, somersaulting in the air, barrel-rolling over their mother, and engaging in playful acrobatics that were jaw-dropping. Kaia had already perfected a tight corkscrew that allowed her to rapidly descend in place, and Laina had developed the ability to stop so quickly that anyone behind her would hurtle past before they could react. Watching the two play, dive-bombing each other in terrifying maneuvers that elicited little more than laughter from their parents, was extraordinary. Kylan felt like she was seeing the birth of something entirely new for their Kind.

"Do you see that elk down there?" Talan murmured.

"I do," Raine said. "Do you think it's time for some practical exercises?"

"Yes," the dragon rumbled.

"Kaia! Laina!"

The baby dragons wheeled about and came close to Raine, paralleling her movement on the back of Talan, their small wings flapping away.

"Do you see that elk down there?" Raine called out to them.

The two little heads dipped as Talan made a wide circle about the area. They turned bright eyes back to their mother.

"I want you to take it down."

The two little ones felt a thrill of excitement as Talan continued her wide, leisurely circle about the area. She was high enough not to disturb the elk and maintained a position to where her shadow would not cross over the beast, considerations to which she was certain her offspring were oblivious. The two briefly came together, then with no planning at all, dove down toward the animal.

It was a testament to their raw talent that they nearly got the elk, despite their many mistakes. But their shadows spooked the animal, and as he leaped sideways, then sprinted into the undergrowth, Laina barely managed to avoid a tree trunk and Kaia crash-landed into a pile of dirty snow. Kylan's chuckle drifted over on the wind to Raine and Talan.

"So close and yet so far," Raine said under her breath.

The children regrouped and flapped upward to their parents, catching an updraft which eased their ascent.

"And what did we learn?" Raine prompted when the little ones were gliding next to her once more.

Neither had yet mastered human speech, or even spoken a word, but they were both expressive. Laina began honking out a litany of excuses while Kaia muttered and growled overly critical pronouncements of their actions. Raine stopped them with a raised hand.

"You're both wrong."

The two babies looked to their mother as their wings fell into a rhythm with Talan's.

"Kaia, you're too harsh, and Laina, you're making too many excuses. It is what it is. And you must see through to that. Now what did you learn?"

The wind whistled past them as Talan flapped once to the twenty flaps of the little ones, who were deep in thought. They wheeled about in a wide arc over the trees.

Kaia muttered a few growls, and somehow Raine interpreted this baby dragon-speak.

"Yes, you're right. You approached from the wrong angle and the deer saw your shadow as you came in."

Laina offered a few more growls, higher pitched and a bit more sing-song than her sibling, but just as clear to Raine.

"Yes, you're also right. You should have coordinated your efforts and approached from different angles. And you should have anticipated your post-attack trajectory."

"There's another one," Talan rumbled, changing course.

"Alright," Raine said, "I want you two to formulate a strategy, then I want you to go get it."

The two babies peeled off as Talan again began a wide, high circle, and they hovered as they discussed their plan. When it was set, they separated, and Raine watched intently.

Laina dove downward, directly in the sun's path so that her shadow passed over the beast, but this time, when the elk tried to escape, he leaped right into the path of a swooping Kaia, whose jaws closed around his throat and took him to the ground. The yelping beast disappeared into a spray of blood as the two baby dragons pounced on it.

"Hmmm," Talan said apologetically. "That's the dragon in them."

"I don't know," Raine said with a sigh, "it might be the Scinterian in them as well."

But despite the bloodbath, Raine could not hide her pride. Not only had the girls learned from their mistakes, they had used their knowledge to induce the deer into a fairly complex trap. And when the babies were done with their frenzy, which had little to do with hunger, Talan glided in and landed beside them.

Laina took stock of her sister's bloodied condition, then glanced down at her own scales, slick with blood. She was a little embarrassed and studied the moss on the tree next to them. Kaia, too, assessed their behavior, and was belligerently uncertain how to feel.

"There's nothing wrong with bloodlust," Raine said, strolling towards them. "You get that from both sides of your family. It's a natural state for a dragon, and Scinterians have long given in to it in the heat of battle. The trick is," Raine said, glancing down at the mauled deer, "it must serve a purpose, and it must be controlled."

The two babies pondered this statement while a bright flash of yellow light brought their mother in human form to them. A flash of white light followed, and all three adult women could now fit in the clearing with the baby dragons.

"But you brought us dinner," Raine suggested, nudging the deer carcass with the toe of her boot. "Might we share in the spoils of your hunt?"

Both Kaia and Laina bounded about in excitement. The thought that they could provide food for their parents and for the blue dragon filled them with joy.

"Then I'll make a fire," Raine said. "We can probably camp here for the night, if you want."

The thought of an overnight outing caused yet another flurry of excitement, and the babies bounded about the small clearing.

"Why don't you two go rinse off in that stream?" Talan suggested, and the babies sprinted off.

"They'll sleep well tonight," Kylan observed, watching them go.

"Yes, they will."

Raine found some cuts of meat that were not completely mauled and prepared dinner for the three adults. She allowed the little ones to chew on the carcass and watched as they both prepared the venison to their liking. Laina barely seared the outside with a quick puff of fire while Kaia sustained the heat slightly longer for a more medium rare cut, then both set to gobbling the meat down. It was not long before they settled around Talan drowsily, nosing her limbs so they could get close. And it was not long before Talan, too, drifted off to sleep, leaning back against a tree, a child under each arm.

Raine poked at the fire with a stick, gazing into the flames. She looked across the flames at her lover, sleeping peacefully with their children. It was a beautiful sight, but her expression was more one of resignation. Her eyes drifted to Kylan, who was not watching the fire or Talan, but was watching her. And as their eyes met, Kylan knew the Scinterian understood.

Raine poked the fire again and returned to staring into the flames.

Chapter 17

Y'arren, the elven matriarch, arose early as was her custom. She nodded to her acolytes and set out for a walk in the nearby forest, as was also her custom. She would make the rounds of the nine altars that surrounded the wood elf encampment, meditating at each one, before returning to the village.

Her meditations, however, were cut short this day, indeed, were never started at all. As she approached the first altar, an object attracted her attention, an onyx box placed carefully in the very center of the altar. She slowed her step, then stopped.

She extended her senses outward toward the strange object. It was magical and yet not, radiating enormous power, but from an unknown source. It did not seem evil or good, just profoundly neutral. She resumed her approach, her wooden staff making a hollow sound on each stone step.

She stopped at the top and leaned forward on her staff to examine the object more closely. Strange markings were engraved in the glossy blackness, words and glyphs that had no meaning to her. This itself was momentous, because no one in this realm knew more of language and lore than her. The markings looked familiar, however, as if they were related to something within her great extent of knowledge, although not present themselves.

There was a piece of parchment placed beneath the corner edge of the black box, and Y'arren hesitated to touch it. Something was at work here, but for the life of her, she could not determine what. The box was not large, was rectangular in shape, and utterly obsidian in color. Its gloss created an illusion of depth, as if one could stare down into the glyphs far past the box itself.

Y'arren shook her head. Part of her wanted to leave the box where it was. But she could not do so without risking harm to someone else if the object was dangerous. She reached out her gnarled hand, but again hesitated and the hand hovered in the air. At last, she pulled the piece of parchment from beneath the edge of the box.

Now these were marking she understood, ancient elvish, the old tongue, a language that few in the world still spoke. This made her think she was the one meant to find it, because there were only a handful in Arianthem who would even recognize the language, let alone be able to read it.

She read the note slowly, her lips moving as she translated the ancient words. She frowned, and then read the words again. Her eyes returned to the black box, still uncertain. At long last, with great misgivings, Y'arren picked up the onyx coffer, tucked it beneath her arm, and started back towards her camp.

Chapter 18

"Can you see him?"

The two girls stood perched on the parapet, eyes straining at the horizon. They were both so taut with excitement that Laina had already fallen off once and had to loop back around to land, ready once more.

"There he is."

The girls leaned forward, wings held close to their bodies, eyes still straining. They could not see what Raine had spotted. They shifted from foot-to-foot impatiently, willing the black dragon to appear.

And then they saw him, the sleek silhouette visible at last. The baby dragons trembled with excitement, their shifting increased, and their little necks wove back and forth in a serpentine dance.

"Hold on," Raine said, "he's not close enough."

Laina nearly tumbled off again, and for a moment her little claws scrambled for hold as she backpedaled furiously. But her forward motion was halted when Raine reached over and grabbed her with one hand, stabilizing her.

"He's almost here," she murmured.

Both little dragons thought they were going to die, so fiercely were their little hearts pounding in their chests. They had been waiting for this.

"Alright," Raine said, "Go get him!"

The babies shot off the balcony like miniature missiles, wings flapping furiously as they raced one another toward their big brother. A roar of joy echoed back to them as Drakar recognized his little sisters and the two baby dragons roared in response. They were wingtip to wingtip as they neared him, two little specks in the sky as they peeled apart and darted about him. Raine could see the whiteness of his teeth even from that distance as his great jaw widened into a smile.

The three siblings engaged in an extended display of acrobatics, and Idonea was remarkably cool on Drakar's back, given the forces she was likely experiencing with the jolting changes of direction. Her laughter drifted back on the wind. Finally, Drakar leveled out, and Laina drifted inward, plopping down on his neck in front of Idonea, who embraced her both with her arms and with the spell she was using to maintain her position. Kaia drifted off to Drakar's left wingtip and stoically powered on until they reached the courtyard, at which time she glided into an almost perfect landing. Drakar followed her lead, coming to rest next to his little sister.

Laina scrambled from his back and both girls galloped over to Raine, who caught them mid-air in their leap, then hugged them tightly. Raine set them down and they bounded over to Talan, nudging and head-butting her while she stroked them with proud affection.

Idonea slid from her brother's back, then Drakar disappeared in a flash of red light, and the twin beauty of the dragon's elder children emerged arm-in-arm.

"By the gods," Drakar commented, slightly out of breath, "how in the world did they learn to do that?"

"It's a long story," Talan said, giving him a kiss on the forehead, "and Raine is an excellent teacher."

"I would say so," Idonea said, leaning forward, and Talan lightly kissed the cheek she proffered. "They could barely walk last I saw them."

Kaia frowned, for that certainly wasn't true, which made Idonea laugh. Kaia slid a side-long glance at her twin and took from Laina's expression that Idonea was teasing them. She turned back to Idonea and reared back, blowing a small funnel of fire in her direction which Idonea laughingly deflected with an impromptu magical shield. The two twins were wide-eyed at this feat, which was much more impressive to them than being able to fly or breathe fire. They bounded over to her and scurried about, effectively communicating their fascination and admiration for this ability.

"And how is Madame Directorate?" Raine asked cheerily.

"She's well," Idonea said, stroking the wriggling little bodies bumping up against her legs. "She sends her regards to both of you, deeply regretting that you could not visit yourselves."

"I thought I told you to take care of them," Talan said to Drakar.

"I did my very best, mother. There are dozens of elven ladies far happier now than when we arrived. But the Directorate seems to desire only her little scholar, although she speaks lustfully of Raine."

"Who doesn't?" Talan said with a sigh.

Kylan caught the tail-end of this conversation as she entered the courtyard. "Ah, my liege," she said kissing Idonea on the cheek and hugging Drakar, "all of Arianthem went into mourning the day you and Raine found one another."

A delightful dinner passed with Drakar regaling all with his adventures in the elven capital, the more ribald tales censored due to the presence of the young ones. Kylan enjoyed the recount of his misadventures, particularly when her imagination could fill in the missing parts. When he was finished, Idonea discussed what little had been learned regarding the second prophecy, relaying what had already been revealed by Y'arren.

"And what makes Kiren believe this prophecy is related to the first?" Talan asked.

"I'm not certain," Idonea said, "I'm not nearly the scholar that she is. But something in the pattern of the words, the phrasing, is like the first."

"Even though those words are unknown?" Raine asked.

"Yes. Kiren had difficulty explaining it, but there was almost a rhythm that was reminiscent of the lines of the previous prophecy, absent that final line that no one could translate. Well, no one but the two of you."

Raine glanced at Talan. They had known the final line that had spelled out Raine's fate, and thus had been able to circumvent it. But now they had several lines that could not be translated.

"I took a rubbing of the actual artifact," Idonea said, removing a piece of parchment from an inner pocket of her robe. "I understood none of it, but Kiren is certain the third line reads 'to defeat that which cannot be defeated.'"

"And how would she understand even that?" Kylan asked. "With so little to go on?"

"The history of Arianthem is one of bloodshed and conquest," Idonea explained, "and some words have been handed down over generations with little change. Language can be a form of subjugation, determined by the victors, and therefore constant across cultures. Words such as this are likely to be similar or the same."

Talan held out her hand and Idonea passed the parchment over. The dragon examined the strange markings. Four lines of equal length, the first line in two parts. Although the markings bore a clear resemblance to ancient elvish, they were different enough that the words were incomprehensible. She could see the similarities to "defeat" in the third line, but that really meant nothing to her. In the common tongue, "gorge" could mean a narrow valley, or what her children did at the dinner table. She was reluctant to give this prophecy any credence at all.

Raine was pressed to her side, looking over her shoulder, and Talan passed the parchment to her. Raine set the cloth upon her knees and stared at the ancient markings, a look of concentration on her face. Talan felt an odd tension, and glanced to her companion, whose striking good looks were highlighted by the flickering light of the fire. Raine chewed her lip, a gesture which normally would have produced nothing but desire in the dragon. Now it filled her with a slow-growing dread. Raine reached out to touch the third line, her fingers lightly brushing across the raised lettering. The fingers brushed the second line, so similar in diction to the third, but so frustratingly unknown. And then the fingers settled on the second word of the first line.

"This is 'child,'" she murmured.

Idonea leaned over to see where she pointed. "Yes," she said, surprised, then reminded herself that Raine was one of the few in Arianthem who spoke Ancient Elvish. "That was the only other word Kiren could translate."

"And the second line does mirror the third," Raine said, her fingers again brushing the parchment, a gesture that felt like fingers brushing up and down Talan's spine while the word "child" was a whispered echo in her ear. "At least in pattern."

The tension Talan felt seeped into the rest of the group. The strange shadows that flickered across Raine's face made Drakar uneasy, as if they were cast by entities not present in the room. Idonea was troubled that Raine seemed to have made some sort of connection with the words when she had hoped the prophecy would have no credence at all. And Kylan felt the tautness in her liege and friend as if the strain were upon her directly. The two little ones hunkered close to the ground in front of the fire, tails and necks tightly intertwined.

"Enough," Raine said, abruptly breaking the spell that had fallen on all. She was tempted to throw the parchment in the fire. But she had burned many copies of the previous prophecy, and it had done nothing to change fate. She handed the parchment back to Idonea, aware that two tiny dragons were staring at her somberly, sensitive to the mood that had fallen on the group. She stared at them sternly.

"Go," Raine said, and two little dragon heads perked up, "get the book."

There was a mad flurry, then a scramble as sharp nails tried to gain traction on the stone floor, which once achieved, resulted in a headlong sprint for the door. The two little reptilian bodies disappeared, there were several large metallic clatters in the distance, then Kaia came racing through the door slightly ahead of Laina, the Elven Book of Lore in her jaws. Laina would have none of this, grabbing Kaia's tail, which caused her to jerk to a stop but the book to continue in a straight line into the fire, or it would have had not Idonea raised her hand, instantly stopping the book's forward progress. It floated in place as the two baby dragons looked on in chagrin, and then the book gently floated over to Raine's waiting hand.

"Really?" Raine said as Talan looked at the ceiling and Kylan hid a smile. The mood had utterly changed and Drakar breathed easier.

Both girls scurried over to Raine, swarming her in mortification be-fore settling down on each side. Kaia rested her chin on Raine's leg and Laina nudged her side, but as always, Raine was more entertained by her children than angry. They were dragons, and she would always judge them by that unruly metric.

"So, where were we?" Raine said, opening the great book, and two little heads snaked over her shoulder. "Yes, we were here."

Talan leaned over to examine the elaborate illustration, and Idonea did the same from the other side. Drakar made a note to look through the book later, and Kylan could picture the page, having already spent hours poring over the magnificent tome.

The page depicted a Scinterian battle formation. Great flags flapped in the breeze, carried by standard bearers who, unlike most in that position, were well-armed for they could wield the sharpened poles with ferocious dexterity. The drummers stood apart, their pointed drumsticks as much weapons as instruments, the drums themselves less musical than violently utilitarian. The troops themselves stood in unconventional arrays based upon individual skills, the sword, the shield, the lance, the bow, all covered in the blue and gold markings raised upon their skins so brilliantly illustrated they looked as if they could leap from the page. And at the very top of the cliff stood the horn blower, the Scinterian who would sound the battle cry.

"This one here," Raine said, tapping the horn blower, "this would be the commanding general."

The girls glanced at the fierce muscularity of the men and women on the page, enraptured.

"He or she would blow the horn, calling all the Scinterian to battle, but this was no normal battle cry."

Both dragons looked to their mother, again highlighted by the flame from the fire. "The Scinterian horn sounds much like this."

And then an unearthly, ethereal, noise came from Raine, beginning somewhere low in her diaphragm and landing precisely in her vocal cords to produce an eerie, modulating sound somewhere in the vicinity of several minor chords. The call was not loud, but somehow echoed throughout the hall, folding back upon itself in stunning, terrifying harmony. It descended in a disorderly manner that was gorgeously discordant. It hummed inside the two baby dragons with a vibration that touched every bone and membrane. Both Kylan and Talan were startled, but Raine was oblivious to this reaction, so intent on the girls was she. She looked down at the two wide-eyed dragons.

"And once the horn was sounded, the drums would begin."

Raine began tapping her fingers on her leg, at first a slow, gentle patter, the emphasis on the first beat. The little dragons stiffened. Somehow, they knew this song as if it was a part of them.

"This beat calls the infantry to formation."

The rhythm pulsed, and after a few repetitions, Raine increased the tempo and shifted the emphasis to the second beat, striking her legs a little harder. The baby dragons understood this ancient, primal rhythm, and their hearts began to beat in time.

"This one calls the cavalry."

After a few rounds, Raine increased the tempo once more, her strikes heavier and faster, the emphasis now on the third beat as the slow growing crescendo inexorably swelled. She smiled a fierce smile.

"This one calls the archers."

The fourth beat became the emphasis as the pace again increased, steady and unrelenting.

"This one calls the dragons."

When the emphasis finally shifted back to the first beat, it was a different song entirely, the rhythm unstoppable and merciless, declaring victory before the fight had even begun. Shadows flickered on the walls surrounding them.

"And this one," Raine said, "sounds the charge."

With a final violent slap on her knees, Raine finished the percussive symphony. The two tiny dragons trembled with excitement, filled with an energy that made them feel as if they would explode.

"Go!" Raine encouraged, laughing aloud, and the two little ones scrambled about, plowing right through the fire and sending embers in every direction. They sprinted from the room, taking flight before they were even at the door. They had no idea where they were going or what they were doing; they just knew they needed to move and burn off the energy that threatened to consume them.

Raine chuckled at the destruction they left in their wake, brushing some embers from her clothing. She caught Kylan's eye across the fire, and Kylan's enigmatic expression caused Raine to glance over at Talan, who bore the same look. It took Raine a moment, but then she understood.

"I'm sorry," she said, coughing a little, "I forget there are those here who have heard the real thing. I apologize if I did it poorly, or if it brought back unwanted memories."

Kylan stared at the youngster in front of her, quite certain the girl understood nothing. Raine had performed the battle call perfectly, and the rhythm of the drums had been so precise, Kylan half-expected a Scinterian army to appear. Although Raine had brought back many memories, none of them were unwanted. It spoke of a glorious, violent time when the dragons and the Scinterians united to save the world, and she yearned to join the twins as they raced around the castle.

"Where did you learn to do that?" Talan asked, quiet wonder in her voice.

Raine flicked another ember from her shirt, as if to brush away the question. But Talan leaned around to capture her gaze. "Where did you learn that?"

"My uncle taught me," Raine admitted, brushing one more nonexistent ember away. "Apparently it was my father's wish that I learn them even if there were no more Scinterians to call to battle."

Talan pondered this admission, marveling that there were still things she did not know about her Scinterian.

"Your father would be proud," Talan said at last, and the words brought comfort to Raine.

"I think I'm going to go find those little monsters," Drakar said, rising to his feet. The drums had affected him as well. "Maybe we should go burn something to the ground."

It was late at night when the twins finally settled in. Raine had been wrapped drowsily around Talan for a while when the two little girls burrowed in the blankets next to her. The silver-haired woman was sleeping peacefully and barely stirred at the intrusion. Soon, soft snores and little puffs of warm breath told Raine the little ones had followed their mother into sleep.

Raine was drowsy but not sleepy. Her mind was a little too active for slumber just yet. Perhaps it had been the strangeness of her reaction to the parchment bearing the prophecy, the unwelcome connection to words she could not even understand. Or perhaps it was the beat of drums that still pounded in her chest and throbbed in her veins.

Raine rolled over on her side, slightly dislodging Laina, who gave a little honk of protest in her sleep. Raine grabbed the little tail and wrapped it back around her waist, and the baby dragon twitched happily next to her.

Raine positioned her arm beneath her head so she could look at her love as she slept. The regal features, the long dark eyelashes, the slight lines about her eyes and mouth, all filled Raine with a fierce longing coupled with a growing melancholy she could no longer ignore.

She sighed and rolled over onto her back, staring up at the ceiling as Laina adjusted her tail once more. The real reason she could not sleep was the weight of the unspoken conversation that lingered between her and Weynild, and she made up her mind that they would speak tomorrow.

Drakar was back in dragon form, his sleek black outline a contrast against the light snow in the stark morning light. Kaia and Laina bounded around him, playing tag around his legs while his serpentine neck chased them. Idonea was glowing with a soft light generated by the spell that kept her warm despite her minimal clothing. Raine adjusted the straps on her armor, more out of habit than necessity since it was so well-fitted. She checked the fit of her two short swords in their sheaths, the presence of the weapons also likely unnecessary since she was heading out with five dragons and a mage. Still, she pulled them out halfway, then re-seated them, satisfied with the action.

Kylan and Talan came out into the courtyard, and Kylan's expression made Raine take a closer look at Talan. The silver-haired woman was as gorgeous as ever in the early morning light, but there was something about her that finally forced Raine's hand. She approached the two women, Kylan in her blue armor and Talan in her red.

"Kylan," Raine said, "I know we were planning on an all-day outing, but Talan and I have had little time to ourselves. Do you think you could take our children," Raine paused, mentally adding Idonea and Drakar to the group, "well, all our children out for a flight, and we'll join you soon?"

Kylan was not fooled for an instant, and Talan's side-long look at Raine told her she was not fooled, either.

"Of course, my dear. I imagine you've had little time to yourselves since the twins were born. Join us whenever you're ready."

Raine felt a pang as the blue dragon transformed and the little ones now bounded over to play in her enormous shadow. She suppressed the flutter of anxiety she felt knowing that neither she nor Talan would be with the babies. But as the little ones frolicked about the two massive dragons, one as black as night and a colossal one that twinkled like the starts, Raine knew they would be safe.

"We won't go far," Kylan promised, sensing Raine's apprehension.

Idonea watched the exchange curiously. Her first thought had been that her mother and Raine intended to dive into bed, but as Raine took her mother's hand and Talan said not a word, Idonea revised her opinion. She was not certain what was going on, and the inscrutable look on her mother's face as the two turned back towards the castle did not set her mind at ease.

"Let's go," Kylan directed, and the blue dragon's tone only furthered Idonea's unease.

Raine and Weynild walked through the castle holding hands, neither saying a word. They were used to comfortable silences, but this was not comfortable. Raine felt as if she were bearing an enormous weight, most of it pressing down on her heart. She had to remind herself to breathe.

They went into their private room, and Raine stirred the embers in the firepit back to life as Weynild settled in front of the flames. The kettle was still warm, so Raine prepared them both tea, handing a cup to Weynild as she settled next to her, angling her body on the couch so she faced Weynild's profile. Weynild took a long drink from her cup, the amber eyes glowing as she stared into the fire.

Raine tried to take a drink, but her throat was thick with unsaid words and ached with pent-up emotion. She could not swallow and set the cup aside. Her eyes began to glisten, and then slowly, a beautiful purple tear escaped and began to roll down her cheek. Weynild sighed.

"Raine."

Raine closed her eyes as she fought for, then regained control. Weynild did not need to say anything more. Her resigned tone as she spoke her name told Raine everything she did not want to hear. Raine took a deep breath and steadied herself, preparing to speak the words she had avoided for months.

"You need to sleep."

"Yes," Weynild said simply, reaching out and taking Raine's hand. "I do."

Raine clenched the hand, willing the conversation and all its meaning to just go away. Weynild was not speaking of just any sleep, but rather the Great Sleep of the dragons, crucial for their renewal and longevity. It was not a choice, but an inevitability. Not a matter of "if," only "when" and more importantly, for how long.

"This is my fault."

"What?"

"If only I had been more powerful when we fought Hel," Raine said. "If I had more magic, it wouldn't have drained you so."

"If it weren't for you, I'd still be encased in amber," Weynild said, dismissing Raine's self-recrimination. "And it was only the power you were able to give me through our bond that defeated her. This is not your fault. You could as much blame it on me for giving birth to two dragons instead of one, and yet there's nothing I would change or trade for them in all the world."

Raine had not thought about that. It was likely the combination of the battle with Hel, then giving birth, that had led to Weynild's need for the Deep Sleep.

"It could be for only a few months," Weynild said.

"Or it could be for a century," Raine said, her voice cracking, "or more."

Weynild did not argue this point. Dragons could sleep for centuries.

"I'll be without you," Raine said, staring into the fire. "For years. Possibly decades."

Weynild was silent for a moment, then spoke quietly. "And I may awaken, and my children will be fully grown."

This silenced Raine. She had not thought of that aspect of it. Her own suffering had occupied her mind because she imagined Weynild blissfully sleeping while she endured her absence. But Raine had not considered the dragon's side and was now ashamed of her self-absorption.

"I've been selfish."

Weynild pulled Raine to her.

"You're never selfish. You're the most selfless person I've ever met. And the only thing that keeps me from utter grief is knowing you'll be here with the girls while I sleep. You will raise them. You will teach them to be Scinterians, and you've already shown you can teach them to be dragons. They'll keep you company. Kylan will be here. Drakar and Idonea can come and go. And you can sleep every night at my side."

"I will protect you," Raine said fiercely.

"I know."

Weynild kissed her deeply, and it was not long until the sorrow transitioned to anguished passion. The dragon and her lover spent hours exploring one another, as if for the very last time.

Kylan was unsurprised that Talan and Raine did not join them on their outing, and she and the children returned to the castle in the early afternoon. The babies raced through the halls and swarmed their mothers, chittering and growling their rendition of the day's events. Raine was animated as she asked for details, and Talan nodded her approval. But both Kylan and Idonea observed the resignation that permeated Talan and Raine as they went about preparing some food, noting that although the two were somber, the strain had dissipated. Acquiescence to some unspoken truth had taken hold, relieving the tension but adding a sense of melancholy.

Empathy was not Drakar's strong suit, but even he sensed the mood of his mother and Raine. He sent several questioning looks Idonea's way, and she silently communicated her own uncertainty accompanied by the unspoken agreement they would talk later.

But that would not be necessary, for Raine had thought at length on how to explain this to the girls, and in her musing had gone to the Book of Lore in the off-chance that Y'arren had included this aspect of dragon history in the tome. But of course, the elven matriarch had done far more than that, and as Raine caressed the pages she needed, those near the end of the book, it became apparent that Y'arren had once again seen events long before they transpired.

After the baby dragons were fed, Raine motioned for them to join her near the fire as Talan settled between Idonea and Drakar, and the three quietly discussed events from Alfheim. Kylan sat halfway between the two groups, interested to see how this would unfold. Raine dragged the book to her lap and began thumbing through the pages, stopping when a little nose would nudge Raine regarding some item of interest, and the three would explore and discuss the pictures. Kaia was greatly intrigued by the dwarves, and Laina spent a lengthy amount of time examining the numerous drawings of the Ha'kan. Raine explained the various clans of dwarves, then the difference between the warrior, scholar and priestess castes of the Ha'kan, deliberately vague on the description of the priestess caste as her daughter gave her a wry, skeptical look that reminded Kylan so much of Talan, she muffled laughter.

Finally, Raine turned to the page depicting a sleeping dragon. The behemoth was curled up in a cave, much like the mountain keep in which the children had been born. And the fire in front of the beautiful red dragon cast iridescent flickers upon her scales so that she appeared to glow with a gentle flame as she peacefully slept. Both little dragons leaned closer, for the rendition was perfect and the dragon unmistakable.

"Now, this is important," Raine began, and her tone was such that it caught the attention of both Drakar and Idonea.

"Dragons are immortal, so they can live forever as long as they don't become sick or injured. And unlike the sons and daughters of men, they become stronger, and bigger as they get older. A dragon can be killed in battle, but as long as they have some life force left, there is a chance they can recover."

Raine's finger absently caressed the red dragon on the page. "But in order for dragons to live so long, to remain immortal, sometimes they need to sleep."

Kaia furrowed her brow. She slept every night, but that didn't seem to be what her mother was talking about.

"And not just any sleep," Raine said. "The Deep Sleep of the dragon, the 'Dragon's Night,' can last a very long time."

Idonea had a sudden sense of unease, as did Drakar. Raine was not telling a simple story.

The finger caressed the fiery red dragon again. "The Dragon's Night can last for years, decades," Raine cleared her throat. "Even centuries."

The two baby dragons stared down at the red dragon on the page, then looked to one another. Amber eyes and blue eyes flitted to Raine, troubled, then returned to the page, staring at the sleeping dragon. Finally, as one, they both looked to the golden eyes of their mother across the room, whose heart was breaking even as outwardly she was impassive as could be.

"Yes," Raine said, seeing that they understood. "Your mother needs to sleep. And soon."

The babies' attention returned to the sleeping dragon on the page, their hearts heavy. They could not comprehend even a year apart from their mother, let alone a decade. And the time span of a century was equivalent to forever in their young minds.

"She's not going away," Raine said firmly. She knew how to halt their negative thoughts because she had already fought this battle with her own. "She'll be here. Right here. With us."

Both little ones stiffened as this thought took hold, and Raine pressed forward. "And it will be our duty to protect her."

When Raine spoke these words, her purple eyes burned with a violet fire that no Arlanian had ever displayed, but that fire was matched by the burning violet in the eyes of her baby dragons. They posted up on their sturdy little legs, wings slightly spread, tails alert, gazing across the room to their mother with a fierce fortitude that made Talan's heart swell to bursting.

"Every day," Raine said, as if announcing an edict, "we will guard this castle with our lives to protect the Queen of all Dragons."

Both Kaia and Laina bobbed their heads, as if this duty were inevitable.

"And every night," Raine continued, "we will sleep wrapped about her to keep her warm."

Again, both baby dragons nodded fiercely, ignoring the reality that the body mass of all three would scarcely cover Talan's right foot.

"And we will never be apart."

The two little ones bounded from Raine's side and sprinted to Talan, smothering her with love and imagined protection. And Talan hugged her babies as she gazed upon her lover who somehow had managed to relay grim knowledge in an almost victorious manner as Idonea and Drakar struggled to absorb this news. Kylan felt the glisten of tears, certain she would cry even though tears for a dragon were rare.

Raine's eyes still burned with a purple fire, for although her little ones might contribute little, she spoke the truth when she said she would protect Talan'alaith'illaria with her last breath.

Chapter 19

It will be soon."

"Yes," Talan said, her arm draped about Raine's shoulder as they sat on the low wall, their backs to the thousand-foot drop that bordered the north side of the castle. They sat hip-to-hip as the two little dragons frolicked in the snow in front of them. Drakar was throwing snowballs at them which they gleefully incinerated in mid-air. Idonea sat on a bench near the doorway absently casting spells with her left hand as she read from an ancient book. When the castle had belonged to Talan, the great library in the eastern wing had been established, and when Kylan became possessor of the keep, she had both maintained and expanded the collection. The assortment of books, tomes, manuscripts, scrolls, and letters rivaled both the elven library in the Alfheim capital and the Ha'kan collection in Haldis. It was Raine's intention to begin exploring the collection, and to teach the girls to read in another year or two.

This thought caused an ache in Raine's throat, for her love should be present for that. Talan squeezed her shoulders, sensing the distress that came and went with the arbitrary flitting of Raine's thoughts. But she could not and would not lie to her, not to bring a comfort that would be painfully temporary.

"It will be tonight," Raine said quietly, "won't it?"

"I believe so."

Raine suppressed her Arlanian emotion with Scinterian pragmatism. "Is there anything you should eat before you sleep?"

Talan squeezed her shoulders again. "No. My sleep will be so deep I'll need nothing."

"Is there anything I should—"

Raine broke the sentence off. It sounded foolish, asking her if there was anything she should do in her absence when that absence could be a hundred years. The Arlanian ache in her throat returned.

"I don't know if it would be better or worse if I knew how long you were going to sleep."

"I know," Talan agreed. "I try to pretend I'll see the children in just a few months, and then I wonder how it will be if they're fully grown by the time I awake."

Raine mulled the many partings they had been forced to endure. They had spent far more time together than apart, but it never felt that way. "I know it's been two years, but I feel like I just got you back from another sleep."

This thought also weighed on Talan. They had been separated by the capriciousness of Hel and by entombment and captivity. At times that felt like yesterday.

Talan stood, taking Raine's hand. "Let's go inside."

Idonea's hand paused in mid-spell as she watched her mother and Raine enter the castle. She, too, knew it would be tonight.

Evening came far too soon, and as the sun went down and the castle dimmed to the light of fire, a somber mood settled on all. Talan could not help but think how different this was from her last Great Sleep, when she had dozed off without a care. This time she left so very much behind, and although she did not deign to pray to the gods, she sent a silent supplication to Sjöfn, the Goddess of Love, to make this sleep brief.

The children were uneasy, picking at their food, and after several fitful starts of conversation, the adults fell into silence. After the extended silence grew oppressive, Talan had enough and stood up.

"I'm merely going to sleep," she said. "I'm not dying, and I have two dragons, a powerful mage, and the greatest warrior in all Arianthem to make certain that doesn't happen." She moved to Kylan. "You're my friend and my second, and I'm grateful you'll care for my family. No," Talan corrected herself, "I'm grateful you are my family." The two elegant women hugged one another, and Kylan bowed to her liege when they separated.

"Drakar," Talan said, taking her son's hands in her own. "I'm so very proud of you. You take good care of your sisters."

"I will, mother," Drakar said, hugging her fiercely.

Talan turned to Idonea and embraced her. "My beautiful daughter, blessed and cursed to be so much like me. Keep an eye on that one," she said, nodding to the little red dragon with the amber eyes.

"Oh, don't worry," Idonea said, "anything she tries, I've done before."

This brought about low laughter from Talan, welcome to the heart-stricken group. "Well, keep an eye on that one, too," she said with a head toss in Kaia's direction. "She'll find new and interesting ways to get in trouble."

"Now come my love," Talan said, taking Raine's hand. "And come on you two," she said to the little dragons, "let's go to bed."

And the four walked from the room.

Talan had chosen the far end of the grand room with the forge for her place of rest. It was deep within the castle, protected, and very warm, although this last feature was not necessary for her, but would make it more comfortable for Raine and the children, given their intent to sleep with her every night.

"I can stay in my current form for the time being, if you like," Talan said. "I'll change naturally when I fall asleep."

Raine shook her head. "No, I want you to transform and get comfortable. Besides, you know I love you just as much in your natural form. Possibly more."

The silver-haired woman smiled, stepped back, and then disappeared in a brilliant flash of yellow light. The two little ones scurried about as the enormous dragon circled once, then twice, then settled down on her belly, snaking her neck around to rest upon the floor. After she shifted a few times, scraping against the tiles of the floor, Raine climbed up onto her neck and sat behind her head, leaning back against the great girth of her body, her legs dangling above the floor. The baby dragons scrambled up, flapping their wings to get a little lift, then settled in the warm crook on both sides of Raine. Talan's breathing slowed, and her great eye half-closed as the small dragons nestled in.

"Let me tell you a story," Raine began, and the babies fluttered happily.

"The first time I met your mother, I had to climb up the entire side of the mountain to get to the cave where you were born."

The girls greeted this feat with snorts of admiring disbelief, emitting tiny puffs of smoke. Raine's hand absently stroked Weynild's warm, reptilian skin, and the dragon gave a low rumble of satisfaction.

"I know. It took me forever to climb all that way. And when I finally reached the top, I found this beautiful red dragon. But to be honest, I half-thought she was going to eat me."

This brought about giggling from the two of them.

"But I didn't care," Raine said, "because the minute I laid eyes on her, it was love at first sight…"

Chapter 20

The next morning, Raine's eyes opened. She was laying on Weynild, the two little ones curled up next to her. The red dragon slept peacefully, the slow rise and fall of her chest gently rocking the trio. The breathing was rhythmic, but already slower than normal. Weynild had explained that as time progressed, her breathing and heartbeat would slow and almost stop, but this was no cause for concern. As her sleep deepened, she would enter a state of hibernation in which all her functions would nearly cease.

Raine climbed down, careful not to dislodge or waken the little ones. She gazed upon the red dragon and tried to fathom the strangeness of it. Her love was here, but not here. She felt a great loss, but it was hard to maintain the feeling or plumb the depths of the emotion because Weynild was still right here. She could touch her, and she could feel her presence far more than when Hel had entombed her. It was difficult to sort out what she was feeling right now, and the fact that Weynild could awaken in a few weeks or in a century made it all the more difficult to sort through her feelings.

Raine moved quietly through the castle and out on to the courtyard, somehow surprised that the sun was indeed rising, the orb oblivious to the fact that a large part of her world had stopped. She leaned on the stone wall, gazing out over the gentle slope of the mountainside that went on for a thousand leagues. The frozen stone of the wall was painful to her hands and that pain began to leech up her arms.

"I know the Scinterian in you likes to suffer when the Arlanian in you aches," Idonea said, coming up behind her, "but losing your hands to frostbite is probably not a good idea. I would warm you with the spell I use," she said, handing her a cloak, "but we all know how well magic works on you."

"Thank you," Raine said, pulling the cloak about her shoulders and tucking her hands inside its warmth. "I feel so numb, I guess I was just trying to feel anything. Or maybe I'm feeling too much and was seeking numbness of another kind."

"Likely both," Idonea said, "because you are you."

Birds began to chirp, the hardy little finches and robins that somehow survived and even thrived on the top of the mountain. Squirrels jumped from tree-top to tree-top, dislodging white powdered flakes, and a white fox trotted across the field beneath the castle, leaving a trail of pawprints in the otherwise pristine snow. It seemed impossible to Raine that life could just go on as normal.

"I wonder if it's my destiny to be both most blessed and most cursed by the gods."

This was an unusually morose thing for Raine to say, but also unusually apt.

"The last two years have been the happiest of my life," she continued, "and for them to end this way seems so unfair."

Idonea could not disagree with this statement. Raine and her mother were a perfect match, two halves of the same whole. But time and again they had been called upon to fight for Arianthem, even against the gods themselves, and this usually resulted in their separation. Now that they were at last together, a happy family, a simple characteristic of dragon biology separated them.

"At least you have the little ones," Idonea said. "And thank the gods they have you, because they'll miss our mother terribly."

The word "our" reminded Raine that once again, she was being thoughtless. Weynild was also Idonea's mother, and she would suffer from her absence.

"Years ago, I don't know that I would have missed her that much," Idonea mused. "But you came along and healed our relationship, and now I'll miss her terribly."

Raine thought back to when she first met Idonea. "You would have missed her then."

"Yes," Idonea admitted. "But I would have pretended not to."

The chirps of birds and the chatter of the squirrels filled the gap in conversation, and then Raine squinted her eyes.

"Do you see that?"

"Not yet," Idonea said, scanning the expanse of the sky to see what Raine meant. "Only your great raptor has eyes better than you."

"Funny you should say that, because I think that's who's coming."

Idonea saw a speck in the crystal-clear sky, but it was some time before she could even identify it as a bird. Soon the wings became distinct, even though it was some distance out. Finally, the outline resolved into the shape of a great hawk, and as it neared, its size became apparent. It let out a piercing cry, circled the castle once, then glided into the courtyard to land on the wall near Raine.

"Hello, Gersem'i," Raine said as she approached the bird. It would have been her height standing on the ground and it dwarfed her on its perch. But the raptor lowered its head, and Raine reached up to scratch the back of the bird's neck where the feathers were ruffled, awaiting that hand.

"What's this?" Raine asked, lifting the leather bag that hung about the hawk's neck. She looped the strap over the head to free the bird from its burden, then set the bag on the wall. She removed a small scroll from the top of the pack.

"It's from Y'arren," Raine said, identifying the seal as she unrolled it. "And she didn't want anyone else to read it because it's written in the Ancient tongue."

"What does it say?" Idonea asked curiously.

"She's enclosed something. A box she found on one of the altars near their camp. It had this note attached."

Raine pulled out another piece of parchment and felt an odd tingling, much like when she had touched the parchment with the rubbing of the prophecy on it.

"I don't like that look on your face," Idonea said.

Raine examined the piece of cloth. It had only a few words written on it, again in Ancient Elvish.

"I've been practicing the Ancient tongue," Idonea said, "but I'm not nearly as proficient as you. I recognize your name, but nothing else. What does it say?"

"Not much," Raine said, "only four words. 'A gift for Raine.'"

"A gift for you? From whom?"

"It doesn't say." Raine glanced back at the scroll. "And Y'arren doesn't know, either."

Raine set both the scroll and parchment aside, and with some degree of disquiet, reached into the pack and pulled out a black box. It was smooth, dark as night, shiny, made of some unknown material that gave the illusion of depth. One could peer down into it as if the box were far deeper than its dimensions allowed. Idonea leaned closer. There were a few markings on the lid of the box, imprinted rather than engraved and perfectly flush so they did not mar the smoothness of that surface.

"Can you read those glyphs?"

Raine shook her head. "I don't recognize any of them. You?"

Idonea also shook her head. "No, they're not familiar. Is it magic?"

"If it is," Raine said, "then I just disenchanted it. Do you feel anything?"

Idonea laid her hand on the lid of the box. "I don't," she said, "not magic, anyway. But it does feel powerful. Which makes no sense at all," she admitted, "if it's not magic. Can you open it?"

Raine examined the box from different angles, holding it up in the sunlight. There were no latches, hinges, or locks. Only a thin line around the center gave any indication that it was not a solid block. She tried to lift the top off, but it would not budge. "I don't see any way to open it. Perhaps it's some sort of puzzle."

"A mystery indeed. Does it feel dangerous?"

On the face of it, the question might have been ridiculous. But Idonea had learned that Raine had instincts about these sorts of things.

Raine turned the box over, running her fingers over its smooth, flawless surface. She could see her reflection in the black depths.

"No," she said at last. "Something. But not dangerous."

She sighed, then placed the box, the scroll, and the note back in the leather pack. "I'll put it away for now. I'll have plenty of time to explore this mystery later."

The twins arose mid-morning, and although initially dejected, their exuberance overcame their sorrow, and soon they were racing around the castle. Raine did catch Kaia gently nudging Weynild to see if she could awaken her, but the great dragon slept peacefully on, oblivious to the little head butting up against her. Kaia started guiltily when she saw Raine.

"Don't worry, little one," Raine said, "I tried the same thing this morning."

Somehow the day progressed normally, as if Weynild were just out for a hunt rather than sleeping for possibly the next hundred years. Raine went through moments where everything was alright, but because everything made her think of her love, her thoughts returned to Weynild often, which made the pain of her absence even more acute.

While Raine sat on the retaining wall, Idonea entertained the two little dragons with various spells while Kylan made frost patterns in the air. Laina was particularly fascinated by the magical spells, watching her older sister closely. It was interesting to watch the little dragons in their natural form because they were so intelligent and coordinated even at that age, which carried over into their infant forms in a distinctly unnatural way.

"I wonder if Laina will become a mage," Drakar pondered aloud, at Raine's elbow.

"Is that even possible?" Raine asked. She knew quite a few dragons and they were all imbued with dark magic, but she didn't know any of them to be mages.

"It's not impossible," Drakar said. "We're full of magic, but very few are capable of controlling it enough to cast spells. That's why Idonea is so powerful, and so very unusual."

Drakar's admiration for his sister was for once free of the lust he normally displayed. He tended to be a little more circumspect around the two little ones, saving his inappropriate behavior for when they were not there.

"But she's not a dragon."

Drakar made a rude noise. "By the gods, she might as well be. And it wouldn't surprise me if that one," he said, nodding towards Laina, "turns out to be one of the few of our kind capable of spellcraft."

"And what about that one?" Raine asked of Kaia, curious to know what Drakar thought of the little blue dragon.

"Ah," Drakar said, "do you need to ask? That little monster is going to be the fiercest warrior in this realm." Drakar paused, then amended his statement, "Present company excepted, of course."

"No, no, you were right the first time, or at least that's my hope," Raine said. "That's the hope of every Scinterian parent; I'm no exception. I hope these little ones exceed their parents in every way."

Drakar laughed. "The Divine help Arianthem."

Chapter 21

As the week progressed, Weynild's breathing reduced, her heartbeat thudded ponderously slow, and except for the sluggish, intermittent rise and fall of her chest, the great body ceased to move as she fell into a deeper sleep. Raine, Kaia, and Laina attempted with some degree of success to find normalcy. Raine spent the days playing with them, although to Idonea's eye, the "play" was thinly disguised training. True to their Scinterian nature, the girls loved it. Whether they were tracking Raine as she hid from them, flying through obstacle courses set up around the castle, or hunting in the surrounding forest, they approached the lessons with gusto.

Raine had, with some caution, mounted Kylan so she could join the girls in flight and was relieved that she did not respond to her as she did Weynild. This seemed to amuse Kylan, who had never doubted for an instant that Raine would remain true. Although Raine had a weakness for dragons, and Kylan was certain she could seduce just about anything that moved, neither would cross that line out of love for Talan. So, it was with relief and joy that Raine swooped about on Kylan, still able to cavort with the girls.

Drakar, surprisingly, was the most morose at Weynild's absence, and Raine began to understand that Weynild's baby boy was far more attached to her than he would ever let on. When he fell asleep one night in the great room, sprawled next to the firepit not far from the sleeping dragon, Raine did not have the heart to wake him. The next morning, Kylan approached Raine.

"That boy needs to have sex."

"All right," Raine said mildly, accepting the pronouncement with the full understanding that dragons handled their emotions via sex almost as much as the Ha'kan did. "Are you volunteering?"

Kylan broke into tinkling laughter. "Of course not. The boy would lose his head if I slept with him and I promised Talan years ago I wouldn't break his heart. He just needs to go find a tavern wench or five and get it over with. It's not good for dragons to remain pent up."

"And what about you?" Raine asked. "You sent all your paramours away before we arrived. You must be a little 'pent up' as well."

"A little," Kylan said, "that's the understatement of the year. I confess at times it's hard being around you, although your constant maternal instincts seem to take the edge off my lust. But I could use a tavern wench or five, a few stable boys, perhaps a dragon or two…"

"Well, this sounds like an interesting conversation," Idonea said as she neared.

"We were just commenting that Drakar needs to 'let off some steam,' so to speak," Raine said. "And Kylan as well. Which brings to mind your current condition. I've not known you to be celibate for any length of time."

"Hmmm," Idonea said, "I am due for a romp with my knight commander."

"Nerthus?" Raine laughed. "I'm sure she's pining away for you. And that will serve two purposes. It'll satisfy you and make Drakar jealous, and he'll end up bedding half the imperial capital."

"The imperial capital," Kylan said with a gleam in her eye. "A stealth visit for some debauchery sounds like an excellent idea. But what will you do?"

"What will I do?" Raine repeated. "I'll spend a few days with my babies in this nice warm castle at the top of the world."

"And you don't have needs?" Kylan asked curiously.

"You have to remember," Raine said, "I was celibate the first 300 years of my life before I met my love."

Idonea and Kylan were both silent, then Kylan turned to Idonea.

"I can't even imagine," she said, and Idonea burst into laughter.

"Neither can I," she agreed. "But will you be all right for a few days on your own? Not in terms of protection, of course," Idonea clarified, "I pity anyone who would threaten my mother or those two little ones."

A spark of violet fire flamed in Raine's eyes, a new and terrifying phenomenon that occasionally manifested since the birth of the children. Idonea surmised it was the combination of the extraordinary love Arlanians felt for their children coupled with the Scinterian's fierce need to protect them. It was the only time the purple in Raine's eyes inspired more fear than desire, at least in those wise enough to interpret that violet flame.

"Oh, I'll be fine," Raine said. "I think I'm going to begin teaching the girls to read. They're already so smart I think they'll learn quickly."

Kylan was having second thoughts. She had promised Talan she would watch after the girls, and perhaps it was not a good idea to leave Raine in the mountain castle without an adult dragon.

"Kylan," Raine said, tilting her head as if she read her mind, "Do you doubt me?"

It was then that Kylan recalled this was the creature who had twice defeated a Hyr'rok'kin invasion, had saved the mortal realm, and had conquered the Goddess of the Dead to take control of the Underworld. It was easy to underestimate her, given her lovely appearance and easy-going manner. But all who did so paid a price, and for most, that price was death.

"Nooo," Kylan said slowly, "I think you'll be fine for a few days."

Chapter 22

The three cloaked figures made their way through the bustling marketplace, the business district of the imperial capital. Tent-covered displays brimmed with wares: armor, weapons, furniture, jewelry and clothing. Food carts were overflowing with fresh fruits and vegetables. The smell of fresh bread blended not unpleasantly with the smell of hay. Peace was good for the people of Arianthem, as was the generosity of the Ha'kan, who had opened the trade routes to facilitate the commerce so evident in this city square.

The lack of conflict in the realm, however, did not create total complacency. The three cloaked figures stood out in the free-wheeling openness of the trade center, the opposite of what they were hoping to achieve. The eyes of the imperial guards stationed about the square began to follow them. One broke away from his post and began trailing them at a distance.

"Well, this isn't working," Idonea said. "You two can shapeshift; I can't. Why don't you turn into something nondescript and lower your hoods?"

"I think that's a good idea," Kylan said. She had no concern for her welfare; everyone around them was in more danger from her than she from them. But life was easier when they did not attract attention. And they were being followed by more than the guard. A shadowy figure tailed them at a distance far more covertly than the imperial soldiers.

Kylan concentrated, trying to contain the light of the transition within her cloak, then lowered her hood. Her fine, elegant features had changed to the plain, course features of a farm wife they had passed on their way through the gate, and her hair was now a washed-out gray. The illusion was easy for her to maintain since the woman's face was fresh in her memory.

Drakar, on the other hand, emitted a great deal of red light from beneath his mantle, then removed his entire cloak with a flourish, revealing a buxom bar maid he recalled from a previous fling. It was evident he remembered parts of her anatomy better than others as his breasts were three times the size of a normal woman's.

Kylan sighed.

"Drakar," Idonea muttered under her breath, trying to suppress her laughter. "You're such an asshole."

Drakar's dramatic presentation attracted the attention of not just the guards, but nearly everyone around them. And to make matters worse, he had dressed himself in a blouse with a tight belt about his midsection that pushed the gigantic breasts upward and created a canyon of his cleavage. Some tried to act casual, averting their eyes, then glancing back surreptitiously. Others just openly gaped at the near-comical display.

The imperial guard following them was in the latter group and stopped in his tracks. He stood gawking with all the others.

"Hey, sweetheart."

A man from the crowd staggered toward Drakar. He slurred his words and Idonea could smell the beer on his breath. She had the sudden premonition this was all going to go horrible wrong. She raised her hand, but the sheer absurdity of the slow-motion disaster hindered her response.

"How much to touch one of those?"

The man was so intoxicated, he tripped as he reached outward and went face-first into the mountain of flesh that so mesmerized him. The crowd started to laugh. Or they did so until the large-breasted woman grabbed the man by the back of his neck with one hand, then threw him over five rows of tents and halfway across the busy square. The eruption of laughter abruptly silenced, and the clanging metal, squawking chickens, and loud exclamations of fright and anger were easily heard from across the square, despite the distance from the hard landing.

"Drakar," Kylan said, sighing again.

The imperial guard behind them drew his sword fearfully, as did the multitude of others that began to close in on the trio. They did not know what they were dealing with; no human had that kind of strength, not even vampyre. Who knew what this creature really was?

Kylan took a deep breath, preparing to expel a little frost to cool everyone off when Idonea raised her hand.

"I've got this," she said.

She waved her hand about, making a few circles in the air, and as the guards neared, they lowered their swords, coming to a stop in confusion. They felt calm, unwilling to raise their weapons in anger. It muddled them and they stood there uncertainly, the swords dangling from their hands.

"What is going on here?"

An exceptionally large woman in heavy armor pushed through the crowd, accompanied by more imperial guards. Her fair complexion was ruddy with anger as she thrust one of the frozen guards aside and entered the impromptu circle that had formed about the three interlopers. She put her hand on the hilt of her greatsword, taking in the unlikely scene of the grotesquely breasted bar maid, the conspicuously plain farm wife, and the mysterious, still-hooded third figure.

"I'm not going to ask again," the Knight Commander said, partially drawing the greatsword from its sheath.

Tinkling laughter drifted from the cloaked figure, and the heart of the Knight Commander gave a little leap.

"Oh my," Idonea said, "just who I was looking for."

Idonea lowered her hood and Nerthus struggled to maintain her composure. Her fair skin flushed to the roots of her fair hair. The imperial soldiers were astonished, partially at the beauty of this woman, and partially at the reaction of their fearsome commander. Nothing fazed the Protector of the Empire. She was stoic, unmovable and unflappable in the face of everything. To see her react to anything or anyone in this manner was extraordinary.

Nerthus gathered herself. "Idonea," she said gruffly, "it's a pleasure to see you."

"The pleasure'-s all mine," Idonea said in a sultry manner that made the Knight Commander's men glance from the dark-haired beauty to the imperial commander, then back again. Their astonishment was transitioning to understanding, and then to enormous envy.

Nerthus re-seated her sword in its sheath and attempted casualness.

"And what brings you to the imperial capital?"

"Like I said, I came to see you."

Nerthus' eyes flicked to the comically-breasted bar maid. "Then let me guess who this is."

A flash of red light enveloped the bar maid, then disappeared to reveal the striking, dark-haired man. Gasps came from the crowd. Drakar's expression was sardonic as he smoothed his thin mustache.

"Knight Commander," he said, bowing effusively. Nerthus knew the young man well enough to detect his mockery, and well enough to ignore it.

"Drakar," she said, mirroring his slight sarcasm. "Couldn't arrive in the capital without making a scene?"

"The man touched my breast," Drakar said with mock indignation. "You of all people know how insulting that is."

Nerthus grew red again and her men paled at the comment, for beneath the Knight Commander's heavy cuirass were a pair of very large breasts that she took pains to conceal and they took pains not to notice. Only Idonea could take the sting from the off-hand remark, and she took a step toward Nerthus and slid her arm beneath the Knight Commander's.

"As I said before, Drakar, you're such an asshole."

The rebuke and attention soothed the knight commander, so much that she glanced down at the onyx star she wore to detect magic.

"As I've said in the past, any effect I'm having on you is not due to magic," Idonea said, and Nerthus was once again faced with the irony that she, formerly the most prominent mage-hater in Arianthem, had fallen quite hard for one. Her onyx star would tell her if magic was being used against her, but as always, it was inert in Idonea's presence. This mage did not require magic to cast a spell on her.

"And who is this?" she said, turning to the very plain woman in the superbly fine cloak.

"Just a friend," Idonea said.

"Really?" Nerthus said skeptically. These two did not travel with "just a friend." Their friends were the royalty of Arianthem, political leaders, or heroic figures from the pages of history itself. But the Knight Commander knew she would have no more luck trying to force an answer from them than she would attempting to take them on in battle. And she was more interested in getting Idonea alone in her quarters than she was figuring out who this third person was. Whoever traveled with the dragon's children was no danger to the Empire.

"The Empress will wish to see the Baroness of Fireside."

Drakar snorted and the sultry laughter sprang forth once more. "I keep forgetting that I have a title. Tell her majesty we'll call upon her tomorrow. Until then, we'll be staying at Raine's–," Idonea corrected herself, "my estate."

The two dark-haired beauties, male and female, raised their hoods once more. The plain farm wife gave Nerthus an amused look, and the Knight Commander again tried to determine her identity. She was so familiar, not the face but rather the expression, but Nerthus could not place her. It was not Idonea's mother, she knew that much, for that dragon inspired a terror in all forms that Nerthus was unable to suppress. No, this was not Talan, but something likely as spectacular.

"Feel free to stop by tonight," Idonea said over her shoulder, leaving the knight commander with a resigned look on her face and all others in stupor.

Kylan, too, raised her hood and followed Idonea and Drakar. A glance back told her the shadowy figure had disappeared.

"Why in the world would Raine live in that cave when she could live here?"

Idonea frowned at Drakar. "Do you really need to ask that?"

Drakar thought for a moment, considered Raine's priorities, which were so very different from his, and shook his head. "I guess not. And she really gave this thing to you?"

This "thing" was the most impressive mansion in the imperial capital, an estate that for years was shrouded in secrecy, its owner unknown, its servants unaware of their employer's identity. For decades they possessed perhaps the easiest job in all the empire: maintaining a house that required no attention and serving a mistress who was never there.

"In theory," Idonea clarified. "She gave it to me because she needed me to be the 'Baroness of Fireside,' and handle her social duties at court. I enjoy toying with those fops whereas Raine has no patience for that sort of thing. But I consider Fireside more of a loan than a gift."

"I wouldn't mind being the Baron of Fireside," Drakar said, his lips on the verge of a pout.

Kylan entered the room, returned to her usual form and wearing an elegant blue gown that twinkled like stars. She put her hand beneath Drakar's chin, and squeezed his cheeks, causing the pout to manifest fully.

"You are the son of the Queen of all Dragons and will be an Ancient Dragon yourself, and you want some silly imperial title?"

Kylan released him, and the pout turned to a look of chagrin. "Well, not when you put it that way." He sprawled onto the sofa. "I'm assuming there's something to drink in this place?"

"There's a full wine cellar and just about every liqueur and type of spirit you could want in the kitchen," Idonea said.

"Good. I need to imbibe. I'm always trying to be on my best behavior around mother," he said, leaping to his feet and heading into the kitchen.

"As if she doesn't know that," Kylan murmured.

"Will you be going out this evening?" Idonea asked.

"I don't think so. It's late. I believe I'll rest. I'll need all my wits about me tomorrow."

It was a curious comment, especially for Kylan who could be as wild and unrestrained as Drakar if the mood struck her. It made Idonea think that Kylan had come to the imperial capital for more than just a fling, although she would likely not pass up that opportunity if it presented itself.

"And I fully expect that you'll be receiving a visit from your knight commander," Kylan continued, "so the capital will only have to survive the onslaught of your brother."

"Hmm," Idonea said, "then there's a chance it will survive."

True to Kylan's prediction, Nerthus appeared shortly after she retired for the evening, ushered in by one of the very discreet staff that Raine employed. Nerthus stood stiffly while the servant prepared drinks, then relaxed when he bowed out of the room.

"Not wearing my phylactery these days?"

"What?" Nerthus exclaimed, startled by the question.

"You would have known I was here if you had it on."

Nerthus sat down heavily. "Actually, I was going to get to that, but since you brought it up," she said, flushing again.

Idonea examined the woman across from her. The knight commander was formidable, and attractive in a fierce sort of way. And when she removed her half-ton of armor and shelved that perpetual frown, she was even more attractive. Idonea enjoyed the knight commander because she had a streak of wildness completely at odds with her cold, professional demeanor, and Idonea enjoyed that contradiction, as well as the passionate sex that resulted from it.

"You broke it," Idonea concluded.

"It was an accident!" Nerthus said. "I was training. I've been without it for six weeks, and—"

"And what?"

Idonea had that slightly expectant look on her face that both infuriated and aroused Nerthus, as if some things were utterly predictable to the mage.

"And I've felt its loss every day."

That was the other side of the knight commander that attracted Idonea, a slightly unhinged romanticism the woman kept well-hidden from those around her. Nerthus had once gathered vials of blood from the imperial mages, knowing that she could track them if they ever went rogue. None of them had ever done so, but she collected them all the same. In one of their first sexual exchanges, Nerthus had taken Idonea's blood, but not for those reasons; she knew trying to corral this one was impossible. She had taken it so that she could find Idonea if the mage ever needed her.

"If I remember correctly, you didn't have my permission to take my blood. You took advantage of me when I was exhausted and weak."

Nerthus rolled her eyes. "If I've learned anything, it takes more than the defeat of a Marrow Shard and Reaper to exhaust you."

"I was talking about the copious amount of sex after the battle. When you took me to that chantry and had your way with me."

"Well, something like that," Nerthus said. "In hindsight, I'm not sure who was having who."

The sultry laughter spilled forth once more as Nerthus continued.

"Besides, your mother threatened to annihilate me when she found what I wore around my neck."

"She is protective," Idonea admitted.

"So, will you give me another one?"

And this is the other part of the knight commander that so attracted Idonea. The woman was aloof, reserved, difficult to read, yet displayed a vulnerable side to Idonea that was endearing. Idonea was glad she had not met Nerthus in her youth, for she had often been careless with the feelings of others. Although she could not promise exclusivity, she was gentle with the knight commander. And although Nerthus had resigned herself to the fact that Idonea would never be hers, she consoled herself with the fact that Idonea would never belong to anyone.

Idonea stood and took Nerthus' hand. "I think we should probably get you out of that armor, and if you can 'exhaust' me, I'll let you have whatever you want."

Chapter 23

The sun had been up for quite some time when the knight commander clanked into the throne room. She somehow managed to look disheveled although her armor was polished to a sheen as usual. Bristol eyed his counterpart suspiciously. She had left her post early yesterday, which she never did, and there was only one thing in all the realm that could fluster her so. As Nerthus avoided his gaze, he suspected they were going to have visitors.

The Empress Aesa also examined her formidable knight commander. The woman was implacable, almost infuriatingly so, and to see her unnerved, on the verge of agitation, gave her pause. But the response of her other knight commander, the giant redhead who was Nerthus' opposite but complement in so many ways, provided solace. Bristol seemed entertained by the knight commander's deportment. The fact that yesterday, Nerthus had acted as if she had news for her, then abruptly cut herself short, piqued the curiosity of the Empress further.

The business of the court progressed as usual, boring and at times petty. Various nobles came forward with problems or issues that were of utmost importance to them, but in the larger scheme of things, mattered little. Nerthus guarded the throne with typical vigilance, her skill and experience compensating for her current inattention. Her mind was elsewhere, but she could still disarm any threat that walked through the door.

But the threat that walked through the door disarmed her. As every eye turned to the smoldering vision of loveliness that sauntered into the throne room, the vial of blood resting comfortably between Nerthus' breasts grew warm. The Baroness of Fireside had been amused at her presumption when she presented the tiny vial the night before, already connected to a carefully measured gold chain.

Aesa smiled, for this one brought dark energy, and a fierce, unrepentant sensuality that overshadowed every noble in the room. They faded into a gray background as Idonea left a trail of fire and anguished desire in her wake, and the Empress welcomed one who shared her penchant for the atypical.

Idonea curtsied before the throne, the slight movement barely a nod to convention, but one that caused her breasts to nearly spill forth from the ensemble that scarcely contained her curves. The slight movement was paralleled by the noticeable lean of those in the courtroom that yearned to see the exposure. But their lean was for naught, because Idonea's demeanor promised much, but delivered little, and the frustration was palpable.

Drakar, like everyone else, had glanced to his sister's breasts, but his lust warred with his anger. With so many others eying his sister, his natural protectiveness joined with his unnatural jealousy, the two stemming from disparate origins but similar goals.

Kylan put her hand on Drakar's shoulder, knowing the boy could not yet contain the lust that dominated dragonkind. It was unfortunate that lust had been unknowingly directed at Idonea at such a young age, for dragons most wanted that which they could not have. But the touch was enough to calm the young man.

The touch also brought the unintended consequence of the scrutiny of the knight commander. Kylan inwardly sighed. She could barely remember the face of the woman she had imitated the day before, and she had done her best. But it was clear, judging by Nerthus' expression, that she had not succeeded and looked markedly different.

Aesa stood, and in complete breech of protocol, walked down the steps and clasped Idonea's hands.

"Baroness, we're honored at your presence."

"Thank you, your eminence," Idonea said, returning the breech of protocol by kissing the Empress on the cheek.

"And this is your ridiculously handsome brother, is it not?"

The complement soothed Drakar, as did the smoldering look the

Empress cast his way. Were she not the property of the most dangerous vampyre in Arianthem, and undead herself, Drakar would have considered an attempted liaison. But even he was not so stupid to tempt the anger of the head of the Assassins Guild.

"This is Drakar, my older brother and eldest son of Talan'alaith'illaria."

The illustrious title had the counterintuitive effect of humbling Drakar, and he struggled with the unfamiliar emotion.

"You're a dragon, are you not?"

Drakar was mute, but Idonea had anticipated the momentary hiccup in Drakar's response. "He is, your majesty, an Ancient Dragon in the making."

This brought many "oohs and ahs" from the gallery, which under normal circumstances would have caused Drakar to preen. But perhaps it was his newfound responsibility with the little ones that caused him to feel exasperated and slightly stupid. He was becoming far too noble for his own liking. Kylan enjoyed every minute of it.

Aesa's eyes drifted to the plain woman accompanying them, but something stayed her commenting upon her presence. She merely nodded to her, then took Idonea's arm.

"I'm fatigued. Would you care to join me for afternoon tea?"

When the sun set again, Idonea found Nerthus and enticed her into a sexual encounter in a little-used wing of the imperial library. The possibility of discovery merely heightened the deliciousness of the experience, and as Idonea lay on her back staring up at the paintings on the ceiling, her fingers entangled in the knight commander's hair, she marveled at the tortured desire she could pull from this woman.

Drakar barely dodged the husband he had just cuckolded as he snuck away from the chambers of the lovely young thing who had slipped a scented note in his hands earlier that day. He was now on his way to the quarters of the Minister of Industry, who was away on business, according to the earlier, off-hand comment of his shapely wife. His teeth gleamed white in the darkness as he smiled at the ridiculous intrigues of the court. These women had all competed for his attention this afternoon. He could only imagine the conversations tomorrow when they sought to subtly crow over their conquest, only to learn that he had enjoyed them all. He adjusted his trousers, which were already growing tight in the front once more.

Kylan, on the other hand, slipped quietly through the bowels of the castle, passing cellars that had once served as barracks and dungeons. Although allegedly unused for decades, the hallways showed signs of recent and frequent passage; sconces burned at even intervals down their length. Kylan was unperturbed when ahead of her, a figure slipped from the shadows into the light of one of these torches.

The woman was lovely, deadly, a slightly mocking look upon her face, and Kylan thought it likely this was the spectral figure who had followed them through the market square the day before.

"Hello, Malron'a."

The vampyre bowed to the rather plain-looking farm wife, knowing that what stood before her was neither plain nor a farmer's wife. And although she was one of the deadliest creatures in all of Arianthem, second in command of the elite arm of the Assassin's Guild, she also knew she was no match for the being in front of her.

"My Mistress would like the honor of your company."

"Well," Kylan said, "that is why I'm tramping through the basement of the imperial castle."

"Of course," Malron'a said, "please follow me."

Kylan suppressed a sigh. She had sworn off vampyre, but they could be so incredibly attractive. Dangerous and sensual, they were far sturdier than the sons and daughters of men. They just brought about so many complications, wanting to drink her blood and all that. Not that she was opposed to the occasional sanguinary perversity, it was just that once they got a taste, they wanted more. And for Kylan, the opposite was true. Once she got a taste, she generally was done. There were exceptions, of course. Talan had been a repeat lover over the years, until the Queen had found her Arlanian, and there was bevy of her kind she kept around because they entertained her, but when it came to commitment, she was as bad as Drakar. No, she thought to herself, possibly worse.

The beautiful vampyre escorted her into chambers that were surprisingly luxurious given their location. Of course, it was likely the empress spent significant time down here, given her own undead situation. Her escort excused herself and disappeared.

A woman sat in a throne-like chair decorated with skeletal filigree. She wore a dark cloak that draped down around the legs of the chair, but not a great deal else. Pale cleavage glowed in the dark and emphasized the breasts that thrust upward in the tight-knit bodice. Kylan idly let her gaze rest upon that valley. This casual, fearless scrutiny made the woman smile, revealing white teeth and the slightest of fangs. She was gorgeous, terrifying, a manipulative mastermind who ruled the Assassin's Guild. She was ruthless, cruel, as brilliant as she was merciless. She was also the Empress' lover, or perhaps more accurately, the Empress was hers. She had once been hired to kill Aesa, and had made the young woman undead, technically fulfilling her contract.

This woman also saw deep into the reality of things, and made this ability immediately known.

"Hello, Kylan."

With a wave of her hand and a flash of white light, Kylan transformed into her usual elegance.

"Hello, Pernilla."

The woman's pale, blue-green eyes caressed the loveliness of the figure before her, and Kylan could almost feel fingers upon her, tendrils of an invasive plant brushing up against her skin.

"And why are you here, dragon?" the vampyre asked, her words liquid like honey mixed with hemlock.

"You're an Oracle. You tell me."

The startling pale eyes examined the ancient creature in front of her. The dragon came for information, but she would trade for something in kind. She had sensed something she could not see but guessed at its source. She wanted to know if her supposition was correct.

"Talan sleeps."

Kylan was quiet a moment, then saw no advantage to hiding the truth. Her only solace was that Pernilla valued information more than gold, and therefore guarded it more closely.

"Yes."

The vampyre's gaze grew distant. "So, the Queen enters the Dragon's Night."

Kylan carefully controlled the emotions this phrase stirred. She had done her best to put on a brave face, but she missed her liege as much as anyone. Even when she and Talan were far apart, on different sides of the continent, she could always feel her Queen. But now it felt as if she were very far away. Not quite as far as the Underworld, but close.

"And what of Raine?" Pernilla asked, her pale eyes re-focusing on the one in front of her.

"What do you think?" Kylan asked. "She guards her lover in hiding."

Pernilla folded her hands together, then placed her index fingers against her lips, deep in thought.

"Then the defenders of Arianthem are absent."

Kylan did not know what to make of this statement. Without the equalizing force of Talan and Raine, the Assassin's Guild could run rampant. Indeed, the entire underbelly of Arianthem could rise up, and although the forces of good were formidable throughout the realm, it was always nice to have an unstoppable ally at your side.

But somehow Kylan did not think that was what Pernilla meant. Indeed, it seemed the vampyre was digesting this news with a great deal of contemplation and a degree of misgiving.

"This is not good timing," Pernilla said at last, and this was what Kylan had come for. Pernilla paused while she sought words for sensations, attempting to describe what was discernible only from the shadow it cast.

"Something is stirring."

"Your Mistress, perhaps?" Kylan suggested.

"Perhaps. The Goddess is not happy with anyone in this realm right now. And I dare say she would take vengeance even against me, despite my many years of service. But it's something else. Possibly something that's guided by her."

"But not Hyr'rok'kin," Kylan said. "I haven't seen any since the battle in the Underworld."

"Nor I. No," Pernilla said, "this is something different."

Kylan had the distinct feeling that, although it was "something different," Pernilla had an idea what that might be. But before she could ask, the vampyre abruptly changed the subject.

"And what is this I hear of a new prophecy?"

Kylan sighed. "I see your spies are as efficient as always. There's only one phrase that's been translated."

"Yes, 'to defeat that which cannot be defeated,'" Pernilla said, demonstrating just how good her spies were. Her gaze absently settled on Kylan's cleavage, for even when focused on other things, habits were difficult to break. Kylan sarcastically took a deep breath, causing the breasts to rise and the vampyre to smile as she looked away, polite but unrepentant.

"Pernilla," Kylan said, having had enough. "Tell me what you see."

"Raine is dreaming of the Goddess."

Cold fingers whispered down Kylan's spine. "Yes."

"Raine is in great danger. Talan's magic won't protect her much longer."

"But they're only dreams."

"Dreams," Pernilla mused. "The domain of witches, especially necromancers."

Kylan was getting angry. "Speak plainly, vampyre. What do you see?"

Pernilla shrugged. "Unfortunately, I see very little."

Kylan's anger spiked, then waned as she realized there was an undertone to what the woman was saying. "Your vision is being blocked."

"Or at least interfered with, to a degree," Pernilla agreed. "And it would take a being, or beings, of enormous power to do so."

The dragon now knew where Pernilla was going with this conversation but refused to believe it.

"You can't be serious. They were utterly defeated by the Scinterians centuries ago, banished from this and every other realm."

"Yes," Pernilla said, "they were."

Tomb-like silence settled between them until it grew too oppressive for Kylan.

"Then what should Raine do?"

"I don't know," Pernilla said.

The matter-of-fact response chilled Kylan to the bone. If the master of machination had no ideas, then things could get very bad.

"I do know this," Pernilla said. "Even when this prophecy is fully translated, it could have multiple meanings."

"Why do you say that?"

The striking, pale eyes did not blink. "Well, think about it. 'To defeat that which cannot be defeated.' The only thing in Arianthem that 'cannot be defeated' seems to be Raine."

Chapter 24

Raine glided over the snow at a decent clip, keeping pace with the little ones skimming low over the ground. The day before, she had fashioned a pair of skis from a downed tree, and now was careful not to venture too far downhill since she had no dragons to pull her back up. The upward hike would be good exercise, but who knew what trouble her children would get into as she slogged back up the mountainside. She did ponder some sort of arrangement in which the girls could pull her back up, and the resulting mental picture so entertained her she determined to put some effort into it later. It seemed she could repurpose the halter-and-strap contraption she had created to help their early flying lessons.

But right now, she was covering a lot of ground without them, stabbing her poles into the ground with an alternating rhythm, her powerful arms thrusting her forward across the snow. Kaia and Laina swooped about her, occasionally diving down into the snow to see how far they could skid along on their bellies before they leaped skyward once more. Flurries flew out in their wake, dowsing Raine, who only laughed at their antics.

When they got close to an area with a thicker forest, she glided to a stop, unlatched her skis and motioned the tiny dragons near. She leaned the skis against a tree and turned to her expectant little ones. Kaia nudged the folded bow at her waist, which really was her favorite weapon out of Raine's arsenal, and Raine complied by pulling it from her belt. With a flick of her wrist, she snapped it out to its full length, an absurdly casual maneuver given its difficulty and the sharpness of the weapon's leading edge. She pulled an arrow from the quiver at her side and sighted at a fox across the clearing in front of her. She deliberately missed, causing a pile of snow next to the creature to explode, resulting in a leap straight upward before the poor animal landed and sprinted into the underbrush. This evoked peals of laughter from the girls.

Kaia galloped off and returned with the arrow in her mouth. Raine re-slotted the arrow and took aim at a pinecone so far away it looked little more than a dot, the shot more intuitive than technical because it really was impossible to complete. Nevertheless, the pinecone was speared through, much to the delight of the baby dragons.

"When you're a little older, and can control your shapeshifting, I'll teach you how to use this. We might have to get the dwarves to make you smaller ones to start out with, but we'll see."

Raine continued to pick out impossible targets around the clearing, and the girls bounded through the snow to chase down her arrows while she considered her last statement. Her "little ones" might be able to use the larger bow from the start, once they were a little older, just based upon their dragon development, which would greatly surpass their human form.

Talan had explained that dragons had something of a default form when they transitioned, and she, Kylan, and Drakar looked much like a human version of their dragon selves. They were able to radically alter their appearance, but this illusion required effort, whereas maintaining the "default" required no effort at all. All three adult dragons were gorgeous creatures and therefore gorgeous in their natural transformation. Raine had no doubt that the toddler versions of her girls were their default, as close to a "true" human appearance as they would ever have. The fact that Laina already favored Talan's human state and Kaia favored her, lent credence to this belief.

However, her children were not human, and they would possess all their dragon strength and intelligence even as infants. This set up the interesting possibility that these children would be reading before they could talk, running before most children could even stand, and would likely be using that bow long before most children could pick it up. The thought filled her with excitement. It also made her remember a time when her uncle had expressed amazement at her strength and agility, given that she was a "half-breed" and smaller by far than most Scinterians.

A fat squirrel dislodged a pinecone from a nearby tree and Raine absently fired off another shot, impaling the object and pinning it to the trunk before it had fallen halfway to the ground. Kaia did a somersault in the air and Laina hooted her approval. Both raced to the arrow, swooping about one another. Raine admired their brilliant colors, the deep blue of Kaia and dark red of Laina bright against the white snow. Their drab baby colors had quickly given way to the iridescence of fully-grown dragons, another anomaly that Talan had commented upon.

They reached the arrow at the same time and began fighting over it, tussling in a blue and red ball of fury that made them look purple from the distance. Snow flew until they began blowing fire at one another, at which time water began to spray about. Raine just shook her head and began to strap on her makeshift skis. She glanced down at the castle. She had purposely worked her way up in elevation so that her return trip would be downhill, and now she had a good slope to build up some speed.

"I'll race you back!" she cried out over her shoulder, pushing off.

The two little dragon heads jerked upward, their bodies half-buried in snow. They jumped up, little claws scrabbling to gain traction as they stepped on and over one another. At last they were free and sprinted across the snow to gain momentum before they launched themselves into the air, furiously flapping to catch their mother who was already halfway down the mountainside.

The race was close, but it was Raine who reached the wall first, using a small snow bluff to ramp over the edge and into the courtyard. The two babies swooped in behind her, skidding on the icy tile. Kaia slid for some distance, spinning about in circles, and Laina plowed into the back of her, causing Raine to double over with laughter.

They dusted themselves off, then Raine strolled through the castle with the little ones ambling along behind her. They were all pleasantly tired. A pot of venison stew was boiling over the low embers of the hearth, and the delightful smell filled the great room.

Raine glanced over at her love, who was peacefully sleeping. Her heart ached to be so near and yet so far away. She felt a small tug on the leg of her breeches.

"What is this?" she asked in surprise.

The girls had transformed, and now looked like toddlers, both standing upright but barely coming to her knee. They each hugged a leg, and a pair of blue eyes and a pair of amber eyes looked up at her expectantly until both turned purple. She reached down and wrapped an arm about each little waist, lifting them up so she could hold them.

"Need to get a little closer?"

She had at first thought the girls transformed solely for her, but then realized they sometimes did so because she could hold them in ways she could not when they were dragons. She did so now, a girl on each hip, and they happily snuggled into her side as she went about preparing dinner. When she needed a free hand, they were strong enough to wrap their arms about her neck and support themselves. Indeed, they were able to clamber about her almost like the monkeys that inhabited the lowland swamps in the south.

She prepared one big bowl and then settled in front of the fire, a girl on each leg and the bowl in the middle. She handed them wooden spoons and the two little ones gazed at the implements in consternation until they watched her, then began mimicking her actions. At first their efforts were comical, and more of the soup wound up on the floor than in their mouths. But in an astonishingly short time, they were manipulating the utensil with a degree of dexterity that was otherworldly.

"Uh-huh," Raine said, taking a spoonful, "you guys aren't going to fool anyone."

Laina cocked her head to the side, the gesture far more dragon-like than human, merely confirming Raine's assessment. Her children were extraordinary and would not pass for human any time soon. But it was sheer joy to hold them like this.

"Do you think you can talk?" Raine asked conversationally, taking a spoonful of broth.

Kaia frowned, her expression far too thoughtful for such a tiny human. Laina was busy with her spoon.

"Can you say 'Raine'?" Raine asked, taking another spoonful and blowing on it.

Kaia looked to Laina, and Laina stopped, her spoon hovering in the air. The two seemed to communicate on an unspoken level even beyond that which they shared with their mothers. Something passed between them and two pairs of violet eyes turned to Raine.

"Mama."

Raine stopped, for her heart lurched in her chest at Kaia's words. Carefully balancing the children on her knees, she set the bowl on the floor, then gathered them to her.

"Mama," Laina repeated as she snuggled beneath Raine's chin.

Raine could feel her heartbeat in her chest, so powerful were her emotions. She loved her babies in any form, but to think that she could have them in both filled her with a joy so enormous it was almost painful. She hugged her children to her, kissing the fine hair on their heads, rocking their little bodies until their breathing slowed and they were fast asleep in her arms.

Raine struggled to awake, feeling an enormous weight on her chest. She was also cold, which was unusual given the temperature of the room when she fell asleep. When she opened her eyes, she realized why this was so. The sense of disorientation, the strange constellations of stars in the sky when the sky should not be visible, all told her she had not awakened.

The Goddess of the Underworld sat across from her on her horrible throne, elbow propped on the elaborate arm, chin propped in the hand, finger tapping on the cheekbone, lips pursed in thought.

"Hello, my love."

Raine said nothing, merely gazed at the personification of evil before her.

"So rude," Hel said sarcastically, "when I've missed you so."

"What do you want, Hel?" Raine said, struggling to keep her tone even.

As always, the disrespect infuriated her. "What do I want?" Hel said, sitting upright, "what do you think I want? I want Talan dead, and you chained to my bedpost for all eternity."

The tone of the Goddess was dangerous, but Raine's response was even more so.

"You don't want Talan dead."

The anger of the being in front of her seethed across the space between them. While imprisoned in the Underworld, Raine had correctly deduced that Hel still harbored feelings for the dragon, a fact that made her own position all the more precarious. Hel's infatuation with her was fueled as much by jealousy and revenge as lust.

"Perhaps not," Hel said dismissively, "Perhaps just entombed as before. She was my favorite decoration." The Goddess adjusted her position with these words, causing her cleavage to rise. Raine's eyes inadvertently followed the movement, causing emerald eyes to gleam.

"So, how are you doing this?" Raine asked, waving her hand in a general direction, trying to change the subject.

The attempt merely made Hel smile. "I am capable of things you can't imagine."

"I thought the Allfather forbid you from the mortal realm."

"I'm not in the mortal realm right now, am I?"

Raine was not certain of the truth of that, because Hel's presence felt very real.

"Besides," Hel said with a wave of her own hand, "the Allfather is busy at the moment."

Hel's dismissive tone was again on display, but this comment filled Raine with dread. Although there were other gods who had come to her aid, it seemed the only one who could truly keep Hel in check was her grandfather. And if the Allfather was gone…

Hel stood, as if to press the advantage she sensed. She took a step forward.

"It's only a matter of time–"

The Goddess stopped, puzzled. Something was blocking her path, something that was between her and the Arlanian. She reached out to feel the outlines of the invisible barrier.

"What…?"

Raine's dread grew, for she knew what lay between her and the Goddess, and as the air between them flickered, the Goddess understood as well.

An outline of Talan in human form was between them. Raine's heart ached as she took in the beauty of the ephemeral sleeping form, hands folded peacefully over her chest in repose.

"What is this?" Hel asked, reaching out to touch the sleeping figure. But she could not, for the creature was both solid and intangible, a translucent image that was also completely impassable.

Hel could not fathom this manifestation, but when she looked to the sadness on the Arlanian's face, dawning understanding took hold, and a small thrill traversed her spine.

"Talan sleeps."

The second word was drawn out, the beginning and ending sibilant like the hissing of a snake. Raine did not respond, truly did not need to, for it was clear the Goddess understood the full implications of the "Dragon's Night," including a few that Raine was just beginning to realize.

The Goddess gazed down at the creature she both loved and hated, stroking the cheek she could not actually touch.

"So, her battle with me was not without cost. The Dragon's Night can last a thousand years."

It was a cruel exaggeration, but not entirely untrue. It could happen.

"And even now she fades."

The translucence of the body was pronounced, and although still a barrier, it was not one that would last much longer. Hel verbalized this fact with pleasure.

"The deeper she sleeps, the less protection her magic provides." She turned to the Arlanian. "Soon, she'll not be able to protect you at all."

Raine took a deep breath, then exhaled, her lack of response merely confirming Hel's pronouncement. She gazed at the fading body, her sadness palpable, and it was at last that sadness that was enough to begin to awaken her.

"Goodbye," she said as the Goddess watched her disappear.

Chapter 25

Raine stood on the parapet, staring out at the empty blue sky. She did not know when Kylan and the others were returning; they had left for "a few days," and this was only the sunrise of the third. Her children lay snuggled on top of Talan's great body, tucked between the scales behind her head. Upon awakening, she had clutched them to her, unable and unwilling to return to sleep, but it was not long before restlessness overcame her, and she carefully placed them on their mother's neck. She then padded silently across the floor and left the warmth of the great room.

She had stood in the darkness of the courtyard, staring up at the glittering stars, welcoming the familiar constellations. When she had been imprisoned in the Underworld, that faux sky had been filled with strange patterns of stars, creating an existential dread within her, a feeling she was very far from home. The few times Hel had appeared to her in her dreams, this same dread had overtaken her, a feeling that she was someplace else, someplace foreign and wrong. As much as she welcomed the familiar stars in the courtyard, she welcomed the light of day even more.

Raine tried to think through the various ramifications of the presence of the Goddess in her dreams. Were they only dreams? They felt so real, and upon awakening she was as ice cold as if Hel had been standing right next to her. And she knew in her heart that Hel spoke the truth when she said Weynild's magic would not protect her much longer.

Could Hel sense what was around her in this world? If so, then perhaps she should no longer sleep with the children. This thought broke her heart, but if it kept them safe, she would tuck them in with Weynild each night, then leave to sleep in another part of the castle. Kylan could stay with the girls as well.

And what did the absence of the Allfather mean? Where was he? Would any of the other gods act to keep Hel in check? The God of War had come to her aid at the end of the battle in the Underworld, as had Sjöfn, the Goddess of Love. Both had done so because she was the sole survivor of their most honored and beloved children, the Scinterians and Arlanians. But Raine wondered if they would do so again. The gods were a mercurial lot, and she could not say that she cared much for any of them. If she were to worship a deity, it might be Saga, the Goddess of Wisdom, but Saga did not wish to be worshipped and kept her own council, which was probably why Raine liked her.

Raine's thoughts returned to the dream. When she had been apart from Weynild on the hunting trip, and again when Weynild had left her in the keep, Hel had been able to touch her, even kiss her, which brought up the very unpleasant possibility that once Weynild's magic faded completely, Raine could be raped nightly in her dreams. Given that Hel seemed to have a great deal of control over her in that world and she was unable to fight back, this would be almost as horrible as being back in the Underworld for real.

Raine sighed. She was already composing in her head the missive to Y'arren requesting help. If anyone could figure out a way to protect her, it was the elven matriarch, and Raine turned back towards the castle. She might as well begin writing the letter before the girls were out of bed.

It was with a certain amount of dread that Raine watched the sun go down, given that Kylan and the others had not returned. She and the girls had spent the day in their usual fashion, running pell-mell through the castle and surrounding countryside, playing, hunting, napping, then playing some more. The activity allowed her a degree of respite, the physical exertion shutting off the uneasy ruminations of her mind. But as the shadows grew long, her heart grew heavy, and with one last wistful look at the sky, she went inside.

She did her best to hide her unease from the little ones. The two ate ravenously, and Raine tried to match their enthusiasm, but picked at her food. Despite her efforts to hide her feelings, the little ones were aware of her distress and nuzzled her. Finally, Raine settled with them before the fire with the Elven Book of Lore, and it was enough, at least temporarily, to distract them all.

But as the fire burned down to embers and the eyelids of the little dragons grew heavy, Raine knew she could delay the inevitable no longer. She set the book aside and the three padded over to the great red dragon in the corner, climbing up onto her leg where they could sit in the crook between her neck and belly. The two little ones fluttered contentedly while Raine stroked beneath their wings where it was most sensitive. She stared across the great room, willing herself to stay awake, but the warmth of her love and the closeness of the two little dragons curled about her made it difficult, and she felt her own eyelids grow heavy.

Raine opened her eyes, and realized she had not opened her eyes. The Goddess sat before her, an expectant look on her face. Raine struggled to move, and with great effort, got to her feet. Hel also stood, her dark robes flowing around her. Everything surrounding them was pitch black, no form or feature anywhere, an oppressive darkness hiding everything but that which softly glowed between them. Raine shivered.

Weynild's body shimmered softly in front of Raine, flickering. The dragon in human form was translucent, barely there, the absence of her presence already well known to the Arlanian. Hel reached out to touch Talan, and her hand passed through the ephemeral form as a muscle in Raine's jaw twitched. The Goddess smiled, and it was not pleasant to see. With a deliberate move, Hel stepped forward, passing through the translucent image, and Weynild's body disappeared.

The room around them began to materialize, and to Raine's horror, one-by-one she saw the features of the Great Room of the castle begin to appear, as if willed by Hel.

"Ah," Hel said, looking about, "you're in Talan's old castle in the mountains."

The muscle in Raine's cheek spasmed as she clenched her jaw. Somehow Hel had managed to do far more than appear in her dream. As casually as possible, she glanced behind her. The great red dragon slept peacefully, curled up against the far wall. There was no sign of her children. Hel followed her gaze.

"Such a beautiful creature," she said.

Raine could not breathe. She had never felt such terror before, her fear entirely for her children. When she forced herself to exhale, her breath came out as frost. Hel examined the phenomenon with interest.

"It's almost like I'm here." She glanced around the room, pleased at the level of detail. It was difficult to move, but surely it would become easier with time. She took a step toward the dragon.

"Stay away from her," Raine said through clenched teeth.

Hel whirled upon her. "Or what?" she demanded. "What is it that you think you're going to do to me, Arlanian?"

Raine's jaws ached with the strain of keeping her teeth from chattering. "If you do anything to harm her…"

"Quite frankly," Hel said, almost bored, "I'm not sure I can. It's your dream. Right now, you're the only one I can affect." She glanced back at Talan. "But that might change, given the amount of time I intend to spend here. I shall have to decide what I'd like to do to that dragon."

Raine cried out in rage, lunging toward the Goddess, but Hel stopped her with the lift of a finger. Raine hovered helplessly, paralyzed by the power of the one who stood before her. The finger moved beneath her chin and Hel forced her to look up. Cold emerald eyes examined the refined features, the lovely mouth, the long dark eyelashes that framed those violet eyes. The insolent inventory was prolonged and ultimately brought great pleasure to the Goddess. This creature was as gorgeous as ever, and Hel's desire was even more inflamed by the fact she knew the mortal's true identity, although "mortal" was no longer an appropriate descriptor. Taking the Arlanian to her bed before had been a blow against Talan; now there would be many who would suffer at the girl's forced liaisons. Those who had stood against her would pay for that interference, and this one would pay most of all.

Hel leaned down with the intent to kiss Raine when an odd sound stopped her descent. Her head slowly raised back upward, a puzzled look on her face.

Raine, however, knew exactly what the sound was, and her heart pounded in her chest so loudly she felt certain the Goddess could hear it. But Hel's head was cocked sideways, as if trying to decipher the strange noise.

"That's the oddest thing," Hel murmured. "I can't quite place it, although I'm certain I've heard it before." She turned towards the door of the great room, as if expecting something to appear.

Raine also was expecting something to appear and she closed her eyes, praying to every god that wasn't Hel. Perhaps the prayer was answered, or perhaps her desperation was at last awakening her, but just before the little ones appeared in the doorway, Raine's body began to fade away in Hel's grasp.

"What is this?" Hel asked, turning back to the girl in her arms. The firmness of the flesh was giving way to nothingness, and as the body dissolved, so did the room around her. Suddenly Hel was back in her chamber in the Underworld, staring at the black silk sheets of her bed. Feray, her chief handmaiden, braced herself for the anger of her Mistress, for the Goddess had expressed optimism that tonight would be the night she would take her Arlanian, and she had returned far too soon for that to have occurred.

But Hel was not angry, merely puzzled. She sat for a moment in the bed, silent. She rose, still thoughtful, and as she drifted out toward the garden, Feray was grateful for her Mistress' distraction. Somehow that volcanic rage had subsumed into a reflective preoccupation.

Hel plucked a piece of night jasmine from its vine, inhaling deeply from the petals, noting neither the texture nor fragrance of the plant in her contemplation. Twice now, the Arlanian's response had been most intriguing. Hel rubbed the plant between her fingers. The girl was hiding something, that was clear, but she could not fathom what that something could be. Could she be cheating on Talan while the dragon slept? The thought threatened to reignite her rage, but that ember flickered out. That was so unlikely it fell into the realm of impossible. The Arlanian had slept with none but her and Talan, a fact she had confirmed through numerous spies.

Could it be something about Talan? Perhaps the dragon was more than sleeping, perhaps she was injured. But the lovely body that hovered between them, the manifestation of Talan's dark magic, had been in relaxed repose, and that beautiful monster in the corner had been peacefully sleeping.

Hel settled onto a bench beneath the great trees in her courtyard, all which glowed with a soft yellow light. She rolled the powder from the night jasmine between her fingers. No, it was something else. The Arlanian was hiding something, something of great importance to her. This brought the faintest of smiles to the face of the Goddess. She would find this secret, for whatever the Arlanian held dear could be used as leverage against her.

Laina was standing on her chest, her face inches away when Raine opened her eyes. The little dragon peered down at her mother in consternation. Kaia did the same, although she appeared upside down to Raine, as she stood above her head. Both baby dragons had intense frowns on their faces. Raine clutched them to her, overjoyed to see them safe and unharmed. Her reaction, however, did not set their little minds at ease. Their mother's distress in her sleep had been obvious to them, and they had done all they could, short of lighting her on fire, to awaken her.

They were content, however, to nudge her for a bit, then curl about her body, blowing warm little puffs of air that gradually leeched the freezing cold from her bones. Laina rested her head on Raine's thigh and Kaia shifted her torso so it rested against her side. It was not long before their eyelids grew heavy once more, their breathing grew deep, and both babies drifted off to sleep, Laina with a tiny snort, and Kaia with one last troubled look at her mother.

Raine stroked the brow of the little dark dragon, comforting her and easing the frown in her sleep. Laina's tail twitched, then curled about her waist. The unconscious gesture soothed and pained Raine, for she welcomed something she was inevitably soon to miss. Her grief nearly overcame her at this thought, but her expression hardened as the Scinterian rose inside her. She would do anything to protect her children.

Anything.

Chapter 26

The great blue dragon alighted, and the white light had hardly dissipated before Kylan noted the look on Raine's face.

"What has happened?"

This attracted Idonea's attention, who was sliding from the back of her brother, who disappeared into a flash of red light once freed of his passenger. The two dark-haired siblings gazed with consternation at Raine, and both heads swiveled as one to their younger siblings, who were tumbling about in the snow behind her. Once assured that the children were unharmed, the heads swiveled back to their mother.

"It—," Raine paused, searching for words. "It's complicated. Let's have dinner, then once the children are settled, I'll tell you."

Raine's stew was not quite as good as Talan's, but she had made remarkable strides in the absence of her lover. Possessing few domestic qualities and even less desire to develop them, things had changed when the children were born. It was startling what a difference little ones could make.

"This is quite good," Idonea said, unable to disguise her surprise.

"Thank you," Raine said with mild sarcasm. She tempered her response. "Necessity breeds competency."

"More than competent," Kylan said. The stew was delicious, the venison fresh, the spices perfect and on point.

"Thank you," Raine repeated, this time with no sarcasm at all.

Drakar brought the girls over, the two little ones shuffling behind. Raine was grateful, for he had played with them non-stop since his return, which meant they would fall asleep quickly after they had eaten. He, too, was tired, given his long flight from the imperial capital, then the exercise with the baby dragons. As he spooned stew into his mouth, he decided it was likely the latter that had so exhausted him. Those two were a handful.

Kaia buried her face in a bowl, and stew flew everywhere. Laina was no less barbaric in her table manners, which caused Raine to cover her smile with her hand.

"By all the gods," Idonea muttered as she leaned to wipe Kaia's face. Laina presented a mouthful of teeth, which Raine surmised was a smile as she awaited the same treatment. Her big sister leaned forward and sponged away the detritus of the meal.

"You two need to go to sleep," Kylan said.

Laina started to protest, but a simple glance from the Ancient Dragon stopped her objection. She lowered her head and her belly scraped the ground. Kaia padded over to her and nudged her head.

"Yes," Raine agreed, "you two need to go lie down with your mother. She misses you and needs your warmth. Come along now."

The three about the fire watched as Raine accompanied the two baby dragons over to the giant red creature in the corner, all three having the similar thought that no one moved with the deadly grace of the Scinterians. It was not always evident which of Raine's personas was dominant at any given time, but right now it was evident the Scinterian was in control.

The baby dragons settled on the great girth of their mother, both attempting to expand their diminutive wingspan to provide cover. Raine nodded her approval, and the tiny creatures fluttered happily as they settled in. It was likely both were sound asleep by the time Raine returned to the fire pit. With one last glance over her shoulder to confirm their slumber, Raine sat down next to Drakar. She opened her mouth to speak, then clamped it shut, staring morosely into the fire. The crackling of the flames was loud in the silence.

"Raine," Kylan prompted at last, the prompt gentle but firm.

"Hel can find me in my sleep."

The statement was unclear and horrifying, and the others hoped clarity would lessen that horror.

It did not.

"Talan's magic no longer protects me, and Hel was here."

"What do you mean, she was here?" Idonea asked.

"She appeared to me in my sleep last night, and she could see the great room. She knew where we were. She knew it was Talan's old castle, and she could see my love sleeping in the corner."

"Did she see the little ones?" Drakar demanded, trying to control the hysteria in his voice while asking the question on everyone's tongue.

"No. She didn't," Raine said. "I was able to hide them from her. But I won't be able to hide them much longer."

An oppressive silence settled on the group as all thought through the ramifications of Raine's words. It was Raine who broke that silence.

"I don't think she can affect Talan, she said as much. I think she can only affect me."

Kylan's ice-blue eyes held a pair of equally blue ones. "It doesn't matter if she can affect the children. She must never know of them."

"I know."

Raine's words were simple and absolute.

"They can't stay here."

Idonea's thoughts raced, trying to come up with any sort of solution to this terrible conundrum. "You could stay in another part of the castle, keep the children separate from you when you sleep."

Raine shook her head. She had already thought this through.

"It will only take once," Raine said. "One time where they come to me when I'm dreaming, and they'll be discovered. Hel was here. I can't let her see them, especially while Talan sleeps. I can't protect them both, my love and my children.

"Then leave the children with Talan," Kylan said, a brutal suggestion. "At least they could stay with her. You could draw the Goddess away while we watch them here."

"That was my original plan," Raine said. "But now the Goddess knows where Talan sleeps."

Kylan saw the flaw in her proposal, and Raine's reasoning. "And if you left, she would wonder why, knowing you would never freely leave Talan's side. And she would also believe that Talan was helpless, no longer protected by you."

"Yes," Raine said. "And she would send someone, or something, for her."

"But she won't be helpless! We'll protect her and the children!" Drakar insisted. "We'll stay, Kylan, Idonea, and I!"

"No," Idonea said, holding up her hand. She at last understood the extent of Raine's plan. "The children would still be in danger. But if we leave, Hel won't look for what she doesn't know exists." She turned to Raine. "And she won't attack my mother if she's busy with you."

"Busy," Raine said, the fire flickering in her eyes. "That's one way to put it."

Kylan fell silent, grasping the self-sacrifice Raine proposed. Hel would not bother Talan if she could nightly rape the Arlanian in front of her sleeping body.

"It's the only way I can think of that both my love and my children will be safe."

Idonea slowly nodded. She hated this plan, but it was the only one they had. "We'll take the children away, and I'll began searching for a way to keep Hel from your dreams."

"I've already sent word to Y'arren," Raine said, "asking for much the same. Perhaps together you can find something."

Drakar felt impotent, angry at his powerlessness. But a pair of pale blue eyes turned upon him.

"Drakar," Raine said, "you must protect Kaia and Laina. Kylan will stay here to help me protect Talan. You and Idonea must care for the babies."

Idonea was surprised that Raine would not send the Ancient Dragon with the children. But it made sense, in a way, for Hel would surely concentrate all her attention on this mountain keep now that she knew where Raine and her mother were. And the fact that Kylan did not object, but merely stared into the fire, indicated she agreed with this decision.

Chapter 27

Raine had felt much pain in her life. The blue and gold scars she bore on her back and arms were the greatest physical pain she had ever endured, but that had been dwarfed by the anguish she felt when she had first seen her love entombed in amber in the Underworld.

Now both of those experiences paled in comparison to the agony she was currently feeling. Her heart was breaking. She was separated from her love by the Dragon's Night, and now she was saying goodbye to her children to keep them safe. She hated the gods at this moment.

The two little dragons milled about uncertainly in the courtyard. Drakar perched stoically on the parapet in dragon form, having already said his farewell to Raine. Idonea stood waiting, she, too, having said a lengthy, sorrowful goodbye to Raine.

Raine kneeled as the two little ones came over.

"You know what we talked about," Raine said, stroking their little ridged brows. "You listen to your brother and sister. Hide your eyes as best you can. And stay in human form until Idonea tells you otherwise."

The two little ones solemnly nodded, and Raine fought back tears. "Now I want you to go ahead and transform."

The two little dragons looked at one another, then disappeared into flashes of yellow light. Two beautiful little toddlers stood in their place, and Raine picked them up, one in each arm. Kaia traced the blue and gold markings on her mother's forearms.

"This won't be for long," Raine promised, praying that it was a promise she could keep. "I'll come for you before you know it."

Laina plucked at Raine's shirt front, and Raine kissed her on the cheek. She pressed her forehead against Kaia's, then kissed her as well. Both little ones looked at her somberly, and she squeezed them tight.

"I love you more than life itself," Raine said. "Know that above all."

Raine handed the little ones to Idonea, helping to set them into the slings she had fashioned to allow them to travel on each side of the mage. And Drakar bent his long neck downward so that all three of his sisters could settle comfortably on his back. Once they were secure, he raised his head and nodded to Raine.

"You take care of them, Prince of all Dragons."

Drakar's nostrils flared at the title, and where before it would have stroked his ego, now it strengthened his heart. The ebony dragon again nodded, then flexed his powerful thigh muscles and leaped skyward, his wings momentarily blacking out the morning sun. A last, thunderous roar scattered every flock of birds for miles.

And then they were off, growing smaller with every flap of the black dragon's great wings as Raine stood in the frigid cold until at last, she could see them no more.

The castle seemed unnaturally quiet, and Raine went to take comfort in the presence of Weynild. She was unsurprised to see Kylan standing there before her liege, dealing with her grief in her own way. She adored Talan's dragon babies as if they were her own. The blue dragon simply nodded, then left Raine and her sleeping lover alone.

Raine went about her day as normally as possible, sharpening her weapons, polishing her armor, checking the stores of food and fuel. Several times she went out into the courtyard, staring off into the distance, thinking that perhaps Idonea would come to some solution she had missed and would race back with the girls, but always the sky was empty, and she returned to her chores.

The sun lowered in the sky and the shadows lengthened, and Raine returned to the great room to cook a simple meal over the hearth. Kylan joined her, still silent, bringing some bread and cheese, as well as two flagons of ale. The two ate quietly in front of the fire, the only sound the crunching of the crusty bread.

"Kylan."

The ice blue eyes of the frost dragon in human form flicked to her, and Raine observed how very lovely that form was.

"I've lived with an Ancient Dragon for decades; did you really think I wouldn't notice?"

Kylan sighed, and Raine heard the resignation in that sigh, confirming her suspicion, which she then put into words.

"You need to sleep as well."

"I do," Kylan replied at last. "I didn't know how to tell you. I should have known that you already knew."

"Of course, I knew. I saw the signs of the Dragon's Night in both of you. But I don't think Talan saw yours before she slept."

"I was desperate to hide it from her," Kylan admitted. "I wanted her to believe that I could help keep the children safe."

Raine nodded, comfortable with that deception. She would have done the same.

"It's of no matter."

"No matter!" Kylan exclaimed. "I am sworn to protect my Queen and her children, and I can't even stay awake! I'll be as helpless as her in a few days!"

"It will be sooner than that," Raine said calmly. "But although you'll be helpless, you will not be vulnerable."

Raine stood, and the blue and gold markings rose on her skin and looked to be almost something alive beneath her skin. "You and Talan are the last Ancient Dragons in this world, until my children come of age. It's my duty to protect you."

Kylan finally understood in full the decisions that Raine had made, decisions that had included her as well as her family.

"I am the last Scinterian," Raine said. "Even were Talan not the love of my life, I would have protected you the same."

"You are not the last Scinterian," Kylan said, "not anymore."

This produced a slight smile on Raine's face. "No," she agreed, "not anymore."

That night, at Raine's insistence, Kylan transformed, and the great blue dragon settled next to her liege, their scales scraping as Kylan found a comfortable position. And the Scinterian smiled as Kylan intertwined her neck with Talan's, resting her great head on Talan's girth so that it rose with the slow up-and-down of her breathing. And it was not long before Kylan's breathing synchronized with her Queen's, and the two Ancient Dragons entered the Long Night together.

Chapter 28

S o Raine stands at the top of the world alone?"
Queen Halla had tears in her eyes, and Astrid, her high Priestess, openly wept. The stern general's throat ached with emotion, and Gimle's long lashes fluttered as she blinked to contain her sorrow.

"She does," Idonea said. "She sent a raptor after us to let us know of Kylan's sleep. She was adamant that we not change our plan."

The extent of Raine's sacrifice weighed heavily on the group as the two toddlers played with one another, the lavender in their eyes on full display. Little was remembered about the Arlanians as a people, but their love for their children was as legendary as their tragic sensuality. For Raine to be parted from both her lover and her children at the same time was heart-rending.

"We're honored that Raine sent her children here," Senta said, "and we'll protect them with every sword and shield we have."

Idonea nodded. "Raine believed you would. But she didn't send them here merely for protection. There's an enormous black dragon sitting on the highest point of your castle who will give his life for his little sisters. As will I."

Senta nodded at the wisdom of Idonea's and Drakar's accompaniment, and Idonea continued thoughtfully.

"Raine has many allies and could have sent her children to many safe-havens. But I think she sent them here for a very particular reason."

Kaia sat on the Queen's lap and wrapped her hand around Senta's finger, enveloped in the warmth of the Ha'kan surrounding her. Idonea watched the little one, and the scene only confirmed her thoughts.

"I think Raine sent them here because she wanted them with someone who would love them the way she loves them."

Astrid's tears began anew and this time the Queen joined her. Gimle sought to comfort them both, fighting her own tears.

"Mother, what's wrong?"

The young woman's voice was distressed as she came into the forum, and Idonea noted how very much the Princess was beginning to look like the Queen.

"Nothing," Halla said, wiping the tears from her eyes. "It's nothing Dallan."

Dallan did not see how that could be true, because it appeared the High Priestess and First Scholar were also tearful. Even more disturbing, the First General appeared to struggle with some great emotion. But as Dallan came closer, she began to understand. Her mother held a child, and children could often inspire tears of joy in the Ha'kan. Astrid held one as well. Dallan marveled at the little ones, for the Ha'kan were beautiful without exception, but these children were extraordinary.

Dallan stopped. For the little one her mother held turned to look at her, and Dallan gazed into gorgeous purple eyes. Her jaw dropped as she looked to the second, who also gazed at her with violet eyes, chewing the tiny fist she had stuffed in her mouth. Dallan sought to process this astonishing fact without much success when she felt a tug at her pant leg. She looked down, and Lifa's daughter, who followed her everywhere, gazed at the two newcomers in fascination.

Idonea watched this scene carefully, especially when Kaia's eyes reverted to pale blue and Laina's to dark gold. Dallan marveled at the change of color, unmindful of what that change might mean, whereas Idonea knew full well the girls were startled, having never seen another child.

The little girl at Dallan's side toddled forward, arms outstretched in delight at the two arrivals. Ha'kan children were raised communally from birth, and therefore did not know a stranger.

Laina assessed this improbability with amber eyes as the little girl ambled unsteadily forward. True to her nature, her curiosity overwhelmed any caution she might feel, and she stretched out her hand. When the little girl took the hand in her own, smiling, Laina smiled in return, and chortled a little laugh.

Kaia, on the other hand, was alarmed at the creature's unsteady gait and its contact with her sister. She pushed herself from Queen Halla's lap. The Queen did not expect the unnatural strength and could not hold her, terrified the child would be injured when she struck the floor. But the child did not touch the floor, rather disappeared in a flash of blue light, and a little dragon stood in her place.

Perhaps "little" was not an apt description, at least not to the Ha'kan. The creature was now ten times the size of the child that Halla had held in her arms, the size of a large wolf or a small pony. Its fang-filled head was low to the floor, the tail high in the air, the wings tight against the body, and the little monster looked as if it were about to pounce.

"Kaia," Idonea said with gentle disapproval. Idonea's tone was utterly calm, so the shock and alarm of the Ha'kan eased to a general apprehension. And Idonea held her hand at the ready to produce a ward in case the little dragon accidently breathed fire in her state of disarray.

"By the Divine," Lifa breathed out as she stood next to Dallan. She had arrived just in time to see her daughter toddle toward Astrid, saw the Queen nearly drop a child, and observed the astonishing transformation of the little one she feared would be injured. But although she felt a stab of fear for her daughter, the little dragon did not appear aggressive, rather profoundly wary and even a little embarrassed.

Laina laughed at her twin and the little blue dragon frowned, still pressed to the floor. The unease of the Ha'kan was transitioning to wonder. The little creature was fearsome, but beautiful, and so very expressive, just as much as in her human form, if not more so.

Serene removed her hand from Laina's, and Lifa held her breath as the little girl approached the baby dragon, completely enamored. Unlike the adult Ha'kan, Serene felt no fear, just delight, at the appearance of the creature. She moved slowly, as if sensing the wariness of the dragon, and when she was near enough, she placed her little hands on the sides of the dragon's head. Kaia did not move, merely stared at the little creature, cautious, until the girl leaned forward and kissed her very gently on the nose.

Kaia emitted a little puff of warm air.

The Ha'kan as one breathed out, releasing their tension, all as enchanted with the little dragon as was Lifa's daughter. Lifa was proud of the fearlessness of her offspring, inwardly noting that charm was often as powerful a weapon as a sword.

Idonea just chuckled. Raine would have been unsurprised at this meeting. A pair of amber eyes looked at her questioningly.

"Yes," Idonea said, "you may. Go. Just don't crush the High Priestess."

Laina sprang from Astrid's lap and before she hit the tiled floor, disappeared into a flash of yellow light. Another baby dragon appeared, this one a dark red that appeared to flicker with flame. She rushed off to her sister, and they began to chase one another around the circular forum.

"And be careful with the little one," Idonea called after them. "She's not indestructible like you."

But the two little dragons seemed to realize that, for although they were rough-and-tumble with one another, they were ever-so-gentle with Serene, and her joyful laughter filled the hall as she chased them about.

Dallan sat down numbly, the magical scene almost too much for her to comprehend.

"These can't be your children?" she asked.

"I'm glad you brought that up," Idonea said. "The children are to be kept secret, but if they are discovered, you will say they're my children."

"But they are–?"

Lifa knew exactly who these children belonged to. "These are your little sisters," she said to Idonea, watching the two romp about the room. "These are the daughters of Raine and Talan. The little red one looks just like Talan."

"Yes," Idonea said simply as Dallan's mouth dropped open once more. "These are my little sisters."

And she set about to recount an abridged version of the story to Dallan and Lifa, which the Queen and her staff enjoyed as much the second time.

Chapter 29

Raine stayed awake the first night that Kylan went to sleep, as well as the second. But as the sun rose in the sky the next morning, her fatigue began to weigh on her. She realized it was unlikely she could stay awake another night.

Still, she tried to go about her day as normally as possible, or what had become normal considering she was at the top of the world alone. Physical exertion was her primary activity, and the thick snow provided a rigorous challenge as she ran down the steep slopes, then back up again. The high elevation had at first taxed her lungs, but already she was adapting to the thin air. She dangled a long rope down the precipitous drop on the north side and climbed up and down using arm strength alone until her muscles burned.

She practiced swordplay on the mannikins she had built in the court-yard, but this was the least satisfying of her exertions, so she instead headed into the surrounding woods to hunt, hoping to find some monster to slay. But there were only foxes and hares, and the occasional deer, none of which she would deign to kill.

In the afternoon, she returned to the castle, ate a quick meal, then headed to the library. She longed to look at the Elven Book of Lore, but she had sent it with the girls. The thought of the babies caused an ache to rise in her chest, one she forcefully suppressed.

The ebony box sitting on the corner of the desk caught her eye. She had forgotten all about the strange gift, given the events since its arrival.

But now she had more than enough time to unlock its secrets. She picked it up, noting the same strange vibration as before. She turned the box upside down, right side up, tilted it to the side, but still saw no obvious way to open it. She tried to pry it open with her fingernails, but the lid, or what she assumed was the lid, was too tightly fitted. She traced the glyphs on the surface, which almost appeared three dimensional, floating in the vast depths of the obsidian darkness.

Raine set the box aside. Perhaps the glyphs were the key. She examined the floor-to-ceiling shelves around her. There were books in here that were far older than her, many which had not been touched in centuries. They were in quasi-order by subject, and her fingers drifted over the many titles. "Early Elven Battle Tactics," "Miasmic Eddies of the Deep Woods," "Purification of Alchemical Reagents," and the like. She pulled a few tomes regarding magical symbols and sat down to thumb through them. They were fascinating books, and some showed recent use, probably by Idonea. But many were dusty and faded, the bindings loose, the parchment fragile. Raine turned these pages carefully, lest she destroy something that was likely irreplaceable. It occurred to her she should probably make some effort to duplicate these rare books at some point in the future, lest Arianthem continue to relive a history it had forgotten. Maeva's little treasure, Kiren, would be perfect for that task.

The books were absorbing, and Raine spent several hours poring over the contents. But in the end, she found nothing that looked like the glyphs on the ebony box. She returned the tomes and scrolls to their shelves, and with one last glance at the mysterious object, she left the library and headed toward the Great Hall.

Talan and Kylan were blissfully sleeping, curled about one another. Raine felt no jealousy towards Kylan, perhaps other than she wished that she, too, could turn into a dragon and join them in their peaceful blackness. But as the shadows lengthened, the air grew chill, and darkness spread throughout the castle, Raine knew sleep was coming, and it would not be peaceful.

She stirred the fire to life, the small one that she would cook on, then checked the large one burning in the far furnace. She opened the grate and shoveled fuel into the black maw, welcoming the heat that emanated outward as the slow-burning rocks ignited. It was unlikely the dragons felt the heat or the cold, but she would keep them warm, nonetheless.

She gnawed on a loaf of bread that she paired with a piece of hard cheese, then washed down with a glass of wine. She chewed on some dried plums for dessert, then wiped her hands in the basin of warm water by the fire. And then, because she knew she could not stay awake any longer, she made her way over to the dragons. She pulled herself up onto Talan's neck, finding a space in which she could recline, and let her eyes close.

"So, this is what you were trying to hide."

The words of the Goddess were terrifying and cold fingers gripped Raine's heart as she struggled to open her eyes. It was hard to breathe, and when she exhaled, the air came out as frost. The darkness was complete, but then there was the blurry light from the fire as the room came into focus around her. She looked to her left, panicked—

But the children were not there. Raine's bleary thoughts struggled to focus. Where were the children? Had they fled to another room?

Hel stood before her, examining the blue dragon intertwined with the fiery red one.

"Talan's Second has entered the Great Night as well. How interesting."

Raine's thoughts were still muddled as she tried to adjust to the dream state. She could make no sense of what Hel was saying. Where were the children?

"So, you protect not one Ancient Dragon," Hel mused, "but two."

The room at last came into focus, as did Raine's thoughts. She had sent the children away. Hel was not talking about her little ones; she was talking about Kylan. As her clarity returned, Raine had sense enough to join the Goddess' narrative.

"I am the last Scinterian. I will protect them both with my life."

Hel materialized a throne with the wave of her hand and then settled upon it. "I know where Talan's castle is. I could send every demon at my disposal to attack them."

"Please do," Raine said coldly, "I'm a little bored up here and could use the exercise."

This statement did not displease Hel, and her slight smile filled Raine with dread. She had always preferred the anger of the Goddess over the many other emotions she displayed towards her.

"Come here."

"No."

With a flick of her finger, Raine was yanked from her reclining position and flung at the feet of the Goddess, while Hel merely pursed her lips thoughtfully.

"I seem to have as much power over you in this dream world as I have in every other."

Raine clenched her jaw because that was most certainly true. She tried to tell herself that this was not real, but it did not matter. It felt real, every part of it. And when Hel began disrobing her with mere gestures, she cursed the sensation. If this was happening in her mind, she cursed her own imagination.

Hel watched as the clothing slid away, revealing that perfect body beneath. She caught her breath.

"Ever since the day you betrayed me," she said, "I've dreamed of this moment. So, how fitting it should occur in a dream."

"This isn't real," Raine said through clenched teeth.

"No?" Hel said, getting to her feet. She pulled Raine to her, marveling at the muscularity of the naked specimen in front of her. She ran her hands over the arms, feathering her touch down the silken skin of that magnificent back. "It feels very real to me." Her hand tightened on Raine's arm.

"It's not real," Raine repeated.

"Hmm, well let's see." She lowered her head so that she could whisper in Raine's ear, and that warm tickle felt more real than anything else to Raine. Raine closed her eyes at the sensation, and Hel smiled a wicked smile, knowing she was very close to the beginning of her vengeance. Her eyes drifted to the sleeping dragon, and her smile widened.

"This will be just like old times, me putting you on your knees and raping you in front of Talan."

"Do whatever want," Raine said biting off the words. "This isn't real. I'm at home sleeping with my love, and you're nowhere near."

This infuriated Hel, and she forced Raine face down on the throne. "Really? Let's see how real this feels to you."

Raine struggled with all her might but could barely move. And she could feel the Goddess behind her, moving into position to violate her, and she could feel the blue and gold markings rise upon her skin. But as Hel prepared her instrument of torture to thrust into the one she would claim as her own, the body beneath her grew translucent, began to blur and fade, and instead of the great room in Talan's castle…

She was back in the Underworld, entangled in the black silken sheets of her bed.

The furious scream of the Goddess echoed throughout the great subterranean halls, and even the staunchest denizens of that hideous realm quivered, then slunk back into the shadows. Garmr, the great blood-stained hound that guarded the Gates, whimpered and hid behind a column, burying his head beneath his paws.

Feray saw the sudden awakening of her Mistress and did not hesitate to flee the bedchamber. Although she felt little compassion for Hel's various thralls, she did feel sorry for the one that would serve as an outlet for the livid, frustrated lust of the Goddess. And as Hel snatched the closest thing to her, Feray closed the door behind her, knowing it was unlikely she would see that one again.

All arms and legs were thrashing as Raine felt herself falling through the air. She was stunned by a blow to her head and light appeared behind her eyelids. Her eyes opened, but she could not make sense of the angle of the room, nor what she was lying against. It took a moment for her to realize her face was pressed to the floor, and that she had fallen from Talan and struck her head on the tiled surface.

She slowly pushed herself upright. She was freezing. Her entire body hurt, especially her chest, and the fire seemed very far away. She began to drag herself towards that warmth, and the exertion warmed her, but only a little. When she reached the flames, she got as close as she could without burning herself. She lay there, breathing hard. As her circulation improved, her breathing at last began to ease, and with great effort, she pulled a fur about her to suppress the uncontrolled shivering of her body. It was some time before the pain in her chest subsided. When at last she felt she was no longer in danger of freezing to death, she sat upright, adjusted the fur, and stared into the flames.

The Goddess was terribly angry with her and had nearly succeeded in her attempted rape. But somehow, despite Hel's great power over her in the dream world, she had been able to awaken. Raine pressed her fingers to the tender spot on her temple, trying to think of what had aided her escape. The last thing she could remember in the dream was her markings rising to the surface of her skin. Perhaps it was the violence of Hel's attempted act that had shattered her sleep. Although Raine never consented to sex with Hel, her body always yielded to her seduction. She could not remember Hel ever forcing her against her will; the Goddess just simply waited until that will dissolved into an involuntary Arlanian response.

But is that what had awakened her?

Raine hugged herself and rubbed the feeling back into her arms. As she did so, she felt another tender spot on her body, this one on her upper arm. She raised her sleeve and dumbly stared at the bruise that was already rising to the surface, a bruise much in the shape of a hand. With great disquiet, she lowered the sleeve and pulled the fur tighter about her, returning her attention to the flames.

While asleep, to keep her sanity, she had repeated over and over again that nothing in the dream world was real. It was the one thing she could hold onto, a belief that although Hel could see her, could mentally touch her, the Goddess was not actually there, and nothing she did, no matter how horrible, really happened.

The bruise on her arm tingled, and she looked down at the welt again. The outline forced her to formulate a question she did not want to ask.

If nothing in the dream world was real, then how had Hel left a mark on her?

It was many hours before Feray risked the presence of her Mistress, and she was relieved to see Hel in the bath, deep in thought. She did not see the thrall whom the Goddess had yanked into her bed, but several others were quivering in the alcoves. She motioned for one to attend to Hel, and the young woman fearfully approached, kneeling behind her and dipping a sponge, which she then began to lightly press against the white shoulders. Hel appeared oblivious to the ministrations, which was good news to both the thrall and Feray, for such imperious inattention is what they expected from her.

Faen skulked in, his tail in a heightened state of alert, ready to flee the fury of the Queen. He, too, was cautiously relieved to see her wrath somewhat abated. He settled on a nearby bench, his tail still wavering uncertainly in the air while he waited to see if his Queen had any direction for him. His yellow eyes flicked to Feray, then back to his Mistress.

"I shouldn't have tried to rape her," Hel said at last.

Both Feray and Faen anxiously tried to discern if these words required a response, but the statement seemed directed at no one in particular, so both held their tongues. The thrall was not as discerning.

"You're allowed to do anything you wish, your Majesty."

"Shut up."

The sponge froze, and the thrall sought to undo the damage of her words. "I just meant any would welcome your attentions—"

The woman could not finish the thought, for Hel's hand flashed out and grabbed her by the throat, then shoved her head beneath the water. She held the fiercely struggling creature without effort and with minimal attention to the death throes she was inflicting. When at last the thrall grew limp, Hel threw the body across the room with a mere gesture, into the alcove from which it came. She returned to her dark reverie.

"I brought out the Scinterian in her," she pondered aloud. "That was my mistake."

Both Feray and Faen froze. This was an impossible statement: to agree meant they believed the Goddess had made a mistake; to disagree meant, well, that they disagreed. Both responses would result in death. When emerald eyes slowly raised to Feray, Faen thanked all that was unholy that it was not him who had drawn this lot.

The chief handmaiden smoothed her robes, then spoke quietly. "You always were most successful with her Arlanian side, bringing forth the lavender in her eyes and making those blue and gold scars disappear. She responded to you most passionately."

The silence in the room was pronounced as Feray awaited her fate, but there was a reason why she had been in Hel's service longer than any other.

"Yes," Hel said, nodding. "Yes, she did. And I enjoyed her submission more than I would ever enjoy forcing her. I need only seduce her, and she'll be mine once more."

Feray's heart began to beat again, and she released her breath. The other thralls crept from their alcoves and began carefully tending to their Mistress, who now seemed in a much better mood.

Chapter 30

Raine did not sleep well and was disjointed when she awoke. Although she tried to motivate herself, the activities that normally would occupy her held no interest. The bruise on her arm seemed to throb far more than the one on her head. She had one bright, albeit fleeting, moment. While cleaning the cooking area, a series of scrapes on the tiles caught her eye, causing her to smile, for it was undoubtedly the work of her little ones. She forcibly suppressed the sadness this produced, then sighed heavily. She gave up on her lethargic attempts at completing chores.

She wandered through the castle, and soon her footsteps returned her to the library. Her "gift" sat on the corner of a desk. She half-heartedly began thumbing through some more magical tomes in an attempt to decipher the glyphs on the obsidian box, but nothing looked anything like the symbols. After a while, she gave up on that research, tucked the container underneath her arm and meandered to the courtyard. She briefly considered throwing the gift off the 1000-foot drop to the north, but instead set it on a bench and retrieved her weapons. Perhaps some swordplay would pass the time.

She began warming up with her dual swords, spinning them about her wrists as she worked on her footwork, lunging here, slicing there. It felt good to fight, even with an imaginary opponent. Perhaps it was her recent encounter with the Goddess, but the Underworld was very much on her mind. She recalled the gladiatorial contests in Hel's court, how she had memorized the tactics and techniques of the demons, and how she had devised defenses and counterattacks in her head. She used those memories to invent enemies, and she fought the imaginary hoards with a violence that was visible in her movements.

After decimating several unreal enemies, she paused, spinning her swords about her wrists. She took a stance to begin again, then stopped, her swords paused in mid-air, one guarding, one attacking, both as unmoving as she herself. Slowly, she stood upright, turning her gaze upon the courtyard. She felt a presence, much like when she could sense Hyr'rok'kin or Reaper Shards, but what she felt did not seem evil. She frowned. Nor did it seem good. Her gaze drifted around the vast space. There was nothing in front of her, behind her, next to her; it was as empty as always. She twirled the swords about her wrists, troubled. She examined the sky above, then returned to her perusal of the courtyard.

Her gaze was drawn to the box on the bench where she had left it. Now it was just a white, rectangular outline in the snow. She began walking toward the object, sheathing one of her swords, still twirling the other about her wrist. It was a wonder the box was covered by the white powder, because it seemed to thrum with a vibratory energy. She frowned again. Maybe she was imagining the vibration. Right now, she was not entirely trusting her grasp of things. As she neared the bench, she slowed, then came to a stop in front of the container. She reached down with her free hand, cautiously, and her fingers brushed away the fine layer of snow. She half-expected the glyphs on the box to be glowing, or changing color, or really doing anything at all, but they just sat there inertly.

But strangely, now she could read them, or at least one of them.

"Sentinel," she murmured.

No sooner had she uttered the word than a monstrous black form sprang from the box, moving unbelievably fast. Her second sword appeared in her hand to join the first, just in time to block the blow that would have beheaded her. The demonic attacker wielded dual swords, like hers, except seemingly made from black, smoky air. They slashed at her and that ephemerality was proved an illusion as they contacted her own swords with such force her weapons were nearly jarred from her hands. The black swords came at her in a flurry she could barely defend, and she sought to disengage so she could regroup. She feinted right, dodged left, tried to create space between her and her opponent, but the creature was upon her in an instant, and another furious flurry ensued.

Raine was pressed backward, barely able to defend against the demonic attacker. The man-like shape was a smoky blackness that faded in and out with same solidity and ephemerality as his weapons. The black blades moved with blinding speed and Raine was not so much as anticipating his blows as guessing where they might land. She guessed incorrectly and a smoky blade sliced through the sleeve of her shirt.

Raine jumped over a bench but the creature was there, dual blades swinging at her head. She blocked the attack, her Scinterian blades engaging the smoke blades, making a sound much like steel-on-steel despite their lack of solidity. She moved up onto the wall, and the creature moved with her, still slowly pressing her back. She leaped down, dodged beneath another head-strike, then rolled to her left. She came to her feet, blades at the ready, but still scarcely in time to block the attack. Never in her life had she met a foe even close to her skill, but this creature was trouncing her. It was only a matter of time before one of those blows landed.

The smoky blackness sliced downward, and Raine defended against the strike, but awkwardly, and her right sword went flying. She drew a dagger, and now fought at a disadvantage as the two black swords came at her in a blur. All she could do with the knife was defend, and she wasn't doing that well against the expertly wielded sword. Her own movements were a blur, the contact of the weapons a continuous metallic song, but still the creature increased his speed.

Her other sword went flying, and Raine pulled another dagger so now she wielded two. In a baffling manifestation, the long swords of her opponent transitioned to daggers, so now they were once again equally armed. Or they would have been had the smoky phantasm been less skilled. He engaged her fiercely, and the shorter weapons were just as dangerous. It was not long before one of her daggers went flying and she grabbed the black wrist that flashed downward, stopping the blade just short of her collarbone while her other dagger desperately fought off the second blade. The wrist she held was solid, powerful, and despite her enormous strength, Raine felt her own arm begin to give way.

She allowed it to do so suddenly, twisting out and beneath the downward strike in a maneuver that should have caught the creature off-guard.

But it did no such thing as he whirled about and sent her other dagger flying, disarming her completely. Knowing she could not fight him at distance without a weapon, she closed in and came up underneath his arms, trapping both blades away from her body.

In another bizarre manifestation, the daggers disappeared, and her opponent now chose to fight her hand-to-hand, a form of combat in which he was equally proficient. The two began exchanging blows, fist strikes, punches, elbows, knees, kicks, a black smoky blur of attacks, blocks, counter attacks, feints, and throws. Raine again felt herself at a disadvantage, pressed backward and taking a beating from her spectral opponent.

Raine had no idea how long they had been fighting, but it felt like an eternity. She could feel her reflexes slow and her breathing become ragged. The creature, on the other hand, was not fatigued at all. The monstrosity aimed an elbow at her face, and she went to block it realizing too late it was a feint, and the creature followed through with a spinning, reverse elbow that would take off her head. Raine braced herself for the unconsciousness she knew was coming.

Except it did not.

The black, smoky limb hovered an inch from Raine's face, and she stared at it dumbly. The creature lowered his arms, stepped back, and all tautness drained from his body. He stood upright, not really looking at Raine, not really looking at anything. She still held her arms in a defensive posture, shuffling rearward to create some distance, still in a fighting stance, but now the creature seemed profoundly disinterested in her.

Raine slowly lowered her arms. For the first time, she could get a good look at the spectral being. He was tall, humanoid, his torso possessing a V-shaped taper that implied muscularity, but without any defining features. He had the suggestion of a face, the hint of eyes and a nose, but everything swirled like black smoke, smearing and wispy at the edges. He did not wear clothes, but rather was an obsidian presence, with tendrils of smoke on his head suggestive of wavy hair.

Raine was suddenly annoyed at the outcome of their battle and thought about rushing the creature, but the slightest tilt of his chin in her direction communicated what a terrible idea that was. Raine swallowed her anger and sat down heavily on the bench behind her. The creature made no move toward, her, rather just stood flickering silently.

What was this thing? Why had it fought so fiercely, then stopped so abruptly? Why had he changed his weapons to match hers? Raine's eyes drifted to the cut on her sleeve. Those weapons could do real damage. Her blue eyes flicked back to the flickering presence. This thing could have killed her, a thought she had difficulty grasping. She had never encountered an opponent like this. What had she said before the thing sprang from the box? Sentinel. But what did that mean? Was it a warning? A title? Was it the phantasm's name?

Raine slowly got to her feet, wary of making any sudden moves. The slightest tilt of the creature's head indicated he was very aware of her movement. She backed away from him, circling around until she was outside his field of vision, or what would have been his field of vision had he possessed eyes. She continued to step backward, cautiously, prepared to sprint if needed. The thing did not move, merely stood flickering blackly against the snow.

She reached the door, opened it behind her, stepped through the threshold, then slammed it shut. As soon as she had done so, she felt stupid. She peered through the slot on the door. The creature had not moved, his stoic demeanor increasing her irritation. She slammed the deadbolt over and downward, wondering if it would even stop the creature. She stormed off, uncertain why she was so cross.

Within five minutes, she was at the courtyard window, staring at the smoky presence that simply stood unwavering in the snow. It gazed off at nothing, unaffected by the cold, the wind, the sleet, and most of all, by her.

Raine checked the window with an involuntary regularity throughout the day, unable to curb her obsessive interest in the creature. Every time she did so, the spectral figure was in the same place, in exactly the same position, staring off at nothing. She went to another floor so she could examine him from another angle, and her new perspective offered nothing of value. As the day went on, Raine knew she could not simply leave the dangerous creature in the courtyard, not with two Ancient Dragons slumbering away under her protection. She put on her armor, considered arming herself with every weapon she owned, then, based on the fact the creature seemed intent on matching her weaponry, returned to the court-yard empty-handed.

The black figure still stood unmoving where she had left him. He showed no interest in her return, although somehow Raine knew he was completely aware of her. She walked past him, careful to give him a wide berth lest she trigger another attack. He flickered silently.

The obsidian box was on the bench, again covered in snow. The lid was now open, and Raine was unsurprised to find the container empty. She examined the strange glyph, uncertain what language or culture had spawned it, and more uncertain how she could read it. It was almost as if she were remembering something, although it did not really feel like her memory.

Raine shook her head. That did not make any sense at all. None of this made any sense. But with a growing assurance based on absolutely nothing, she picked up the box. A second glyph made itself known. She mulled the meaning of this second word, as well as its relationship to the first. Finally, still unsure as to whether the box was a peculiar gift or a deadly trap, she spoke the two words.

"Sentinel."

The chin barely tilted, but it indicated the creature was listening.

"Withdraw."

The smoke of the creature swirled into a funnel, shot across the court-yard, and before Raine could even react, the phantasm disappeared into the box. Raine held the object for a moment, stunned, then carefully closed the lid. She set the box down, watched it to see if anything else would happen, and once satisfied that the creature was contained, started across the courtyard.

When she reached the door, she stopped. She turned back to the box. It sat inertly in the falling snow. She frowned. It made no sense at all to go pick up that dangerous thing and bring it into the castle. But unable to deny the strange compulsion, she trudged back across the courtyard. She picked up the obsidian box, tucked it beneath her arm, and headed inside.

Sleep did not come that night, and Raine did not miss it. She sat on Talan's neck with a book, leaning back against her great belly, rising and falling infrequently when the dragon took a breath. Occasionally, she would glance over at the black box that sat clear across the room, then return to her studies. A nearby torch provided light for her to read by, and she was absorbed in a volume on the ancient geography of Arianthem. It seemed that historically, the Ha'kan and High Elves were in much the same place as they were now, although the Empire, at least at the time of creation of the map, did not exist. That piece of the atlas was inhabited by various barbarian tribes.

Raine turned the page. There was a small island off the very southern edge of Arianthem. She turned back to the previous page, noting that it did not appear on that older map. She turned to the following page, and it did not appear on that map, either. She returned to the page with the island and peered closer.

This book was written in a language she did not know, possibly some older version of an obscure Dverger dialect. It resembled the present-day dwarven language, but not enough for her to make out the words. A small pictograph next to it, however, gave Raine some clue as to the island's identity: a pair of violet eyes.

She knew far more of her father's people than her mother's, probably because there were a few Scinterians left when she was a child, but no Arlanians. To her knowledge, her mother was the last living Arlanian, and she had died when Raine was an infant.

Of course, Raine admitted to herself, she had diligently studied Scinterian history, their culture, their values and beliefs, their military strategy, and most importantly, their fighting techniques. She had made no such effort with the Arlanians, and truth be told, half of her knowledge could be incorrect because it had been passed on in rumor and inuendo.

She returned her attention to the book. Could this be the home of the Arlanians? If it was an island, that would explain why they had gone undetected so long, and why they were such an insular people. Raine closed the book thoughtfully. Tomorrow she would begin searching the library for other books on the Arlanians. Kylan had mentioned that this castle was standing before the Great War, which meant it was at least four centuries old, probably much older than that. There might be books on the Scinterians as well, and as studious as she had been in that regard, there were probably things here she did not know.

The light in the far doorway had changed just enough that Raine realized "tomorrow" had already come. She had stayed awake the entire night with little effort and wasn't particularly tired. Her attention returned to the ebony container across the room. She had the beginnings of an idea that was probably terrible, but the compulsion returned, and she could not resist. She trotted across the room, retrieved the box, and headed out to the courtyard.

An arsenal of weaponry lined the wall of the courtyard. Two racks of swords, a rack of bows, an array of lances, a stack of shields, and a trestle of exotic armaments were neatly arrayed along the length of the stone wall. Raine had spent hours dragging the weaponry from the depths of the castle, then carefully arranged the collection. The entire time, the ebony box sat on a bench on the far side of the courtyard, inert.

"This might be the most ill-advised thing I've ever done," Raine muttered to herself.

She perused the armaments, foregoing any of her usual favorites. Instead, she chose a lance, a weapon she was proficient with, but rarely used. It seemed an appropriate choice to test her theory, a theory she had been mulling over ever since the creature had disappeared back into its box. She tested the weight of the spear: it was heavy but well-balanced. It would do fine.

She twirled the lance with one hand, then two, the arcs becoming wider, the swings growing faster, the maneuvers more complex as her body warmed. When she felt she was ready, she took a deep breath and strode across the courtyard, stopping some distance away from the black box. She put her lance in a neutral, non-threatening position, and took another deep breath.

"Sentinel."

The lid of the box opened, and a funnel of smoke sprang forth. But instead of attacking her, the phantasm formed some distance away, facing her, holding a black, smoky lance. The spear was also held in a neutral position as the creature stood waiting.

Very deliberately, Raine moved her lance to a ready position, across her body, in both hands. The lance of the creature snapped into an opposing position with preternatural speed, a speed which nearly made Raine rethink what she was doing. But before she could dissuade herself, she calmly spoke the word.

"Begin."

The creature flew at her, the lance stabbing forward as Raine stepped to the side and parried the lethal blow downward. The other end of the lance came swinging around, but Raine was prepared, blocking that blow as well as the flurry that followed. Footwork with the lance was important, for anticipation and its resulting momentum were key with the longer weapon. She marveled at the intricate movements of her opponent. It was not long until he caught her in a poor position, struck her mid-section with a brutal blow, then stepped backward to a neutral position. She leaned on her lance, gasping for breath. Once her breath returned to her, she stood upright and resumed a ready position.

"Again."

The phantasm did not hesitate but leaped forward in even more brutal attack. But this time Raine did not overcommit as before, but managed to defend against his charge, circling out from range of the lance. She had no time to celebrate her success, however, for the creature was again upon her. It was not long before he swept her feet from beneath her and she landed on her back, blocking the downward swing of the lance that would have crushed her skull. She kipped up to her feet just in time to block another blow, rolled right, and re-gained a more advantageous standing position. Their lances again interlocked in an elaborate, dangerous dance.

Despite the cold weather, Raine was bathed in sweat. She was bruised from one end of her body to the other. Although the creature could have stabbed her at any time, he seemed content to batter her instead. Each time, he gained the advantage, he would simply step back to a neutral position, flickering silently. And each time, Raine would analyze her mistake, catch her breath, then start again.

Finally, the grumbling of her stomach and the position of the sun in the sky told her they had been fighting all morning. The smoky black figure stood silently as she lay her lance on the ground.

"I'm going to get something to eat. I'll be back in a moment."

As she entered the castle, her expression grew wry. There were no indications the creature could understand anything she said, or in fact, was listening to her at all. But apparently, she was going to talk to it anyway. She grew thoughtful. She was likely projecting a great deal on the apparition. There were no indications of intelligence, personality, or emotion, really anything at all beyond a supernatural fighting ability.

She rummaged through the pantry, found some bread, cheese, and jerky, and returned to the courtyard. She sat on the bench, munching on the bread, watching the flickering figure who showed no interest at her at all. He stood staring off at nothingness, wisps outlining his body like little black flames.

The creature could have killed her at any time; that much was obvious. And this fact alone was astonishing to Raine. There was very little in this realm that was even a challenge to her, let alone something that could so soundly defeat her. Nor had she found anything in Hel's realm that was a contest like the solitary figure that stood before her. At first, she had been self-critical, mentally accusing herself of becoming soft the last few years. But that was an inadequate explanation, for previously she had gone years without significant battle, and she had lost nothing in skill for the interruption. This creature was simply her better.

She took a bite of the bread. Where had this thing come from? And what was his purpose here? She was hardly afraid of him; that fear had dissipated with the grasp of his lethality, and his restraint of it. If he had wanted her dead, she would be dead. He could have killed her, both dragons, and then moved on to slaughtering the rest of Arianthem. But instead he stood here, an impassive, improbable, unreadable, man-like column of smoke.

She took another bite of bread, chewing thoughtfully. She had originally thought he resembled Reaper Shards, the Hyr'rok'kin that lived half in the mortal realm and half in the Underworld. But now she saw that those similarities were superficial. He shared the black smokiness of those horrid monstrosities, but where those creatures were semi-translucent, fading in and out, this creature possessed a blackness much like the obsidian box, so dark that light seemed to disappear within him, suggesting endless depths.

Raine tore off a piece of the jerky with her teeth. She chewed on it somberly while she stared at the phantasm, and he stared off at nothing. Finally, feeling her energy somewhat revived, she stood and stretched her limbs. Every muscle in her body hurt. She examined the shields on the rack, choosing a mid-sized one of elven design that would provide a balance between protection and mobility. She drew her own, Scinterian sword, then took a position in front of the creature. The lance he held morphed into a sword much like her own, and a flurry of smoke resolved into a shield in his other hand.

"Sentinel," Raine said, raising her sword as the creature did the same. "Begin."

Sleep would find her this night, Raine knew, for she could not remember the last time she was so tired. Not even the long march across the Empty Land had left her so fatigued, and she had fought several battles on that trek. In fact, as she winced at the various aches and pains in her body, she did not recall ever being this tired.

She heated some leftover stew which she gulped down, and once her bowl was clean, she crawled up onto her dragon lover, patting Kylan's neck as she did so. It was possible that Hel would come for her tonight, but right now, she was just too tired to care. With one last glance at the onyx box across the room, she shifted her position, and wrapped a leg about one of Weynild's armored spikes. Her eyes closed, and within minutes, Raine was fast asleep.

The Goddess examined her prize. At last, she was here, fully present in Talan's castle, every feature of the room in bold relief. The Arlanian lay on the dragon, curled about the dark red barbs on Talan's neck. The blue and gold markings on her arms were prominent. The beautiful body twitched as the Goddess drew near, and the long eyelashes fluttered. Hel waited, triumphant for those eyes to open.

But they did not.

Hel frowned, moving closer. She prodded the sleeping figure. The

Arlanian moaned slightly, muttered something in her sleep, then rolled over, her back to the Goddess. She curled closer about Talan, who did not move at all. The blue dragon let out a soft snort in her sleep.

Hel's fury rose. She went to shake the figure, but this time when she reached down, her hand passed through the body, which was slowly growing more translucent. Nor could she touch either dragon, or anything else in the room.

"What is this?" she demanded, her frustration beyond measure. She finally had the Arlanian where she wanted her, helpless before her in the dream world, and now it seemed the girl had found yet another way to escape her.

"This is impossible!"

Hel's furious proclamation echoed throughout her bed chamber in the Underworld as she awoke. Both Feray and Faen watched her fearfully. They were present with the expectation of her victorious return. Both now regretted that decision as she returned once again defeated and enraged. Hel threw the sheets from the bed, snatched a silk robe from the couch, and stalked from the room as she pulled the flowing robe around her. Everything, living and dead, fled from her path as she entered her garden.

The many Trees of the Dead failed to provide her any solace as they glowed with their vivid amber light. She snatched the head of a night blooming flower and crushed the petals in her hand, flinging the remains to the side. She grasped the thorny stem of a black rose, enjoying the pain it inflicted upon her as she squeezed it tightly.

"Oh, to see you in such disarray, my love."

The mocking tone froze Hel in her tracks. The voice, or rather the one it belonged to, was never welcome in her domain and was especially unwelcome right now. But Hel knew that caution was imperative with this one. She gathered herself, calming her fury, for any display of emotion would be disastrous, a weapon to be used against her. She tightened the sash of her robe, smoothed its silken folds, then turned to the interloper.

"What do you want, father?"

Lok'i eyed his daughter, unfazed by her lack of warmth. His amused expression infuriated her, and she turned away from him again, struggling for composure. He settled onto a bench behind her, toying with the stem of a plant. He let out an exaggerated sigh.

"Still pining over Tyr's and Sjöfn's bastard spawn?"

Hel stared at the tree in front of her as the sardonic question sunk in, trying to grasp the many implications of his statement. She whirled to face him.

"You knew?"

"Of course, I knew," Lok'i said, laughing, "It's my business to know of such infidelities, such indiscretions. Do you think an affair between the God of War and the Goddess of Love would slip my attention?"

"You could have told me," Hel said, unable to disguise the accusation in her voice. She turned away and Lok'i saw his opening.

"It was so much fun watching you figure it out," he said. He stood and slipped behind her, putting his hands on her waist. "She must be incredible in bed," he whispered in her ear.

The inappropriate comment epitomized their convoluted, dysfunctional relationship, and yet it tempted her back to the familiar. Her father would push her to an extreme for his own enjoyment, and despite her best efforts, she would respond. And she did so now.

"You have no idea," she said.

"Hmm," Lok'i said, sensing capitulation. He grasped her hands and turned her to face him. "So somber when you have so many cards in your hand."

"What cards do I have?"

He did not speak, but rather gazed at her intently, and by his look alone she grasped his meaning. She pulled her hands from his.

"No."

He did not respond, merely kept looked at her in an expressive manner.

"No," she repeated. "You would have me unleash something that could destroy us all?"

"Well, you're the only one who can," he said, as if that somehow explained everything.

Hel shook her head. "The Allfather entrusted their imprisonment to me."

"And your dear grandfather isn't here right now, is he? And may I remind you he sided with Sjöfn, Tyr, and their brat, over you?"

That was not exactly the way it unfolded, but hearing the words spill from her father's lips made it seem that way, for that was the power wielded by the God of Lies.

"You do have daddy issues, don't you?" Hel said.

"Hmm, seems to run in the family."

Hel frowned, for arguing with Lok'i was fruitless, and she had no idea why she did so.

"I still won't do what you want me to. I don't know what you would gain from my summoning them, but I won't do it."

"Well," he said, "I'm the Lord of Chaos. I think it's obvious what I would gain. But all that is up to you." He sat back down on the bench, and his tone grew sly again.

"You have another pawn in this game."

Hel crossed her arms over her chest. She did not want to listen to him any longer; she could already feel the honeyed poison of his words seeping into her. Still, she could not stop herself.

"And what pawn is that?"

"That which fled into the darkness, wanders it still."

Hel paused. His words were vague and obscure as always, frustrating riddles, full of loopholes and alternate meanings. But somehow, she knew what he was saying, and what he was saying was impossible. She stared down at the plant in front of her, not seeing it, or really anything at all.

"Is there anything else?" she said at last.

Lok'i merely smiled, knowing that his work was done. "No, my love. I just wanted you to see all your options."

And then the God of Mayhem disappeared.

Chapter 31

The Royal Guard of the Ha'kan snapped to attention. The Queen's garden had been placed off-limits to all but a select few, which included members of the Queen's staff, as well as the Princess and her immediate cohort. This limitation caused much speculation amongst the Ha'kan, for normally the Queen was very accessible and her gardens were open to all. Rumors abounded that the Ha'kan were caring for a grievously injured ally, and the enormous black dragon perched on the parapets seemed to give credence to this gossip, for he was certainly an imposing and protective presence.

But despite the prohibitions regarding the garden, Hildr eyed the small group approaching and made a quick decision.

"I will escort them in," she said to her guards, and they nodded.

Queen Halla sat on a bench beneath the shade of a tree, enjoying the beauty of her gardens and that of her priestesses. Astrid sat next to her, thumbing through a book of poetry while Gimle sat poring over an ancient scroll. Halla's attention was drawn to the approaching party, curious, and when she recognized the visitors, she smiled and stood. She started towards them.

"Y'arren," the Queen said warmly, taking the elven matriarch's hands in her own.

The tiny wizened elf smiled. The Queen of the Ha'kan was now arguably the most powerful leader in Arianthem, yet she was as kind and gracious as always.

"Queen Halla," Y'arren said, "Warmth in winter and cool in summer."

"To you as well," the Queen replied. "First off, we welcome you, and please stay as long as you wish. I can prepare accommodations in the palace, although I know you prefer this garden."

"Your hospitality is most welcome," Y'arren said, bowing, "and I'll stay here in my tent in the gardens, with your permission."

"You have my permission and my blessing." A slight dimple appeared in Halla's cheek. "Now let me guess why you're here."

Y'arren could not disguise her anticipation. "May I see them?"

"Of course."

The Queen and the wood elf walked hand-in-hand through the garden, followed by the Queen's entourage and the few acolytes that accompanied Y'arren. They rounded a hedge, and Y'arren stopped, her green eyes glowing.

Two tiny dragons bounded about the clearing, blowing smoke and fire, chasing the Princess, the First Ranger, and the future First General, all who sought to defend themselves in every way possible. Laughter echoed through the garden at the chaotic play.

A sultry figure approached, and Y'arren's smile grew larger.

"Hello, dragon's daughter."

"Hello Y'arren," Idonea said, leaning down to give the matriarch a hug. "Would you like to meet my little sisters?"

"More than anything in this world."

The participants in the unruly melee paused as Idonea and the wizened elf approached. Dallan, Rika, and Skye all took a step back as the tiny dragons paused, then milled about uncertainly. Sensitive to magic, something enormous, yet enormously different from their mother and sister approached. It was power, but warmth and light, and sundry things that neither could even comprehend. Kaia frowned and Laina was unusually cautious given her personality. Both little dragons were low to the ground, trembling with something neither grasped.

"It's okay, my little ones," Y'arren said in ancient elvish, and it was as if both began to understand. They cautiously stood upright and padded forward. Kaia nosed Y'arren's hand, and she embraced them both, tears in her emerald eyes.

"Did you like the book I gave you?"

Both perked up, for now they fully understood who this creature was. This was their mother's godmother, the matriarch of the wood elves, who worshipped Talan'alaith'illaria, their dragon mother and Queen of all Dragons. They bounded about Y'arren, showing their appreciation in a way that words could never convey. Y'arren chuckled.

"Go play," she said, "I'll not leave you until you're reunited with your mother."

This filled the little dragons with joy, and they sprinted back towards their playmates, hitting the Princess of the Ha'kan square in the chest and flattening her, causing much laughter from her future First General, after she ensured the future Queen was not injured.

"They are a handful," Idonea said.

Y'arren could not stop smiling. This was perhaps the best gift that could ever be given to Arianthem. "I can see that."

Y'arren then grew serious for a moment. "I received word from Raine that both Talan and Kylan sleep, and that Hel threatened her in her dreams."

A significant look passed between Idonea and Y'arren, of which Gimle took note. She had already deduced that larger forces were at work, which now the matriarch seemed to confirm.

"I came here to protect these children." Y'arren nodded to the Queen, and then to Idonea. "I know they're already guarded beyond measure, but I can hide them in ways others cannot."

"Yes," Idonea agreed, "I'm grateful for your magic. The Ha'kan can protect them from a physical threat. But you can disguise them from those who might circumvent my magic."

"Yes," Y'arren said, eying the two little ones in the garden. "That's going to be necessary very soon."

Chapter 32

el stood gazing at the pedestal in front of her, which glowed with a greenish light that bathed her features. Her father's words echoed mockingly in her ear, and she wondered how much he really knew. The timing of his visit was suspect. Or perhaps luck simply favored him. Hel frowned at the thought. When luck favored the Lord of Chaos, it deserted all others.

The pedestal stood inert for a moment while Hel considered her father. Despite her power and their contentious relationship, she did not dare stand against him, for Lok'i destroyed without rhyme or reason, simply for the pleasure of it. And the machinations he set in motion could take centuries to come to fruition. She wondered if she were merely a pawn in his larger game, perhaps a game he had been playing for millennia.

She shook her head at this nonsense. She was the Queen of the Underworld, Goddess of the Afterlife, and the Allfather had tasked her with enormous responsibility, responsibility she had borne flawlessly her entire life.

Until now.

Hel's long eyelashes lowered as she considered her actions. What would the Allfather say if he knew what she had done? Her expression hardened at the memory of her father's words. The Allfather had sided with Sjöfn and Tyr, not her. He had given her little choice in the matter. The eyelashes raised.

"Come forth."

A lovely woman appeared, translucent at first, but gradually solidifying. She wore a shimmering green dress that pushed her breasts together into a valley of cleavage. But Hel had no eyes for this one; that sort of attraction led only to disaster. The green of the dress set off her pale skin and the long auburn locks of her hair.

"You summoned me, my Queen?"

The title was mocking, and the voice fairly dripped with sarcasm. Such sly disrespect would have resulted in the death of anyone else in Hel's realm. It irritated Hel, but she would not be drawn into a verbal skirmish with one who thrived on it.

"Your plan didn't work."

"Ah," the red head said, objecting as she smoothed the folds of her dress, "it was your plan."

Hel's fury started to rise, but she checked her anger. This one was the weakest of all her sisters, but still dangerous beyond measure. And she needed the Green Witch's help, for the enchantress could do things even the gods could not.

The witch watched the Goddess with calculation. She would not push her too far; she was still Hel's prisoner and the Goddess could inflict any number of punishments upon her. But she would prick this one. Not cut her too deeply, just draw a little blood.

"You told me the object of your desire was Arlanian. You didn't tell me she was also Scinterian."

Hel's lack of disclosure was on purpose. The witch and her kind wielded information like weaponry.

"I don't see what difference that makes."

"It makes all the difference in the world," the witch said. Her gaze grew distant, contemplative. "Such a combination, I can't imagine how such a creature came into existence."

The last thing Hel wanted was this succubus contemplating her love. It was one of the many reasons why she had been reluctant to pursue this option. But as her father had so aptly put it, she had few cards in her hands as powerful as this one.

"What difference does it make?" Hel demanded.

"Well," the witch said simply, "Arlanians dream constantly. Every single night. Without ceasing." The witch's pause lengthened as Hel's impatience grew.

"Scinterians, on the other hand, don't dream at all."

The pronouncement stunned Hel. "What?"

"Scinterians," the witch repeated, a contemptuous look in her hazel eyes, "don't dream at all."

Hel smashed the vase next to her. It exploded into a thousand shards. The witch examined the shattered pieces, knowing that she had probably pushed the Goddess as far as was wise. Her next words were matter of fact, a statement of the obvious that would not soothe the seething Goddess, but nor would it aggravate her further.

"I don't know what's going on with your Arlanian-Scinterian. You should be able have full access to her in her dreams. But if she's not dreaming, the only thing I can think of," she said, her hazel eyes glowing, "is that something is really bringing out the Scinterian in her right now."

Chapter 33

Raine stood at the edge of the courtyard staring out over Arianthem. On a clear day like today, she imagined she could see all the way to the land of the Ha'kan, where her children, all four of them, were safe in the land of beloved allies. She imagined the two little ones romping through the Queen's forum, running through the halls of the castle, and tearing about the garden, all under the watchful eyes of their older brother and sister. It brought a smile to her face, then the stab of sadness that always accompanied the reminder of the loss of her children.

She straightened and chastised herself. Her children were not lost, this was a temporary separation. It was likely good for them to be around others. And there were two Ancient Dragons in this castle that required her protection; she needed to continue to prepare herself. She turned away from the panorama and took in a different sight: rows upon rows of weapons that she would spend the morning cleaning and sharpening, then the afternoon dirtying and dulling against her adversary.

Sentinel stood a short distance away, flickering blackly against the light snow covering the grounds. She did not know if that was his name or his title, but it was now how she thought of him. And she thought of him frequently, because when she was not ruminating on her love or her children, she thought only of fighting.

She examined the various weapons at her disposal. Swords, knives, lances, bows, shields, then a selection of more exotic weaponry at which Sentinel seemed equally expert. This fleeting thought led to another, and

Raine turned to the smoky phantasm.

"Sentinel."

The head moved a fraction of an inch, indicating he was listening.

"Choose a weapon."

This was a test on many levels, for Raine was not certain he even understood her. But he extended his arm, and a pole appeared in his hand. Connected at the end of the pole were three chains, and at the end of each chain was an ugly mass of iron bristling with spikes.

Raine frowned. "Wonderful," she muttered. "A flail."

The flail was a weapon she was unfamiliar with and rarely used. She could not help but wonder if that was why the phantasm chose it, although how he would know such a thing was beyond her. But the creature seemed to thrive on finding her weaknesses, although "thrive" was likely an over-statement as he showed no emotion as he pummeled her.

She walked to the rack and found the material version of the object he held. She swung it experimentally, and nearly struck herself in the head. She frowned again. This was going to be a very long day.

Still, as she returned to Sentinel, she felt a shiver travel down her back. It was the anticipation of battle, a thrill that lived in her blood, and one that was always proportionate to the difficulty of the fight she faced. Right now, it felt as if electricity flowed from the back of her head to the base of her spine, and despite the fact she was going to get thrashed, it was an enormously pleasant sensation.

She took a stance across from her ever-present opponent and stretched and cracked her neck. Sentinel raised his flail into an attack position, and Raine smiled grimly. Her last thought as she charged forward with fierce joy was that the onyx box had held the perfect gift for a Scinterian.

www.ingramcontent.com/pod-product-compliance
Lightning Source LLC
Chambersburg PA
CBHW072236170626
46813CB00003B/1244